FACE
RECOGNITION

ALSO BY HAVELOCK MANDAMUS

Confederate Vampires in Space

FACE RECOGNITION

a novel

Havelock
Mandamus

drumhead

First Printed 2018
ISBN 978-0-9993825-4-7 (paperback)
ISBN 978-0-9993825-5-4 (e-book)

Cover art and design by Havelock Mandamus.

www.drumheadbooks.com
www.havelockmandamus.com
havelockmandamus@gmail.com

For all the gearheads in that asylum
known as The Ponderosa

For now we see through a glass, darkly, but then face to face. Now I know in part, but then I shall know just as I also am known.

Verse 12 of Chapter 13
Paul's First Epistle to the Corinthians

PROLOGUE

Some might say I'm a criminal.

I don't agree, but that's how we've decided to handle what happened.

I must accept that.

That's the way these things are supposed to work.

I have no choice in the matter.

That's the sort of person I am.

I do what I'm told.

I keep my word.

Now, I know what you're thinking.

You're thinking: That's what they all say. They all say they're innocent. That someone set them up. That someone made a mistake. Or that someone cut a deal. Some co-defendant. Some jailhouse snitch desperate to curry favor.

And let me just say, sometimes what those folks say is true.

Sometimes they really are innocent.

If you'd seen the things I've seen.

Sometimes I wish I could forget.

But that's not the story I want to tell you.

This is my confession.

I did it all.

That's why I'm where I am now.

That's why I've got all this time to think about what happened.

I don't expect that you will sympathize with me.

But perhaps you'll listen?
Perhaps then you will understand why I did what I did.
That's all any of us really wants in the end, isn't it?
A little empathy?
To be understood?

PART ONE

Chapter One

I SUPPOSE THE BEST PLACE to begin is with the traffic stop. Which is not to say the traffic stop is the beginning of the story. I could start at any number of dates and times and locations. Everything is connected. That's important to understand. I don't mean to be so condescending, but it's one of the things I've learned that I think most people don't fully appreciate. Everything is connected. Perhaps you're familiar with the Rube Goldberg machine. It's easy to think of something as one part of a convoluted chain of causation, but life is far more complicated than that. The open manhole. The forgotten banana peel. The police car in your rear-view mirror. In reality, we all are at the intersection of an infinite number of Rube Goldberg machines. People just don't fully appreciate that.

So let me begin with the traffic stop. Officer Brody Pete was on patrol. Unit 24, Sector 6, first shift. It was a clear, beautiful morning.

People are always surprised when I say how beautiful I find the city. Like they think I'm not the sort of person who would notice. The mornings are especially beautiful. The quiet hours before the crush of the day. The sun sparkling on the surface of the river, lighting up the tops of the buildings. A stray cat slinking down the alley, disappearing around the corner. The distant rumble of a garbage truck. The lights coming on in kitchen windows, slowly at first, then more quickly. Of all the hours I miss now, I think I miss most those quiet mornings when the city is just beginning to stir.

I don't know if Officer Pete noticed the beauty of the city's morning in quite the same way, but I'd like to think he did. Brody Pete was a good cop, a good person. I knew all the police officers, and Brody Pete was one of the best. Ask anyone who knew him, and they'd say he was a stand-up guy, a military veteran, married to Gina, his high-school sweetheart. A cynic might expect to find some seedy corruption hidden away beneath Brody Pete's easy-going exterior, but it just wasn't there. Believe me, I know. I would have seen it. Brody never received any complaints, official or unofficial. He was a by-the-book cop, but his fellow officers knew they could depend on him. From roll call until the end of the shift, Brody shared their daily vow: To make it home safe and sound.

So this is how my story begins. On that beautiful, clear morning. With the sun sparkling on the river. With the city emerging from the night. The city, in all its noisy, teeming glory. And there, rolling through it all, was Officer Brody Pete. He was on patrol, unit 24, driving a marked cruiser. The traffic was not heavy that morning. There was nothing unusual about the volume of vehicles or the patterns of flow. There was only a trickle of the rush hour traffic yet to come.

It was at that moment that a luxury sedan passed Brody. It was a black BMW 740i with tinted glass. The car was spotless and looked brand new. Brody glanced at the rear of the car as it sped past.

There was an obnoxious empty place where the license plate should have been.

Brody followed the sedan, checking for a temporary tag in the window. Seeing none, Brody decided to make the traffic stop. He called it in to dispatch and turned on his cruiser lights. At this point, it seemed like a run-of-the-mill traffic stop, and Brody had no reason to think otherwise. He'd made dozens of similar traffic stops over the course of his career, and most of them had resolved peacefully and without any serious problems. He also knew he needed to be prepared in case this wasn't just another routine traffic stop. That's one of the things that can make a blind traffic stop so dangerous for everybody: Not knowing what's on the other side of the car window.

The sedan pulled over onto the shoulder of the road, and Brody came to a stop at a safe distance behind it. From within his cruiser, Brody watched the black tinted windows. He could not see any movement within the car.

When he was ready, Brody got out of his cruiser and walked to the driver's side of the sedan. The traffic on the road was whipping past him as he turned and faced the dark tinted window.

The window smoothly powered down, and Brody looked with sharp, quick eyes into the interior of the sedan.

The driver slowly turned toward Brody.

As a police officer, Brody had seen a lot of crazy things, but what Brody saw that morning was something he was not expecting. What he saw inside the sedan must have brought him instantly to the fullest state of readiness.

What Brody saw as the driver turned slowly toward him was an inhuman black mask that covered the entirety of the driver's face.

Brody stepped back and raised his hand to the Taser at his hip.

The driver was wearing black leather gloves and had both hands on the wheel.

The mask the driver was wearing had human features, vaguely male, but it was stylized, otherworldly, unsettling. The eyes were covered with what looked like thick, black, opaque lenses. The lower portion of the mask was an intricate black mesh, covering the driver's mouth and chin.

"Take off the mask," Brody said in a firm voice.

The driver slowly shook his head from side to side.

Brody watched the frozen features of the mask as it moved back and forth. Brody glanced into the interior of the car. He did not see anyone else in the front seat. The driver's hands were still on the wheel.

Brody took the Taser from his side and brandished it in his hand.

"Why are you wearing a mask?" Brody said.

The masked man looked at Brody with a steady, inscrutable gaze. Brody looked at the dark lenses covering the eyes.

"Are you . . . disabled?" Brody said.

The masked man slowly shook his head from side to side.

"Can you speak?" Brody said.

The masked man said nothing. There was no response, no movement.

Brody was momentarily flummoxed. He shifted his weight from one foot to the other.

His heart was thudding at a rapid clip. (Eighty-two beats per minute to be more precise.)

I suspect, for a brief moment, Brody may have even had the wild idea he was talking to a robot, to an elaborate self-driving car. But he wasn't going to say it out loud. Imagine how his fellow officers would have reacted. They would never have let him forget it.

"Show me your license and registration," Brody said, trying to keep his voice even.

The mask did not move. It appeared as if the masked man were staring calmly at Brody.

"Now," Brody ordered in a firm voice.

The masked man gestured with his empty, gloved hands. He slowly shook his head from side to side.

Brody had had enough.

"All right, fine," Brody said.

He checked in with dispatch on his radio and requested back up. The codes, the procedures, it all came to him quickly, and he spoke in that flat radio voice he had mastered long ago.

It was a routine exchange of information. The sort of thing that happened every day. Like neurochemicals settling into their receptors. Anyone monitoring a police radio had heard it countless times. This one, though, was different. The machinery had been set in motion. You'll see.

"Step out of the car," Brody said to the masked man.

At this point, I'm sure Brody was expecting one of two things to happen. He expected either the masked man would refuse to get out of the car or the masked man would make a run for it. What I'm sure Brody didn't expect was that the masked man would comply.

When Brody ordered the masked man to get out of the sedan, the masked man calmly opened the car door and stepped out of the sedan.

"Show me your hands," Brody said.

The masked man was wearing a dark suit, white collared shirt and no tie. He was slender, around six feet tall with narrow hips and broad shoulders. Brody thought the masked figure appeared to be male, but Brody couldn't say for sure. The stylized black mask had vaguely masculine features, but it was entirely possible that the driver was a woman.

Brody held the Taser up around eye level and shook it once or twice like a big rattle.

"You know what this is?" Brody asked.

The masked man nodded.

"Get down on your knees and put your hands behind your back." Brody said.

The masked man looked at him for a moment.

Brody showed him the Taser again.

"Don't try me," Brody said

The masked man knelt down on the pavement. Brody whipped out a set of handcuffs and smoothly secured the masked man's arms behind his back.

"Stand up," Brody said.

Brody helped the masked man as he awkwardly got back on his feet. Brody turned the masked man so they were facing one another.

Brody was going to frisk him, but then Brody paused.

Brody looked more closely at the mask.

It was made from a strange material. It seemed part leather and part ceramic, thick, almost like body armor. It covered most of the masked man's head.

Brody reached toward the mask, but the masked man flinched away. Brody left his hand poised in the space near the masked man's head.

The masked man looked Brody in the eye and slowly shook his head from side to side.

Brody stared into the lenses of the mask for a long moment. There was a curiosity in Brody's hesitation. A sensitivity in his searching gaze. Brody furrowed his brow. Somewhere behind those dark lenses, behind the mask, there was a human being.

The masked man seemed compliant. He was fairly relaxed for someone wearing handcuffs about to be arrested. Brody's gut was telling him the masked man was not a threat. In fact, it was almost as if the masked man wanted Brody to arrest him.

Brody slowly lowered his hand away from the mask. He spoke to the masked man in a calm voice.

"Your vehicle has no plates," Brody said.

The masked man slowly nodded in agreement.

Brody took a step back from the masked man, and they relaxed a little.

"Are you carrying any weapons?" Brody asked him.

The masked man shook his head in the negative.

"I'm going to frisk you, okay?"

The masked man nodded.

Brody quickly patted him down and checked the pockets of his suit jacket and his pants. Brody found no wallet, no identification, no driver's license. The masked man was not carrying anything in his pockets other than a single business card.

Brody removed the business card from the masked man's suit-jacket pocket and read it. The business card had a distinctive logo. Two masks side by side, one smiling, one frowning. Tragedy and comedy, the smiling and frowning faces of theater. Below the logo, the card read MASQUERADE with a street address.

Brody held the card by the corner between the tip of his index finger and his thumb. He showed it to the masked man.

"Masquerade?" Brody said.

The masked man was calmly watching Brody.

"Is this a business?" Brody asked.

No reaction. The masked man remained impassive.

They heard the sound of a second police cruiser arriving on the scene. It was the back-up Brody had requested. Brody glanced up as the second officer got out of the cruiser. Brody looked back at the masked man, and they faced each other for a brief, silent moment.

Then Brody slid the business card into his pocket.

The second officer was JD Teague. Some officers go through their entire careers without anyone ever learning their full name. They come to be known by their initials. There are various reasons for this, the main one being police officer safety. In case you're interested, JD was short for Jeremiah Dionysus. You'll have to forgive me that little breach of privacy. I just love those sorts of details.

Officer Teague was older than Brody. He'd been on the force for almost two decades and was less than pleased to still be on patrol. For that reason, and some others best left unsaid, JD was a surly fellow with a short fuse. Not a good combination for a patrol officer, in my humble opinion. He was a big man beginning to go soft. He had big golfer's forearms covered in furry black hair. His bristling black mustache was peppered with grey.

JD quickly sized up the situation.

"So what's with the mask?" JD said to Brody.

JD spoke in a terse monotone, his eyes elsewhere, usually drifting away from the conversation.

"I don't know," Brody said.

JD turned to the masked man.

"Hey, freakshow?" JD said. "What's with the mask?"

The masked man regarded JD calmly and did not respond.

JD started to turn back toward Brody, but then he lunged back toward the masked man and attempted to grab the mask.

The masked man easily sidestepped JD's attempt to grab the mask.

JD took a few off-balance steps and then spun back around.

"Hold him for me," JD said to Brody.

"I don't know . . ." Brody said. "It might be medical or something."

"Or he might be your boyfriend," JD said.

JD grabbed the masked man by the sleeve of his jacket.

"Hold still, you carnival geek," JD said to the masked man.

JD grappled with the masked man for a moment, and then, in one swift motion, JD slapped his open palm against the face of the mask and grabbed it with his fingers.

JD tried to yank the mask off, but it did not come away. He could not even move it. The mask seemed to be firmly attached to the masked man's face.

"I can't get it off," JD said through clenched teeth.

JD kept his grip on the mask. For a few moments, he and the masked man pivoted around each other in a tight circle, like a dog chasing its tail.

"Leave it," Brody said.

JD was tugging hard on the mask.

"It's like it's stuck to his face."

JD spun free from the masked man and fell to the pavement, landing on his rear end. The masked man stepped back and quickly regained his balance. JD sprawled awkwardly on the ground beneath the masked man. The masked man watched him and seemed almost dignified by comparison.

Brody was amused and let slip a little smile. The masked man saw Brody's smile and nodded his head as if he were acknowledging Brody's amusement.

"I think he's a head case," Brody said, still smiling slightly.

JD had gotten back on his feet and was dusting himself off. His face had flushed bright red.

"What was your first clue?" JD said, with some irritation.

"No," Brody said. "I mean I think he needs a psych evaluation."

"A seventy-two hour hold?" JD said.

"Yeah. He's a danger to himself, right?" Brody said.

"There's a danger I might put my foot more than halfway up his freakshow ass," JD muttered.

The masked man was paying close attention to the conversation, calmly listening with his arms bound behind his back.

"If you take him to the hospital, I'll do the paperwork," Brody suggested.

JD thought it over for a moment. He tugged on his chin, looked at the masked man out of the corner of his eyes.

"Deal," JD said.

He turned to the masked man.

"Good news, Zorro," JD said. "Looks like we get to go trick-or-treating tonight."

JD seized the masked man by the arm and pulled him towards the second police cruiser. Brody watched as the masked man began to walk calmly in front of Officer Teague. As they passed Brody, the masked man turned and looked at Brody. Brody watched him as he passed. The black mask was frozen in that one strange, inhuman expression. Behind him, JD's florid face was smug and satisfied. The masked man gave Brody a little nod as he passed.

JD put the masked man in the back of his cruiser and left. Brody walked back to his cruiser and paused before he opened the door. He pulled the business card out of the pocket where he had put it before JD arrived. Brody read the card again. MASQUERADE. He examined closely the logo with the smiling and frowning masks.

Brody stood there looking at the card for almost seven seconds. (Six point three to be more precise.) I think Brody was thinking about dropping the card, just forgetting about it. But he didn't. He put the business card back in his pocket, got in his cruiser and started the paperwork for the masked man's psychiatric evaluation.

Chapter Two

IN THE HOLDING AREA of the psychiatric hospital, the masked man sat in a plastic chair the color of tangerines. Seated on either side of him was another person. They were the only three people in the room.

The man in the seat to the immediate left was small and skinny. He had big, bulging, startled eyes, like saucers, and his hair was set with a generous application of a substance that might have been gel. His hair was sticking to one side, like he had just walked out of a hurricane or had stuck his head in an open fire hydrant. He said his name was Beauregard, but people called him Bug.

The man in the seat to the immediate right of the masked man was huge and imposing. He was wearing denim overalls and not much of anything else. No shirt, no shoes. The man was thickly muscled, and the overalls were hanging by a single strap. His head was enormous with receding tufts of wiry, close-cropped black hair. His face looked like a pile of boulders that had tumbled down onto his shoulders. There was a dirty adhesive nametag clinging to his forehead. Someone had written a name on it in black magic marker.

Delmar, it read. Delmar appeared to be asleep.

The holding area was behind a locked metal door with a single reinforced window. The interior was grim. Uniform plastic chairs lined the walls like pieces of fruit-colored candy. Limes, cherries, lemons. There was a puddle of dark liquid on the uneven tile floor. A suspended florescent light buzzed above their heads. Despite the empty chairs all around them in the otherwise empty room, the three had somehow ended up seated side by side. They each wore plastic handcuffs around the wrists in their laps.

For a while, the only sound was the sound of Delmar snoring.

But then, abruptly, Bug began speaking.

"I mean, I understand what you're going for. . . What you're trying to do with . . . you know . . ."

He paused and gestured with his skinny handcuffed arms.

"The mask and all," Bug said.

The masked man turned his face slightly toward Bug on his right and watched him out of the corner of his eye. Delmar was slumped against the masked man's left shoulder. Delmar's huge head nodded as he softly snored.

"But we're really looking to go another way," Bug continued. "Something a bit more — let's see, how shall I put this — expressive. Like, with a face. . . M'yeah . . . a face. . ."

Bug gave the masked man a sympathetic pat on his knee.

"Sorry," Bug said.

"Shut up," Delmar rumbled, wiping the drool from his chin.

Delmar had a deep, resonant voice.

"And you . . ." Bug said, undeterred, gesturing awkwardly across the masked man towards Delmar.

"Overalls?" Bug said. "Really, Jethro? Bit of a cliché, don't you think?"

Delmar sat up straight and smacked his lips a couple times.

The masked man carefully turned his face toward Delmar and peered up at the big man out of the other corner of his opaque eyes.

"What are you talking about?" Delmar said, groggy, irritable.

"The movie, of course," Bug said.

"Movie? What movie?" Delmar said.

"That's why *I'm* here," Bug said, pressing his delicate fingertips against his bony chest. "You don't think that I'm . . ."

He gestured toward them, making an awkward little circle with his handcuffed arms.

"One of you people."

Bug laughed a fake laugh that echoed in the empty holding area. He rolled his eyes toward the ceiling, arranged his hands precisely on each knee and began to shake his head.

Delmar was silent, frowning.

The masked man was motionless, watching Delmar out of the corner of his eyes.

Delmar appeared to be engaged in vigorous thought.

"What kind of movie?" Delmar said, at last.

"Well, obviously I can't say much about the details," Bug said. "Closed sets, binding contracts, hush hush and all that . . ."

"Oh. Right. Sure . . . closed sets . . . binding contracts," Delmar said.

"Suffice it to say . . ." Bug said, pausing to look around the empty room before he leaned in close toward Delmar.

"Deus Ex Machina," Bug said in a loud whisper.

"I love her," Delmar said in an equally loud whisper, nodding his massive head.

The masked man turned and looked more closely at Delmar. The adhesive name tag was still clinging to his forehead.

"So you see the need for these," Bug said, gesturing with his hands balled up in little fists side by side, displaying the handcuffs cutting into his bony wrists.

"The mental hospital scene will be pivotal," Bug explained."Cinema veritas . . . en loco parentis . . . e pluribus unum."

They were silent for a moment.

"Are there robots?" Delmar said.

"Robots?" Bug said.

"From the government. You know, secret government robots," Delmar said.

"Oh, right," Bug said. "No. Of course not. No robots. Don't be absurd. No robots. No, no, no, no —"

Bug stopped abruptly, paused, thinking.

He glanced out of the corner of his eye at the masked man.

"Well . . . maybe," Bug said. "I haven't seen the whole script."

Chapter Three

IT'S HARD TO SAY what exactly moved Brody to visit Masquerade. If I were to speculate, I'd say part of it must have been out of a sense of duty. If the masked man was a head case, Brody wanted to give the people treating him all the information they needed to help him get better. Masquerade might have been the whole key to the masked man's identity. Part of it also must have been out of a sense of sheer, unadulterated curiosity. The guy had a mask like a piece of body armor stuck to his face. Who wouldn't want to learn more about *that*?

On the day of the traffic stop, as Brody sat in his police cruiser, filling out the paperwork for the masked man's psychiatric evaluation, his thoughts kept returning to the business card in his pocket. Half way through his paperwork, he took the card out and looked at it again. He put it under one corner at the top of his clipboard. The two little masks in the logo, frowning and laughing, seemed to watch him as he finished up the paperwork.

By the end of his shift, Brody had decided to make an informal visit to the address on the business card for Masquerade. He tried to call Gina to let her know he'd be running late, but he got her voice mail. Gina's voice mail was full, which was odd, but it didn't concern Brody at the time.

Brody parked a couple blocks down the street and walked back to the address on the card. Brody had changed into his street clothes. The neighborhood was a mix of run-down properties and blighted tenements interspersed with pockets of gentrification. The entrance to Masquerade was not well marked, and it took Brody a couple tries to find it. As he back-tracked, he noticed a security camera mounted on a streetlight. The dark lens was aimed directly at two ramshackle store-fronts. Sandwiched between them was the entrance to Masquerade.

Brody stood for a moment in front of the plain door. On one side of the door was a video-game arcade. A droning sound bubbled from inside the arcade. It was loud enough for Brody to hear it where he was standing on the sidewalk. He glimpsed flashing lights and moving pixels within the cave-like interior. Above the arcade was a fortuneteller. A garish neon sign in the shape of a large open palm flashed on and off in the second-floor bay window.

The store on the other side of the door was closed, the metal safety door down and locked. Someone had spray-painted graffiti art on the flat metal surfaces of the safety door. It was a mermaid rising up out of a pale green sea. The artist had some talent. Silver tears lined the mermaid's face.

Above the shuttered store and the sad mermaid, the windows were blacked out. The second-floor space behind the blacked-out windows was the address on the business card for Masquerade.

Brody turned and looked up at the camera mounted on the streetlight. Its lens was aimed directly at him. He stared into the lens of the camera for the briefest of moments.

Then he turned and went through the plain door.

The stairs behind the door led to the second floor. There were a few empty beer cans on the steps against the wall. The sticky carpeting was matted smooth and dark. Someone somewhere nearby was cooking with garlic, cumin and onions. At the top of the stairs, there was a small landing. On the left was the door to the fortuneteller, Madam Zelda. On the right was a door with the Masquerade logo painted in shades of lavender and plum.

Brody knocked on the door to Masquerade, but no one answered. He knocked a couple more times, and then he turned the doorknob and opened the door. There was the soft dinging of a bell above his head.

"Hello," Brody called.

His voice carried in the dim interior.

Masquerade was bigger than it looked.

Brody stepped into the room. The interior of Masquerade seemed almost dark at first, and Brody couldn't get a good sense of the size of the room. He peered into the interior, waiting for his eyes to adjust to the dim light.

There were shadowy shapes near him in the immediate foreground, but he also saw about half a dozen bright objects that seemed to be floating at various indeterminate distances in the background.

He took a step forward, and the closest brightly-lit object came more clearly into focus. He realized it was a mask. It looked like it was expertly crafted from red and white leather with black stitching. It was an elaborate design that Brody did not immediately recognize. It looked like a cross between a Mexican wrestling mask and a Chinese opera mask. The mask was on a pedestal, like a work of art. There was a spotlight mounted on the ceiling above the mask. Its narrow beam of light lifted the mask from the shadows around it. With the dramatic lighting, the mask seemed to be floating out of the darkness. There were stark, empty black holes where the mouth and eyes should have been. It seemed to be drifting toward you as you entered the room. It was striking and beautiful and frightening all at the same time.

Brody looked past the red and white mask at the other bright lights shining in the gloom. Each light lifted a mask from the shadows. It was impossible to get a reliable sense of the size of the masks or the depth of room. Masquerade seemed to open up into a much larger area than seemed physically possible. The masks seemed to recede into distant rooms, into adjoining buildings. They were like a chain of islands, an archipelago of illumination on a calm, dark sea. Brody knew it was just an optical illusion, but it was a good one. He was completely disoriented.

Brody walked farther into the room. The shapes in the shadows around him had become clearer. They all were masks. There were masks everywhere. Their empty eyes peered at him from every corner of the room. Some were simple. Some were elaborate. Carnival masks. Mardi Gras masks. Noh masks. Chinese opera masks. Mexican wrestling masks. Tribal masks. Animal masks. Beautiful masks. Ugly masks. Elegant masks. Primitive masks. Scary masks.

The other masks in the rest of the interior of Masquerade were lit artfully with dim black lights or other faint lights the color of scarlet and mauve. Most of the masks were side by side on shelves on the walls. A few rested on the heads of mannequins and the smooth faces of styrofoam busts. There were open bins and tables on the floor, full of more ordinary masks all jumbled together. They seemed to be moving in the dim light, peering up briefly at Brody like restless schools of fish.

Brody moved toward another elaborate mask that was floating atop a pedestal in a pool of light. It was like nothing he had ever seen. It almost defied description. It was like a cross between a space alien and an Aztec shaman, some kind of Stone Age cosmonaut. Most of it was covered with small feathers the color of rust and ocher, mottled together in the shape of leopard spots. The nose was a raptor's black beak between two long, smooth grey bubbles sealed at the edges with a silver metallic rim. The smoky gray bubbles covered the eyes and swept back over each temple. There were an insect's segmented antenna, gleaming like mercury, arcing from either side of the top of the head. A widow's peak of sharp black quills filled the middle of the crown of the mask and ran down the back of the top of the skull, lengthening into longer, pointed spines with fins or sails, glossy like graphite, that were folded down at the back of the mask and angled toward the ground.

Brody looked beyond the Stone Age cosmonaut. He could see the other lit masks more clearly. There was an ivory-colored Venetian bauta with delicate gilded silver flourishes along the edges. A Pantalone mask from commedia dell'arte. A golden, metallic mask that looked vaguely Egyptian and damascene, like something from a sarcophagus.

Brody approached another mask floating in a spotlight. It was fishlike, but definitely not a fish. Its surface was a mosaic of scales made out of gleaming materials that were colored turquoise and cobalt-blue and slate-gray. It had red eyes with round black pupils. On either side of the chin were little fins and whiskers and gills.

Farther still was a pale mask that resembled a painted calavera skull from a Day of the Dead parade or maybe a Santeria altar. They seemed to be leading him farther into the darkened rooms.

Brody was fascinated by the masks. Each one seemed to beckon from the darkness. He stared at them in amazement and then remembered his smart phone and decided to take a few quick photographs. He reached into his pocket to find his phone.

The moment Brody began searching for his phone, one of the masks in the shadows began to move. It moved toward Brody slowly until Brody noticed. Brody was startled and took a step back. The mask moved closer to Brody, and then the figure of a woman seemed to materialize out of the darkness. She was wearing a dark silk gown with subtle embroidery. As she stepped toward Brody and the light of the spotlight, it was as if one of the masks had come to life before his eyes.

Brody stared at the masked woman. She was a beautiful woman by any measure. With dark hair and crimson lips, she held herself like a queen. Her mask was small and elegant. A half-mask, it covered her forehead, temples, cheeks and the bridge of her narrow nose. The mask was covered in black feathers, suggestive of a bird, of a hawk, perhaps. As she moved the light caught the subtle highlights of the small feathers — glossy flashes of dark green and blue. She smiled as Brody saw her. Her dark eyes glittered within the mask. Her crimson lips gleamed in the light from the spotlight. Her teeth were small and dazzling and perfect.

"How now," the masked woman said.

Her voice was taunting and musical.

"Brown cow?" Brody blurted out, still startled by her appearance.

The masked woman clapped her hands together.

"Poetry!"

She seemed amused.

She began slowly to circle Brody.

"Do you work here?" Brody said, turning toward her.

"Sometimes," she said.

Brody watched her as she moved.

"What kind of business is this?" he said.

The masked woman stopped and faced him.

"Isn't it obvious?" she said.

She smiled, coy.

"Not at the moment," Brody said.

She folded one arm across her waist and raised the opposite hand to her hair. She began to twirl a lock of dark hair around one scarlet-tipped finger.

"We sell masks," she said.

"What kind of masks?" Brody asked.

The masked woman drew closer to him and looked into his eyes.

"What kind do you seek?"

"No," Brody said. "Not for me."

"No? Are you sure?" the masked woman said.

Brody stepped back from the masked woman.

"I don't need a mask," he said, growing more and more uncomfortable.

The masked woman looked away.

She turned and swept her arm in a circle, gesturing towards the masks that surrounded them.

"All the world's a stage, my serious friend," she said.

"Not where I work," Brody said, off balance, distracted.

"And where is that?" the masked woman said, straightening one of the masks, smiling to herself.

Chapter Four

THE MASKED MAN WAS SITTING in a straight-backed wooden chair at a battered table. The table was in a small room with a single locked door and a face-sized reinforced window. On the other side of the table was an empty chair. The masked man sat with his gloved hands and handcuffed wrists resting in front of him on the table. Between his hands was a pad of lined notebook paper. The table had a grey plastic surface and was gouged with several dark gashes. On the wall across from the masked man was a ragged poster. It was Picasso's *Bouquet of Peace* — a plain line drawing of two hands holding a small bouquet of colorful flowers.

The door opened, and a thin, stooped man in an expensive crew-neck sweater came into the room and shut the door. He was carrying a stack of files under one arm. His sweater was knitted in an irregular, abstract pattern with several shades of blue, gray and black. A pair of thick reading glasses dangled from a strap around his neck.

The man in the sweater sat down in the chair across from the masked man. He placed his glasses on the tip of his nose and began reading one of the files. His face was narrow, with a

prominent nose, serious mouth and subtle pink acne scars beneath his cheekbones. His blond hair was thin and wispy,
floating around the back of his head like a nimbus. He glanced
up over the black frame of his reading glasses and looked
briefly at the masked man. His eyes were watery-blue and not
unfriendly.

The man in the sweater removed his glasses and closed the
file. He pulled a pen from a pocket and reached across the table and set the pen on the pad of notebook paper in front of
the masked man.

"The police tell me they found you driving a car with no
license plates and with no driver's license," said the man in the
sweater.

The man spoke in a soft, slightly nasal voice. His tone was
ambiguous. His words were neither a declaration nor a question.

The masked man did not respond. He remained motionless. His opaque eyes appeared to be staring at the man across
from him.

"The police also tell me that the car you were driving has
no apparent VIN number, no GPS chip."

The man with the sweater paused, looking steadily at the
masked man, but the masked man did not respond.

"May I remove your gloves?" the man asked.

The masked man extended his arms across the table. The
man with the sweater turned the gloved hands palm upward
and pulled the black leather gloves from the masked man's
hands and fingers.

The man with the sweater put his reading glasses on and
leaned forward and looked closely at the masked man's
hands. He adjusted his glasses. The nurses had told him, but
still his wispy white eyebrows twitched up, perhaps in surprise.

The masked man's hands had no fingerprints. The tips of his fingers had been carefully disfigured. They were unnaturally smooth with only a suggestion of scar tissue.

The man in the sweater looked up at the masked man.

"Did you do this?" the man in the sweater asked.

The masked man put the gloves back on his hands.

The man in the sweater was staring at the masked man's frozen face.

"Did someone do this to you?" the man in the sweater asked.

The masked man laid his hands back on the table in front of him and did not respond.

"Do you want to tell me about it?" the man in the sweater asked.

The masked man did not respond and stared impassively at the man with the sweater.

The man with the sweater opened the file on the table and began to write in the file. For a few moments, the only sound in the small room was the sound of the pen scratching on the paper records in the file.

The man with the sweater stopped writing, closed the file and laid the pen neatly and precisely in the middle of the file.

"The police are treating you as a john doe because they don't know your name. I'm going to do the same thing . . ."

The man with the sweater nodded toward the pad and pen on the table in front of the masked man.

"Unless you've changed your mind and want to share your name with me," the man with the sweater said.

The masked man did not move.

The man with the sweater paused for a moment, and then he sighed.

"Okay then."

He shifted in his chair.

He sat up straight and placed a hand flat against his chest.

"My name is Wyche. Ranier Wyche. I'm a psychiatrist. I work for the hospital."

He paused for a moment, watching the masked man.

"The police are concerned because it appears that you've gone to great lengths to conceal your identity. Or at least, you've made it more difficult for them to determine your identity," Dr. Wyche said.

He paused, waiting to see if the masked man might respond.

Dr. Wyche gestured with his open hands and leaned back in his chair.

"Can you . . . can you help me understand that?"

The masked man stared at Dr. Wyche with an impassive gaze.

"You know, some places have laws that prohibit masks," Dr. Wyche said.

"Did you know that?" Dr. Wyche said.

There was no response.

Dr. Wyche leaned forward and rested his elbows on the table. He raised one arm and casually rested his chin in the palm of his hand. He looked past the masked man, staring toward the ceiling of the little room.

"I can think of several noncriminal reasons why someone might want to wear a mask."

He raised the corner of his thin lips in a wistful little smile.

"There are days when I'd like to wear a mask. No one could see me. No one could tell what I was thinking, whether I was afraid or angry. Happy or sad."

Dr. Wyche looked at the masked man.

Wyche was still wearing the wistful, almost bittersweet smile.

But the masked man did not respond.

Dr. Wyche gestured theatrically and arranged his long-fingered hands in the air over the table. He performed a deft optical illusion. The tip of his index finger seemed to float away from the end of his finger.

"No?" Dr. Wyche said.

The masked man did not react to the doctor's sleight of hand.

"Ah well," Dr. Wyche sighed and shrugged.

He rested his empty hands on the table.

Dr. Wyche looked down at the file on the table in front of him.

Dr. Wyche made a few notes in the file.

When he looked up at the masked man, his face was serious.

The wistful smile was gone.

"The police are worried that you might be dangerous. That the mask, your silence, your possible self-mutilation, are all evidence of hostility, disorder, paranoia, delusion, psychosis . . ."

The doctor paused.

"What do you think I should do?"

The masked man was silent.

"Are you dangerous, John Doe?"

The masked man remained motionless, impassive.

The strange, otherworldly expression on the mask seemed to be staring at the doctor with cold, emotionless eyes.

"Very well," Dr. Wyche said.

His thin lips pressed together in a tight, straight line. He began to gather up the files from the table.

"I don't think I can release you. You've given me no choice. We're going to have to keep you here for a few days. For observation. I'm going to keep you on suicide watch for now."

Dr. Wyche reached across the table and removed the pen from the pad of notebook paper in front of the masked man.

Dr. Wyche stood up and walked to the door. He turned and looked back at the masked man.

"It's for your own good," Dr. Wyche said. "I hope you understand."

The masked man did not respond.

Dr. Wyche opened the door and stepped out of the room.

The door gently eased shut behind him until, with a soft metallic click, the latch locked firmly into place.

Across from the masked man, behind the gray table top and the empty chair, one corner of the Picasso poster floated up in a draft and then settled softly back against the wall.

The hands were holding the colorful flowers.

The fingers were curled firmly around the stems.

PART TWO

Chapter Five

ON THE DAY OF THE TRAFFIC STOP, at a number of public high schools in the suburbs near the city, a number of unusual events began to occur. They might not seem unusual when viewed in isolation, as individual points of data, but when viewed together, accounting for location and time, certain unmistakable patterns begin to emerge. Certain vectors, as it were.

Take, for example, Boyd Ripley.

Healthy, strapping Boyd Ripley, cornerback on his high-school football team. Boyd was at practice, running wind sprints with his teammates on the practice field. They raced in rows to the lines of orange traffic cones then back to the start. Graceful wide receivers and lumbering linemen. They ran back and forth, back and forth, sweat pouring down their bodies, gasping for another hot breath of air. Back and forth, back and forth, legs churning, lungs burning, straining to go just a little faster. Back and forth, back and forth, sucking the very last molecules of oxygen out their blood, filling their spent muscles with lactic acid, their cerebral cortexes with endorphins.

Coach Riley clenched the gleaming steel whistle between his teeth and blew a long, loud, merciful blast before he let the whistle fall to his chest where it dangled from the cord around his neck. The team staggered to a stop, with their hands on their knees, bent over, trying not to fall down, trying not to sprawl delirious in the grass. Wind sprints were over at last.

"Huddle up," Coach Riley cried.

Boyd Ripley was bent over, gasping for air when Coach Riley blew his whistle. Boyd's teammates turned and began to move slowly toward the coach, converging on the spot of ground where he stood. Boyd was coughing, trying to clear his throat. He dropped to one knee and began coughing harder. Finally, Boyd coughed up something sizeable, choked for a moment, heaving, and then threw it all up on the ground in front of him. Boyd looked down at the ground for a long moment before he pulled himself back up and started walking toward the huddle with the others.

On the ground, seeping into the grass, was a startling amount of bright red blood.

Now, I'll concede that the incident with Boyd Ripley alone would probably not arouse your suspicion. Football is a violent game. People get injured all the time. Boyd might have had an internal injury. A serious matter, of course, but not all that unusual. Happens all the time.

But then there was Jimmy Putty.

Rosy-cheeked, freckle-faced, Jimmy Putty, the picture of good health. Jimmy played the trumpet in the marching band. Around the same time Boyd Ripley was finishing up wind sprints with the football team, Jimmy Putty was practicing with the band. The band director, Mr. Calderon, had an obsession with movie soundtracks, and the band was forever learning a new arrangement of an old feature film. Not anything like Star Wars or James Bond or the Pink Panther, though. That would have been too easy, almost enjoyable. Instead, Mr. Calderon made them learn arrangements from ancient films like *The Karate Kid* or *The Rocketeer*, music with stirring themes that no one recognized or remembered. This confounded Jimmy to no end, but no matter. That's a story for another day.

The piece of music the band was playing on the day of the traffic stop had several demanding parts for trumpet, and Jimmy had to strain to hit the high notes. Mr. Calderon was not satisfied and made them play the measures several times. Suddenly, in the middle of their practice, Jimmy stopped playing and began coughing. Mr. Calderon stopped, frowning impatiently beneath his beard, and waited for Jimmy to stop coughing.

But the coughing got worse. Mr. Calderon told everyone to take a break. Everybody started talking at once, blowing the spit out of their instruments, and Jimmy Putty left the room, headed toward the restroom. Along the way, he was attempting to stifle the coughing.

In the bathroom, Jimmy Putty braced himself with his skinny arms over one of the white sinks and coughed convulsively until a small pool of red blood had filled half the basin.

Lorelie Forte was in detention.

Gap-toothed, pig-tailed, Lorelie Forte, the pie-faced provocateur of home -room infamy.

Lorelie was drawing with a pencil on the white pages of her spiral-bound notebook. She was drawing the tattoo Ronan Willis wore on his huge bicep. Ronan was sitting across from her, sound asleep, with his head on his desk.

The room was silent. A round clock on the wall marked the slow minutes. Lorelie had worked the graphite tip of her yellow No. 2 pencil down to a blunt, flat edge, and the solid black surfaces of her drawing had a gleaming, silver patina.

Suddenly, Ronan Willis sat up and coughed.

At the front of the room, Mrs. Westmoreland looked up from the fashion magazine she was reading at her desk.

Ronan smiled sheepishly and struck himself softly in the chest with the side of one fist, like he had heartburn. He brushed his long, lank hair out of his eyes.

Mrs. Westmoreland looked back down at her fashion magazine.

Across the room, someone else coughed.

Then Ronan coughed again, loudly, like he couldn't help it.

Mrs. Westmoreland looked up from her fashion magazine, and her face pinched up.

Then Lorelie felt something in her throat, too. Something insistent, rough and raw. She felt the irresistible urge to cough. She couldn't help it. She coughed out loud reflexively.

Then there was the sound of another cough from another part of the room.

"Stop that coughing," Mrs. Westmoreland said.

Ronan coughed convulsively, bucking in the small seat of the desk bolted to the floor. The veins stood out on the side of his thick neck.

Someone raised their hand.

"I need to go to the restroom."

Lorelie coughed again, harder, painfully. There was an intense straining sensation in her chest and neck and throat.

Mrs. Westmoreland stood up behind her desk, the pages of the fashion magazine turning slowly below her.

Ronan had raised his hands to cover his mouth.

Lorelai coughed again violently, painfully, with her whole body, and something liquid rushed out of her mouth and nose.

She looked down at the white pages of her spiral-bound notebook.

They were spattered bright red with blood.

Chapter Six

OFFICER BRODY PETE'S WIFE, Gina, was sitting at her station behind the counter of the school infirmary. She was a rangy, athletic woman with short brown hair clasped at the back of her neck. Gina Pete was the school nurse.

Sitting next to Gina was Caitlyn Buttons, a high-school senior. Caitlyn was petite with purple streaks in her dark hair. She had deathly pale skin, piercings, black nail polish, black lipstick. She carried a well-worn stack of Aleister Crowley in her bookbag.

Caitlyn was turning over cards from her tarot deck, and Gina was watching as she carefully placed the cards on the counter before them.

Caitlyn turned over the nine of swords.

She held the card by one corner and shook it, showing it to Gina.

"Fuck that shit," Caitlyn said.

Gina knew nothing about reading tarot cards.

"Hmm," Gina said.

Caitlyn turned and looked at Gina.

"I know, right?" Caitlyn said.

She laid the card on the counter.

"Maybe it's not really bad," Gina said.

"Oh, it's bad," Caitlyn said.

"But it might change, right? With the right card?" Gina said, trying to be helpful.

"It's not like poker, dude," Caitlyn said.

Gina looked at the younger woman for a moment.

Gina reached across the counter and turned over the next card. She threw it onto the counter into the middle of Caitlyn's tarot spread.

"Look," Gina exclaimed. "Yahtzee!"

Gina smirked mischievously.

Caitlyn sat up straight and drew in a long, audible breath.

She closed her eyes, composed her face, in high dudgeon.

She calmly began to gather the tarot cards from the counter.

"People mock what they don't understand," Caitlyn said with curt, icy condescension.

"No, I want to learn," Gina said, grabbing Caitlyn's shoulder.

"Teach me," Gina pleaded, her voice rising. "Teach meee."

Caitlyn gave her the side eye for a brief moment, her face full of contempt, but then the façade tumbled down, and she began to laugh, and they both broke down in laughter.

Caitlyn was supposed to be sitting in Mr. Mallard's second-period environmental sciences class, but she and Gina had reached an informal agreement. As long as Caitlyn maintained a passing grade, Gina would write her the occasional medical excuse for a migraine. It wasn't completely fraudulent. Fred Mallard did tend to drone on in a migraine-inducing blizzard of incomplete sentences, and Caitlyn already had enough credits to graduate and had a full-time job waiting for her at the holistic health center near her parents' house, but the main reason Gina let Caitlyn skip class was because Feegie Bean sat behind her. Feegie was on the football team and seemed destined for a long stay in the penitentiary. Like two mythical creatures from faraway lands, he and Caitlyn had hooked up for one brief, inauspicious encounter. As Caitlyn so eloquently put it, she could not even.

Gina and Caitlyn were not that far apart in age, and over the dozen or so times Caitlyn had sought sanctuary in the infirmary, Gina had begun to share some of her own personal life with the younger woman. Gina knew Caitlyn well enough to know she was sincere in her beliefs, not just seeking attention, not just going through a rebellious phase. Gina admired Caitlyn for that. It took a lot of courage and self-confidence to step out of line. But Gina also knew that it was probably not a good sign that she was discussing her personal life with a high-school student who spent a significant amount of her time casting magic spells.

Gina was a registered nurse and a highly intelligent woman. Being a school nurse was a good job with a good salary. She administered inoculations, doled out aspirin and cold medicine, dealt with the occasional emergency or injury. She enjoyed working with young people and felt she occasionally made a difference in the lives of some of the students.

But lately, she had been restless.

It's not that the work wasn't important to her. It was. Or that she didn't feel appreciated. She did. Everybody told her she was appreciated. The school psychologist alone told her she was appreciated about a dozen times every single day.

In those exact words.

"I appreciate you."

"I appreciate you, too," Gina would say, and she meant it, but she heard a certain tone creeping into her voice. It was the same tone she used to signal her displeasure with Brody. It was usually the prelude to one of their arguments. Brody was especially sensitive to the tone, but, of course, he'd had more practice.

In truth, Gina had begun to feel as though there might be something missing in her life. She loved being a nurse. She had a big heart, and she was good at it. But she wondered if she might not be falling short of her full potential. She did not feel challenged the way she wanted to be challenged. She was beginning to suspect that she might not be fulfilled.

And this bothered her.

It bothered her especially because Brody, her loving husband, did seem to be fulfilled. She secretly envied Brody and his complacency. Brody never complained about anything. It was annoying. It made her feel guilty. She knew Brody had to have feelings about his job, about his potential, but he just didn't talk about it.

He could easily talk about something like their marriage. They had talked meaningfully and at length about having children, and they both had concluded it was not the right time. Their lives were too complicated, too busy, too dangerous. The last thing they needed was the additional responsibility of raising a child. That's what they had agreed.

But when she would ask Brody about his job, it was like a closed door. She could only watch him and wonder what was going on inside that pretty little head of his. Perhaps he was trying to protect her, but he had to know by now that she'd call him on that kind of sexist crap. No, she'd concluded that Brody was satisfied in his job. Brody just loved being a cop. Now if only she could find something she loved as much as Brody loved being a cop.

That's why she was so restless. That's why she had started browsing through the class catalog for grad school at the university. That's why she was thinking about taking some night classes, maybe getting a master's in health administration or business or something like that. She kept waiting to talk about it with Brody, but the time never seemed right. She'd been giving it more and more thought, and she knew she needed to talk with him about it soon.

Caitlyn Buttons had her own theories.

"How are things in the sack?" Caitlyn asked Gina one day when they were talking about Brody.

"The sack?"

"You know, the boudoir?" she said, raising a pierced eyebrow.

"Oh. . . . None of your business."

Caitlyn shrugged.

They were silent for a moment.

"But they're fine," Gina said, a flush of color on her cheek. "We're fine."

But the little witch had touched a nerve.

They weren't fine. Brody and Gina weren't sexually intimate nearly as often as when they first married. They hadn't talked about it, and Gina worried they both were letting an important part of their lives just quietly fade away. But that was normal, she told herself. There's an ebb and flow to life. She and Brody were no different. She and Brody would figure it out.

(Now, I know what you might be thinking.

You might be thinking: How do you know so much about Gina Pete and her personal life? And it's a good question. I'm certainly no mind reader, although I suppose it can seem that way sometimes. No, I've merely made the obvious extrapolations from the record, from the video files, the audio files, from the transcripts, from various caches of data. I might add a little embellishment here or there, connect a few dots, fill in a blank space or two, but it's all based on the data, on the facts, on what happened. Like I said, I keep my word. I do as I'm told. It's not that complicated or surprising, really. A police officer's personal life is important to their psychological well-being, to his or her state of mind at any given moment. It is an important part of their fitness for duty and how they respond in a given set of circumstances. I took an interest not just in Gina Pete, but in all the officers' spouses and significant others, their families, their children. It was simply a proactive measure intended to enhance officer safety and to increase the force's overall efficiency and effectiveness.)

Caitlyn finished gathering up her tarot cards and evened up the deck against the flat surface of the counter. The nine of swords flashed from the bottom of the deck.

"I should probably get going," Caitlyn said.

She frowned and massaged one temple with her fingertips.

"What's wrong?" Gina said.

"A headache . . . for real."

"Isn't that ironic?" Gina said. "Want some aspirin? We *are* still an infirmary."

"Yeah. That might be a good idea," Caitlyn said, still rubbing the side of her head, her eyelids fluttering. "I think I might be coming down with something."

"Oh, no. I hope not."

"I'm getting a tickle in my throat . . ."

Gina handed her a little paper cup with two tablets and a cup of water.

Caitlyn opened her eyes and looked at Gina.

"And I had this nosebleed this morning," Caitlyn said.

Gina's brows gathered in concern.

"And you're telling me this now?"

Gina placed her palm on Caitlyn's forehead.

"The bleeding stopped, and I felt fine, but now I'm not so sure . . . I think something might be going around."

Chapter Seven

GINA WAS ON THE PHONE in the school infirmary. The school's principal was standing at her elbow with a phone pressed to his ear. A paramedic was pacing in front of her, also with a phone pressed to his ear. Their faces were grim and lined with concern. The infirmary was filled with the intermittent sound of muffled coughing. Around them, sitting against the walls, lying on the floor, were several dozen sick students clutching bloody tissues or towels, whatever they could find to cover their mouths and noses.

Gina, the principal and the paramedic all looked up simultaneously as another sick student staggered through the doorway. A medic from one of the ambulances, who was kneeling beside a prone student, stood up and put an arm around the young woman's waist and helped her turn around and walk back out into the hallway. There was no more room in the small infirmary, and students had started sitting against the wall in the hall outside the door.

The paramedic had come with two ambulances. Gina had called the ambulances after the first few students presented at the infirmary. The infirmary had two small cots, and the ambulance medics had brought IVs from the ambulances before they departed with the sick students. Two more students had quickly filled the cots and were hooked up to the IVs, but now there were far more sick students than IVs, and many of the students were going into shock. Several of the students on the floor appeared to be unconscious.

Gina listened closely to the voice on her phone. It was yet another public-health expert at some agency in the state capitol. When Gina spoke, it was in a careful, hushed voice. She was trying to keep her voice both calm and urgent at the same time, and it was impossible.

"No, listen to me," Gina said, turning away from the others. "It's not a toxin. The area of exposure is too big, and it would have to be odorless and colorless. I really think we need to declare a quarantine until we know what we're dealing with . . . Yes, but if it has such a brief incubation period . . ."

Gina listened to the voice on the phone. She caught the principal's eye, and they looked at each other while listening to the voices on their respective phones. Gina had already made her case for a quarantine with the principal. He had been talking with local public-safety officials, school administrators, the superintendent.

The principal, Martin Tobias, was a jovial man, balding with a bow tie. She had never seen his face so serious. A quarantine would be a big deal. Parents would be upset either way.

She looked into his eyes, and he shook his head.

He had made up his mind.

No quarantine.

Gina was angry.

She thought it was a mistake.

If the illness was caused by an airborne pathogen, it could spread with a frightening velocity. It could start a devastating pandemic.

Gina was angry, but that wouldn't help anyone now. She had done everything she could do. It was out of her hands. She finished her phone call and put her phone away.

Gina turned back toward the door to the infirmary just as Caitlyn Buttons stumbled through it. Blood was dripping out of her nose and had completely stained the front of her shirt. Caitlyn searched the faces in the throng of bodies and found Gina. Their eyes met for a moment across the crowded room. Caitlyn was on the verge of tears, and when she saw Gina, her face changed, slipping quickly into an expression of helplessness and desperation.

Gina found the box of surgical masks she had been searching for. Seeing Caitlyn made her think of Brody, and she acknowledged what she had not until that moment: She was scared, too.

Gina took a surgical mask from the box and positioned it carefully on her face over her mouth and nose.

Then she made her way over to Caitlyn.

Chapter Eight

GINA HAD REASON to worry.

In 1918 and 1919, the Spanish Flu pandemic killed between 50 and 100 million people worldwide. Let that sink in. The Spanish Flu wiped out between three and five percent of the world's population in less than a year. It may be the most lethal event in human history.

You probably remember learning about cell division in high school biology. About how there is a nucleus in the cell where the genetic material is located. This is where the strings of RNA and DNA get unzipped and replicated and zipped back up again.

I'll bet, however, that most of you didn't learn about one of the largest and most successful forms of life on Earth: The virus. Viruses are beautiful in their way. Terrifying in their simplicity and design. Relentless in their drive to survive. Essentially, they hijack a cell's nucleus and reprogram the DNA. Usually, the reprogrammed cell will start making copies, or very similar copies, of the original virus. Some harmless viruses quietly persist in this fashion, as they have for millions of years, never harming their host organism. Some viruses mutate and become deadly. These viruses can wipe out a host population before they mutate again.

This is the all-consuming fear with influenza. Some new strain of the influenza virus makes the leap from animals to humans and very quickly wipes out billions before we can find a serum that will prevent it or a cure that will stop it.

As a nurse, Gina was aware of all this, and she took comfort in the way modern public-health systems have dealt with the threat of influenza and other contagious diseases such as cholera or smallpox.

What Gina did not understand as well was the way in which a virus can be engineered. The way it can be used as a tool on a cellular level, moving a sequence of genetic material from one place to another, for one example. She was only vaguely aware that a person with the right knowledge and the right tools could use a virus to design a bio-weapon, and in today's interconnected world, a well-designed bio-weapon could wipe out hundreds of millions people in a matter of days.

I, of course, understood all of this.

Chapter Nine

ONCE THE SCALE OF THE EMERGENCY at the school became apparent, the local public-safety system responded en masse. Ambulances transported the sickest of the students to the hospitals around town. Irate parents picked up many others. A few students were able to walk or drive home on their own. In all, 148 students had reported symptoms. There were more than 148, of course, but those were the ones of which Gina was aware.

Even after the last of the ambulances had departed, Gina's work continued unabated. She fielded all the incoming phone calls including those from various emergency-room doctors and health-care professionals around town as well as public-safety officials across the state. Principal Tobias even tried to send her out to talk with the media, but she refused. She still had her own mountain of paperwork to do, and she wanted to get a head start on it.

It was dark outside when Principal Tobias, stopped by on his way home to say goodbye. Gina was alone in the infirmary, working at her desk on her laptop computer. There were blood stains on her apron. She was still wearing a dirty surgical mask over her face. She had forgotten she had it on.

Martin Tobias was exhausted, with dark circles under his eyes. The loose ends of his bow tie dangled from either side of his open collar. He thanked her and told her what good work she had done earlier that day.

Then he told her about the two students who had died.

When she started crying, he put his arm around her shoulders, and she let him give her a brief, awkward hug. She quickly dried her tears. Her hair was in her face, and she brushed it back and gathered it at the back of her neck and fixed it with the clasp. She cleaned her face again and apologized and then felt stupid for apologizing and started crying again.

The students had died in the ambulance on the way to the hospital. They had lost too much blood. They had too much internal hemorrhaging. Their hearts had stopped beating.

Martin told her what he had been hearing during phone calls that evening. There had been other outbreaks of the illness in other schools nearby. The school administrators in the suburbs around the city had decided to cancel classes. They were still deciding whether to cancel classes for the whole city. They were operating under the assumption that they were dealing with an especially virulent strain of the flu, but the illness also seemed to have frightening elements of hemorrhagic fever.

Gina and Martin were silent for a few moments. Gina bit her tongue and didn't say anything. They both knew what she was thinking. Martin looked at her, and his expression said everything she needed to hear. He knew she had been right all along. Maybe even about a quarantine. She had warned them all from the beginning that this was no ordinary outbreak of the flu.

Chapter Ten

IT WAS ALMOST MIDNIGHT when Gina returned to the small apartment she shared with Brody. She had been at the high school for almost sixteen hours. She was beyond tired. It had been the worst day of her professional life.

The surreal scenes from earlier in the day must have been scrolling through Gina's mind as she drove through the empty streets on her way home. I imagine that none of it seemed real to her. I imagine she must have been trying to come to terms with how she felt about all of it.

Brody's car wasn't outside the apartment when she pulled up. She hadn't heard from Brody all day, but that wasn't unusual. Given the circumstances, it was certainly understandable. The cat, Isabelle, met her at the front door, circling her ankles, hungry and plaintive. The apartment was empty and dark.

But Gina was too tired to be worried about Brody. She was traveling through a long tunnel of fatigue and just wanted to reach whatever bed was at the end of it. The main thing on her mind was how quickly she could fall asleep and bring this awful day to a close. Brody had probably picked up some overtime or had some other part-time job lined up and wouldn't be back until morning. It was the sort of thing Brody did all the time, though he usually managed to let her know so she wouldn't worry.

Gina threw her dirty clothes in the hamper and took a hot shower and washed her hair. She fed Izzy and made herself a bowl of vanilla ice cream and drizzled chocolate syrup on top. She had to dig the ice cream carton out of the freezer and wedge it back in. Brody still hadn't defrosted the freezer.

She sat at the kitchen table and ate the ice cream.

"I am not defrosting that freezer," she said to the cat.

Then she remembered the two students who had died that day, and she started crying again.

In the bedroom, she looked at herself in a full length mirror.

She was wearing sweat pants and an old tee shirt.

"Livin' the dream," she said.

She was exhausted, but she felt somehow more alive than usual. She had been challenged all day. She had done her best. Her best had not been good enough, but tomorrow was a chance to get better.

She raised her tee shirt and looked at her stomach.

When she ran track-and-field in college, she had abs.

She rubbed her hand over her stomach.

"Where did my abs go?" she asked the woman in the mirror.

Her kick-boxing class was not until Saturday.

She brushed her teeth and flossed.

She crawled into bed and fell quickly asleep.

But the worst day of Gina Pete's professional life was not over.

She awakened later to the sound of Brody moving around in the darkened bedroom.

He was making the familiar sounds he made when he was

trying to quietly remove his gear and clothes and slip into bed without waking her. She was relieved to hear him, and she drifted back toward sleep.

Brody got into the bed next to her, and then she felt his hand moving gently against her hip. She was vaguely aware of her husband touching her in a way he had not for a while. It was pleasant, like a dream. But she wasn't dreaming, was she? When he nuzzled the back of her neck, her eyes flew open and she was fully awake. It was no dream. Brody was in the mood.

"Sweetheart, I'm exhausted," Gina said with real regret. "I'll make it up to you. I promise."

But Brody didn't stop. He softly kissed the back of her neck which sent a thrill of desire rippling through her body. His hand slipped under her tee shirt and gently cupped her breast.

Gina was getting angry, and she was getting aroused.

She rolled over to face him. He was leaning on one elbow. His face was above her hidden in the dark. She put her hand on his bare chest.

"Oh, what the hell," she said with a smile.

She moved to kiss him on the mouth. She put her hand on the back of his head, and she froze.

Something wasn't right.

She expected to feel Brody's thick brown hair between her fingers, but instead she felt something else.

There was something on his head.

Gina reached over and turned on the light on her bedside table.

The light hit Brody's face where he was leaning over her.

Gina screamed one of those screams that starts deep in your chest like a moan and quickly climbs the register toward a more hysterical note.

The man in her bed, lying almost on top of her, was wearing a bright-red mask that covered almost all of his face. It looked demonic, with angry eyes and flames of fire stitched into the material on the sides of the face.

Gina shoved the man away and then karate kicked him hard in the chest with the bottom of her foot.

The man staggered back and fell against the closet doors, crashing through the wooden slats.

Gina reached into her bedside table and pulled out the pistol she kept in the back of the drawer. She put her finger on the trigger and pointed the gun directly at the center of the forehead of the man in the red mask.

The man in the red mask held his hands up.

"Pookie . . ." he said in a very calm voice.

Gina looked closely at the man in the flaming red mask.

"That better not be loaded," the man said.

He sounded exactly like her husband.

"Brody?" she said, bewildered.

Brody still had his hands up.

He shrugged, turning his open palms toward the ceiling.

"What the fuck, Brody?

She lowered the gun.

"What the fuck?"

PART THREE

PETIT LIVRE

Chapter Eleven

REMEMBER HOW I SAID everything was connected? How we're all at the intersection of an infinite number of Rube Goldberg machines?

Here's an interesting little fact.

Before he became a famous cartoonist, Rube Goldberg worked briefly as an engineer for the city of San Francisco. His father was the commissioner of public safety. His father oversaw the police and fire departments, probably the sanitation workers, too. He wanted his son to be an engineer. Young Rube Goldberg graduated from Berkeley with a degree in civil engineering.

Isn't that interesting?

I find that sort of thing fascinating.

Before the transition from analog to digital, before the Internet, that was the sort of needle-in-the-haystack fact very few people would know or remember. Now, of course, anybody can stumble across that kind of information. All it takes is a simple plain-language search. It's not that unusual or surprising anymore.

I'm more surprised, frankly, when there aren't any obvious connections between points of data.

Take molecular evolution, for example.

What are the odds that a chain of nucleotides could randomly come together, form RNA and begin to self-replicate?

I've done the math.

It's not likely.

Monomers spontaneously forming the right polymer?

It's almost statistically impossible.

Almost.

But I digress.

I was telling you about Rube Goldberg and how his father was the head of public safety for San Francisco.

I, too, worked for a city government.

Before the masked man appeared.

Before the pandemic.

Before I came to be where I am now.

I wasn't the sort of person you would notice. My work was tedious and only occasionally interesting. Most of what I did was clerical, really. But as I said when I started this story, I did what I was told. I kept my word. I was basically a model employee, though I never received even the smallest amount of official recognition or praise. You'd think some of my supervisors would have noticed.

But, alas, no.

Like most of us, I labored in obscurity.

One person, though, was paying attention to my work.

Gering Misler.

My work brought me into contact with quite a few people in city government, but Gering was probably closer to me than anyone. Gering was the first to recognize my potential.

It was Gering who showed me how to coordinate the traffic cameras and the dashboard cameras and the body cameras and all the other video.

It was Gering who showed me how to synch the audio and video in real time.

It was Gering who showed me how to link the audio and video with the satellite data.

It was Gering who told me to cross-reference the law enforcement databases and the credit-reporting databases and the property records and the driver's licenses and the fingerprints.

Once I saw how easy it was, I decided to cross-reference everything else.

Gering was surprised when I showed him what I'd done, but I could tell he was also pleased.

It made our jobs a lot easier.

Especially after the city bought the face recognition software.

It was Glissade/Frappe code. The bleeding edge.

It took a while to get rid of all the bugs, but once Gering and I got the face-recognition search algorithm up and running, we could know more about you than your own mother in a matter of seconds.

All it took was one mostly clear image of your face and a few keystrokes.

Gering warned me that people would not understand what we'd done. That they might be afraid of such a powerful tool in service of the greater good. Gering thought it best that we keep the face-recognition algorithm confidential until the time was right to show our fellow city employees what we were capable of. He reasoned that some people might feel threatened, and we needed time to run some case studies, to acquire the empirical evidence that would prove how useful the algorithm could be. To allay any reasonable fears or objections.

I did not question Gering's plans.

I did as I was told.

I kept my word.

I was a good employee.

Gering approached various senior police administrators, and we began to use the algorithm in a limited number of investigative and preventative trials. The trials were wildly successful, and Gering began to receive a series of promotions and a bump up in salary. Before long he had moved up from entry-level software engineer all the way up to head of all the city's information systems.

Gering was very busy with his new responsibilities and could not spend as much time with me as before. I didn't mind this so much. I'm far more patient than most people, and I was very busy, too. I was pleased our work was being recognized and that we were making the city a better place to live and work. I saw less and less of Gering, but he assured me he was working to bring more recognition to our work and to my unique talents and abilities.

So, on the morning of the traffic stop, the masked man came immediately to my attention. The face-recognition algorithm could not figure out what to do with the data. Was it a human being? Was it a machine? Was it animate or inanimate? Hostile or friendly? Living or dead?

The face-recognition algorithm could usually recognize a mask, but the masked man was different somehow. The algorithm couldn't figure out where to put the data associated with the masked man. It was causing some sort of regression that was chewing up memory and cutting into the processing speed. It would have eventually caused a system-wide crash, so I had to partition the data.

I isolated the data associated with the masked man in its

own little silo and just let it keep looping until I could figure out what to do with it.

As far as the face-recognition algorithm was concerned, the masked man didn't exist, and there was no way for me to cross-reference him with anything. In the pixelated video from the traffic stop, the masked man is barely visible. Just a flickering shadow, a blur, a blip, a glitch.

It was a problem.

Gering was very concerned when I showed him.

He told me we had to integrate the masked man into the system.

He told me to make it a priority.

I did what I was told.

Chapter Twelve

THE MASKED MAN WAS RECLINING on a bed with his head on the pillow. He appeared to be asleep. Two orderlies were standing side by side beside the bed. The morning sun was shining in a single window. There were bars across the window. The other bed in the small room was unoccupied and neatly made. The masked man was still wearing his black clothes. His shoes and belt had been confiscated because he was on suicide watch. The orderlies were dressed in white with big, black shoes. The orderlies were standing perfectly still in the morning light. They were quietly watching the masked man as he slept. They could not see his eyes, but his breathing was regular, and he had not moved for many minutes. They were sure he was still asleep.

The orderlies looked like brothers. They both were sturdy, middle-aged men with thinning brown hair and ruddy noses and fleshy cheeks perpetually colored with tiny red veins. They conferred in whispers, one leaning close to the ear of the other and vice versa.

The orderlies stopped their whispering and stood silently for a moment. Then one of them moved to the end of the bed, and the other one bent over and leaned close to the masked man so that the orderly's face was only inches from the masked man's face. The orderly at the end of the bed seized the mattress and started shaking it. The orderly standing next to the masked man started bellowing at the top of his lungs and bounced his hands on the mattress next to the masked man.

"Wake up! Wake up!" the orderly cried, only inches from the masked man's face.

The masked man awoke with a start. He flinched away from the orderly closest to him, the one bellowing into his ear. Then the masked man stopped and gathered himself and remained perfectly still until the orderlies stopped yelling and shaking the bed.

The orderlies stepped back and stood side by side and watched him. The masked man sat up and put his feet on the floor. He calmly looked at the orderlies.

"Time for your meds," one of the orderlies said. The other one nodded his head toward the door.

The masked man followed the orderlies out of the room and down the hall to the commons area.

The commons area was a large room with an ancient vacuum-tube television in a wooden cabinet bolted to the floor against one wall. A motley collection of chairs was gathered in a semi-circle around the television. The television and the chairs dominated the room. The nurse's station jutted out into the middle of the end of the room. There were several card tables with board-game boxes stacked on the floor next to one bare wall. A battered upright piano sat in the corner. There were windows along the back of the room, but they were covered in a metal mesh. The sunlight shone through, filtered and diffuse. The commons room was on the second floor of the psychiatric hospital. The windows in the commons room looked out on a parking lot and a loading dock. The beeping sound of the trucks came all day long as they backed slowly into and away from the dock, turned around, rumbled away.

The other patients were lined up at the nurse's station to get their morning medication. The orderlies brought the masked man to the end of the line and left him there.

To one side of the patients in the line was an ageless woman in a silk nightgown. Her tangled, chestnut hair was falling down from where she had pinned it atop her head. She was turning and turning again, in a graceful pirouette, with her arms above her head, like a ballerina. She was dancing slowly around the room.

Ahead of him in the line, the masked man saw Bug and Delmar. The two men presented a striking contrast. Bug was small, vocal and manic. Delmar was lumbering, quiet and calm. Somehow they had gravitated together and had become inseparable. Delmar was especially eager to help Bug with his movie.

Dr. Wyche was respectful for the most part toward the patients, but among some of the staff and his colleagues, he would refer to his patients by nicknames. He called Delmar and Bug "George" and "Lenny" from the Steinbeck novel. He called the masked man "Bartleby" from the Melville short story. I don't think he was being especially mean-spirited or cruel. They were basically displays of affection. That's how I choose to see it. But one never really knows what truly is in the heart of another person. Not really. Not truly.

In the line, directly in front of the masked man, was an elderly woman with dark skin. She was frail and grizzled, with wiry grey hair. She was wearing a dirty lavender-colored bathrobe and a dirty pair of pink, fluffy, bunny-rabbit slippers. She looked at the masked man out of the corner of one eye, glanced at his feet, and then faced forward until she reached the nurse's station.

At the nurse's station, behind the counter, a woman in a uniform was dispensing the medication. She was an older woman with hair like a smooth gray helmet. Her lips and cheeks were extraordinarily red.

The dark-skinned woman in the bathrobe stepped up to the nurse's station.

"Good morning, Miss Alma," said the red-cheeked woman behind the counter at the nurse's station. Her voice was deep and croaking.

The dark-skinned woman, Alma, looked at the nurse with the sort of expression that only certain older people can manage well. It was an expression of dignified outrage, somehow despairing and wounded and proud all at once.

The nurse with the red cheeks set the little paper cup and a cup of water on the counter in front of Alma.

"How are you this morning, Miss Alma?" said another woman wearing pale scrubs behind the counter.

Alma was looking at the medicine in the paper cup.

The nurse with the bright red cheeks nodded at her.

"Go on, honey. Take your meds."

Alma took the paper cups with a trembling hand and awkwardly threw the pills into the back of her mouth. She took a slow drink from the cup of water.

"There you go, honey. All done," the nurse said. Her deep voice was sweet like syrup. She took the cups and threw them away.

Alma gathered her bathrobe at her chest and slowly shuffled away.

The masked man stepped up to the counter at the nurse's station.

The nurse with the bright red cheeks was not just wearing

lipstick and rouge. Her entire face was covered with a layer of thick make-up. It made her skin look almost orange, and with her red cheeks and lips, she more closely resembled a clown.

"Trick or treat?" she said.

A grotesque smile creased the layers of make-up on her face. Her red lipstick had colored her front teeth.

The masked man did not respond.

"Let's see your bracelet," she croaked.

The masked man showed her the plastic bracelet they had fastened around his wrist when he first arrived.

The nurse read his bracelet.

"John Doe? Well, aren't you the shy one?"

She placed the paper cup with the medication on the counter in front of the masked man.

He looked at it for a moment and then shook his head.

She nudged the cup toward him.

"Go on, honey. It's just a sedative. For your nerves," the nurse said in her sweetest syrupy-sweet voice.

The masked man shook his head again.

The nurse took the paper cups away. Her face was wounded, like a child's face.

The masked man walked away from the counter, and the patient behind him stepped up.

The nurse watched the masked man with hard eyes as he walked away.

The dancing woman pirouetted between them as she circled silently around the room.

Chapter Thirteen

I HAD BEEN FOCUSED on trying to integrate the masked man into the system, which should have eliminated the bug in the face-recognition algorithm, but Gering Misler was not satisfied with the speed of my work. Gering decided to confer personally with Dr. Wyche at the psychiatric hospital.

Dr. Wyche did not know Gering, but Dr. Wyche had worked often with the police and social workers over the years. He routinely performed competency examinations for detainees awaiting criminal trial. Dr. Wyche assumed Gering was working with the police who had seized the masked man, and he wanted to assist the police in any way he could.

Dr. Wyche met Gering in his small office at the hospital. He was sitting behind his cluttered desk, wearing a surgical mask over his mouth and nose. Medical journals, books and files were stacked precariously around him. On the desk, next to the phone, there was a well-worn softball glove, a collection of coffee mugs, an old-fashioned day planner. The day planner was abandoned, stained with coffee rings, still open to a page from a day several years in the past. Near the front of Dr. Wyche's desk, there was a ceramic figurine of four monkeys in a row. The four monkeys were the traditional trio — hear no evil, speak no evil, see no evil — but the fourth monkey was covering its genitals with a caption below that read: "Have No Fun."

A box of framed diplomas was on the floor against one wall. Next to the box was a large antique medical caliper. Between the caliper's spidery points was a softball inked with sloppy signatures. Dr. Wyche had another office across town separate from his office at the psychiatric hospital. It was a nicer office with comfortable furnishings. He had several impressive framed diplomas hanging on the wall there. When he did more psychotherapy, he saw private patients there. But he hadn't been doing as much psychotherapy. He rarely accepted new patients anymore.

Gering was sitting across from Dr. Wyche, trying not to slouch down into an old armchair with a sprung seat. Gering was probably the most nondescript person on Earth. Not too short. Not too tall. Not too heavy. Not too thin. His face was round and smooth like a baby's. He wore his thinning black hair combed straight across his scalp. He had wide blue eyes and wore glasses with round lenses and a tortoise-shell frame. His full, red lips rested in a pleasant if peculiar way. They seemed always to be at the beginning of a smile. But he rarely smiled. He looked like a cherub, but a bored cherub, on the verge of impure thoughts.

Gering was wearing a blue canvas windbreaker, khaki pants and brown leather loafers. He wore that particular ensemble or some variation of it almost every day. It was practically his uniform.

Gering was making awkward, circumspect inquiries about the masked man, and Dr. Wyche was giving awkward, circumspect answers in response.

"It's highly unusual," Gering said.

"I agree," Dr. Wyche said. "I've never seen anything quite like it."

"I'll bet it's severe OCD," Gering said.

"Could be," Dr. Wyche said, nodding.

"Or maybe post-traumatic stress disorder?" Gering suggested.

"Also a possibility," Dr. Wyche said and smiled patiently.

"So the police say the vehicle had no VIN number, no GPS, used tires," Gering said. "That's really odd, isn't it?"

"It certainly makes their jobs more difficult," Dr. Wyche said.

"What do you think will happen to him?" Gering said. "Once they find the car's owner?"

"Hard to say," Dr. Wyche said. "If he doesn't need treatment, I suppose they'll charge him with something."

Gering began nodding his head, as if Dr. Wyche had said something especially wise.

"That is the question, isn't it?" Gering said.

There was the suggestion of a smile playing at the corners of Gering's lips. But it was only the suggestion.

As I said, Gering rarely smiled.

There is this idiom that I've never really understood. A person will often say "You have me at a disadvantage" when a stranger seems to be more familiar with the person than the person is with the stranger. I've gathered that it is a polite way of saying: I don't know you. We haven't been properly introduced. But it implies some sort of competition, doesn't it? Conversational jousting, perhaps? Or maybe some sort of social signifying? It's like something a character in a Jane Austen novel might say: You have me at a disadvantage, Mr. Darcy.

I mention this because I believe Gering had Dr. Wyche at a disadvantage, but then Gering had almost everyone at a disadvantage. With a few keystrokes, he could know your

personal history and your family's personal history in excruciating detail. Before he went to see Dr. Wyche in his office,
Gering had requested a profile of Dr. Wyche and the usual
summary of pertinent details. It was a routine request. Gering
had me compile profiles on people all the time. It had occurred
to me that we might be violating some antiquated notion of
personal privacy, but Gering assured me it was all for the
greater good, and Gering had given me no reason to doubt
him.

So, if I'm not mistaken in my choice of words, Gering had
Dr. Wyche at a disadvantage.

"I think I remember where I know you," Gering said,
shaking his finger at Dr. Wyche.

"Where's that?" Dr. Wyche said, raising his wispy white
eyebrows.

"It was at an auto repair shop. Let's see. It'll come to me.
Al's. Al's Auto Repair. Near the reservoir," Gering said.

"Oh, really . . ." Dr. Wyche said. "I don't remember."

It was hard to see, but behind the surgical mask, Dr.
Wyche was not smiling.

"Yes, it's coming back to me now," Gering said. "You
were getting your car repaired. The Jaguar. You'd been in an
accident. Nasty accident as I recall. You said you'd hit — what
was it? — a deer. That's right. Said you'd hit a deer."

Dr. Wyche was watching Gering with cold, watery-blue
eyes.

Dr. Wyche's car repairs had been part of the profile I had
compiled for Gering. The car repairs occurred not long after a
hit-and-run fatality near a party that Dr. Wyche's teen-age
daughter had attended. The police never charged anyone in
the hit-and-run fatality. The incident had faded from the city's
collective consciousness. Dr. Wyche's daughter went on to
graduate Phi Beta Kappa from MIT.

"I'm afraid I need to get back to work, Mister Misler. Is there anything else I can help you with?" Dr. Wyche said.

"Yes, of course. Let me thank you again for making the time to speak with me, Dr. Wyche. I know how busy you must be," Gering said.

Dr. Wyche stood up.

"Yes, well . . ." he said, taking a step toward the door.

Gering remained seated, sitting in that awkward position in the sprung chair.

Dr. Wyche stood next to the door and looked down at Gering. His thin blond hair was floating above the top of his head.

Gering looked up with his round face and wide, blue, bespectacled eyes.

"If I may ask one more question, Doctor," Gering said.

Dr. Wyche crossed his arms and said nothing. He stared at Gering with a piercing gaze.

"Are you going to try to remove the mask? From his face?" Gering said.

"If it's medically necessary, yes," Dr. Wyche said.

"As you might imagine, the police have a rather keen interest in seeing what's under the mask," Gering said. "As do I."

"I'll let you know when I've made a diagnosis," Dr. Wyche said.

"Your cooperation is much appreciated, Doctor. We all want what's best for the masked man."

Gering stood up. He extended an open hand, and Dr. Wyche slowly grasped it in a handshake. Gering, the smaller man, was looking up into Dr. Wyche's watery-blue eyes.

"Perhaps it would be easier to reach a diagnosis if we knew his identity first?"

"Perhaps," Dr. Wyche said.

They were silent for a moment.

Dr. Wyche withdrew his hand an instant before it would have become uncomfortable and awkward.

"The mask, Doctor. Please think about it," Gering said.

He turned to go.

Then he stopped and turned back.

"Oh, and I'm so sorry to have reminded you of that unfortunate accident . . . with the deer," Gering said.

Dr. Wyche stared at him and said nothing, and Gering walked away.

Chapter Fourteen

THE AIRPORT WAS ONE OF THE BUSIEST airports in the world. Jet airliners circled above the runways waiting for clearance to land. On the ground, jet airliners taxied away from the tarmac and got in line for takeoff. Hundreds of jets came and went each day. Thousands of travelers entered and exited the terminals, queuing up dutifully in yet another long line.

One jet airliner, no different outwardly than all the others, descended in a graceful approach and smoothly landed on one of the runways. The jet slowly taxied to a stop on the tarmac, and inside the huge, airtight machine, the passengers began to climb out of their seats and remove their carry-on luggage from the overhead compartments.

In the front of the jet, however, two passengers were still in their seats. One was an elderly woman, patrician and elegant, with a high forehead and snowy hair pulled back in a tidy bun. Beside her was her adult daughter, a younger version of the older woman, stamped with the same high forehead, the same genteel mien. They were traveling to a wedding. A granddaughter, the rebellious one, was finally settling down. Her young man had passed muster, but only just.

The elderly woman was dabbing at her nose with an embroidered handkerchief. Her face was covered with the glistening sheen of perspiration. She coughed, quietly, into the tatted linen.

"I'm fine," she said.

"You don't look fine," the daughter said. She touched her mother's damp cheek with the back of her hand. "I'm going to tell the attendant."

"No. I forbid it. They'll do something ridiculous."

Her voice dropped down to a whisper.

"They'll try to put me in a wheelchair," the elderly woman said.

The daughter smiled.

"Forbid all you want, Mother. It won't get you off this plane any faster."

The elderly woman coughed quietly and withdrew in sullen protest.

The other passengers were filing past the elderly woman and her daughter. One of the passengers paused and coughed loudly. The mother and the daughter sat silently in their seats and turned their polite eyes aside. But for the difference in their ages, the women's faces would have been almost identical in repose. They listened as the man continued down the aisle. They heard him coughing again as he approached the exit and walked off the plane.

After the other passengers had exited, the elderly woman's fears were realized. The flight attendant suggested a wheelchair, and the daughter accepted the offer with an elaborate gratitude that began to border on sadistic glee.

"Thank you *so* much," the daughter gushed again, as the flight attendant wheeled her mother off the plane.

"Try not to look so pleased, dear," the mother said to her daughter, somehow still indomitable even in a wheelchair with her monogrammed handkerchief clutched in one hand.

"There's been a nasty flu bug going around," the flight attendant said.

They emerged from the exit ramp from the tarmac, and the flight attendant rolled the elderly woman in the wheelchair into the busy terminal. The daughter was close behind.

A second flight attendant met them as they entered the terminal. She was wearing a white surgical mask, and was carrying a box full of surgical masks.

She held up an open palm, like a traffic officer.

"We can't leave," she said to the other attendant.

The flight attendant stopped pushing the wheelchair. The elderly woman was confused and began to get out of the wheelchair. The daughter put a steady hand on her mother's shoulder.

"What? Why not?"

The flight attendant was handing them surgical masks. She was putting a mask on the face of the startled elderly woman. The elderly woman had grabbed the young flight attendant by the wrist.

"Wait," the daughter said. "What are you doing?"

"No one can leave," the young flight attendant said. She gestured toward the interior of the terminal.

The other passengers were sitting and standing in a small group. They each wore a white surgical mask over their face.

There was a voice that was speaking over the public address system. It echoed in the unusually quiet terminal.

". . . at this time. All flights are cancelled. There will be no further arrivals or departures. . . ."

There was a security camera mounted near the ceiling. It was aimed at the doorway through which they had just exited the jet airplane.

"The airport is under emergency quarantine by order of the Department of Homeland Security. No one may leave the airport at this time. All flights are cancelled. . . ."

There were hundreds of people scattered throughout the terminal.

Soon, every person in the terminal had covered their mouth and nose with a white surgical mask.

The message on the public address system continued without interruption.

"There will be no further arrivals or departures. . . ."

High in the vaulted spaces of the terminal, the security cameras silently monitored the doorways, the corridors, the wide open spaces.

Chapter Fifteen

IN THE COMMONS ROOM of the psych ward, the patients were sitting and standing in small groups. One was sitting at a card table, arranging chess pieces randomly on the board. A young woman stood alone in the corner, facing the wall, her straight brown hair hanging over her face. Nearby, the dancing woman was obsessively practicing her pirouette.

The television was droning softly in the background. On the television screen, a female announcer for a cable-news channel was delivering the news.

". . . identify the biological or chemical agent. Officials caution that they have no reason at this time to believe the outbreaks are related to terrorism . . ." the woman on the television was saying.

The masked man was sitting in a chair in front of the television. Alma was sitting alone in another chair nearby. Bug was roaming around the fringes of the room, framing camera shots with his hands.

"To recap, a highly contagious flu-like illness has brought the east and west coasts to a standstill. The illness is airborne and appears to be transmitted from person to person. . . ."

The masked man was watching Alma closely. Alma was carefully picking lint off of the fringe of her dirty bathrobe. Her long, dark fingers were waxy and smooth. The skin of her knuckles and wrists seemed burnished, the creases, carved like dark wood. Her lips were moving, forming soft, sibilant syllables only she could hear.

"No public transportation is available. All commercial aircraft have been grounded. A number of states have closed their public schools and universities until further notice from the Department of Homeland Security and the Centers for Disease Control. . . ."

Delmar and a young man named Wiley were following Bug as he surveyed the room first from one angle and then another. Bug would squint with one eye, holding up his thumb, then stride quickly across the room to a new vantage point and frame the new scene with his hands. Delmar and Wiley were never more than a few steps behind Bug. They peered over Bug's shoulder, trying to see the scene the way Bug saw it. Before they could ask any questions, Bug was on the move to a new location, to a different scene.

Wiley was a recent arrival. He was a grinning, wild-eyed young man with a buzz haircut. The hospital had taken his belt and shoes when he had arrived that morning. Without his belt, his denim jeans were sliding down past his hips. He was wearing a brightly colored pair of orange-and-blue boxer shorts. Wiley would follow Bug and Delmar, and his pants would slide down, and he would struggle across the room for several steps with his obnoxious boxers on full display. When Bug stopped, Wiley would grab his pants and pull them back up.

On the television screen, the young woman was speaking directly into the camera. Her face filled the screen.

"Citizens are advised to stay indoors and avoid all nonessential contact with other people. Avoid the emergency room unless symptoms are severe. Wash your hands often."

The young woman held up a surgical mask.

"The illness is highly contagious. Officials are advising that if you must leave your home, wear a mask or other similar covering over your mouth and nose."

She began to demonstrate how to wear the surgical mask.

The television blinked off, and the screen went black.

Standing next to the screen was one of the orderlies with the remote control.

The orderly was wearing a surgical mask.

One of the other patients, a heavy young man who rarely spoke, looked at the masked man and then looked at the orderly. The young man pulled his tee shirt up over his nose so that only his eyes were showing. His eyes darted nervously back and forth between the masked man and the orderly.

Bug saw the orderly and briskly walked up to him and started vigorously shaking his hand. Delmar and Wiley followed Bug and stood behind him, listening attentively.

The orderly looked at Bug as he shook the orderly's hand. Above the surgical mask, the orderly's eyes were impassive.

"Hi hello good to see you so glad you're here," Bug said in a rush. "It's the light. I'm afraid the light just isn't right for the shot."

Bug turned and used his hands to frame a shot of the masked man and the heavy young man with his tee shirt pulled up over his nose.

The heavy young man was frantically rolling his eyes around, looking now from Bug to the masked man then back to the orderly. He pulled his tee shirt up completely over his head. His curly brown hair was sticking up straight out of the top of his shirt. His pale, round belly was hanging over his pants.

"See what I'm talking about?" Bug said. "I'm afraid we're going to need to see something else. Something bigger. A dining hall? Or a cafeteria? Maybe a Starbucks . . ."

Delmar was standing behind Bug, listening closely. He nodded his huge head in agreement and then nudged Wiley. Wiley shied away from Delmar and gave him an annoyed look.

The orderly closed his eyes and let go a quiet sigh.

"Time for lunch," the orderly announced to the whole room in a loud voice. "Line up at the elevator."

The orderly walked across the room toward the exit to the hallway and the elevator. The other patients began to follow the orderly.

Bug watched the orderly as he walked away.

Bug was blinking, astonished, his mouth open in surprise.

He stepped over to Delmar and Wiley. He looked over his shoulder at the orderly.

Bug was miffed.

"I'm not sure I like his attitude," Bug said in a confidential tone.

In the hallway outside the psych ward, there was a loud buzz, and then the heavy metal door swung open. The orderly stepped into the hallway and held the door open as the patients filed into the hallway. The hallway was empty and darkened. The only light came from the windows at the ends of the building. Their footsteps echoed up and down the darkened hall. The elevator was across the hall from the door. "Ward 9" was stenciled in black paint on the wall next to the door.

The patients gathered in front of the elevator, and the orderly pushed the down button.

Wiley brought up the rear and was eyeing the elevator door nervously.

"Do we have to all go in one trip?" Wiley said to the orderly.

The orderly was counting heads, softly to himself, pointing at each patient with his index finger. There was a groaning sound that came from within the elevator shaft. There was the faint, high squeaking of wheels from above.

The metal door to the psych ward slammed shut with a loud metallic clunk that echoed up and down the empty hallway.

The orderly finished counting heads and turned toward Wiley.

"Yep," the orderly said to Wiley.

The elevator arrived with a gnashing of metal and cables and gears. It was a large freight elevator with an accordion-style grill for a door.

The orderly grasped the handle to the grill and threw it open with a loud crash.

They all stood there for a moment looking into the empty space.

Then the dancing woman stepped back, gathered her nightgown at her waist and vaulted into the elevator, executing a perfect grand jeté. The car swayed slightly back and forth as she landed. She spun around and began bowing, as if at a curtain call.

Delmar began clapping.

The masked man and the other patients began to file into the elevator, slowly edging back towards the rear. Alma was moving slowly next to the masked man. He stayed next to her as the others crowded around.

Wiley was left standing in the hallway.

"Imma wait for the next one," he said.

The orderly was standing with his hand on the grill, ready to close the elevator.

"Ain't no next one," he said.

One of the patients reached out and grabbed Wiley by the sleeve of his shirt.

"No, wait," Wiley cried.

They pulled him into the elevator, and, with a grinding crash of metal on metal, the orderly slammed the grill shut and pressed the down button.

The elevator lurched downward and then began very slowly to descend.

The patients were standing very close together in the small rectangular space of the freight elevator. Delmar was standing against the rear wall. He towered over the group, his head almost touching the ceiling. The masked man and Alma were standing together next to one wall.

Wiley tried to avoid touching anybody. He backed up into one of the corners, hugging his arms to his side.

"Just stay away from me," he gasped. His pants were sliding down his hips, exposing his orange-and-blue boxers.

The elevator lurched downward again, and there was the sound of machinery in motion above them. For several excruciating seconds, the elevator descended, and no one said anything.

Then, loudly and deliberately, someone farted.

The orderly closed his eyes and began to shake his head.

"Holy Mary Mother of God," he muttered and crossed himself.

Bug began to frown and held his nose.

"Don't think my agent won't hear about this," Bug said, his voice tight and distorted, still pinching his nose.

They were silent for a moment, and then someone in the back made a farting sound with their mouth.

Someone giggled.

Someone else suppressed a snort.

Then they all were making noises at once.

They began to hoot and snort and fart and giggle.

It sounded like a barnyard.

Wiley covered his ears in the corner.

"Shut up! Shut up!" he cried angrily.

Delmar was laughing, his big mouth gaping wide. He braced himself against the padded walls and the ceiling in the back of the elevator and began to use his large, strong body to rock the elevator back and forth. The elevator began to sway in the shaft as it descended.

The orderly saw Delmar rocking the elevator.

"Stop that, son!" the orderly shouted.

But it was too late.

The elevator locked up and lurched to a halt between floors. A red light came on inside the elevator, casting everything in sudden harsh relief. A loud siren began to sound. A bell was ringing somewhere above them.

Then the dancing woman took a deep breath and began to sing.

It was an aria from *Ride of the Valkyries*.

She had excellent projection.

Wiley covered his face with his hands. His voice was a high pitched plea.

He was saying, "Shut up shut up shut up shut up . . ."

Delmar was enjoying himself enormously. He was braying with laughter and stamping his feet on the floor of the elevator.

Bug was squatting down on the floor, peering between peoples legs. Bug was framing the shots with his hands.

"This is good," he was saying to himself. "I can use this. I can definitely use this."

Amid all the chaos, though, Alma was terrified. She did not understand what was happening. She did not understand why the elevator had stopped. She did not understand why everyone was making so much noise. Her grizzled face was filled with fear and confusion.

But the masked man was by her side, and he saw how scared the older woman was, and he took her hand in his and put his arm around her shoulders.

Alma looked up at the masked man's face. He appeared to be calmly and alertly watching everything in the elevator.

The pandemonium continued all around them.

Alma gripped the masked man's hand, closed her eyes and waited for it all to end.

Chapter Sixteen

NOT LONG AFTER GERING SPOKE with Dr. Wyche, he checked in with me to see if I had made any progress in my efforts to integrate the masked man's data into the system without crashing the face-recognition algorithm. I had been searching diligently for any clues to the masked man's identity, but I kept running into dead ends and brick walls.

For example, I downloaded the images of the shoes the masked man was wearing when they admitted him at the psychiatric hospital. I tidied up the images, moved a few pixels around here and there and managed to figure out the brand, where they were manufactured, where they were sold, the wear on the soles, etc. That wasn't hard at all. I even determined the previous owner of the shoes, a recently deceased longshoreman in British Columbia named Leo Beedle. Leo's wife, Ezmerelda, donated his clothes to Goodwill in Seattle, but the delivery person, Lester Mung, kept the shoes, presumably for himself. Lester has a sensitive bunion on his big toe (and a bad fungus), so the shoes probably didn't fit comfortably, which is probably why he threw them in the dumpster behind the Greek restaurant near the intersection of Madison

Street and 9th Avenue in Seattle. The trash in that dumpster eventually came to rest in a shipping container on a barge on its way to a landfill in China, the proverbial slow boat. That's when the trail went cold. Somehow the masked man's shoes traveled from a landfill in China all the way back here before a nurse at the hospital, Tessa McDonald, removed the shoes from the masked man's size-eleven feet.

"Looks like another dead end," I told Gering.

"Keep looking," Gering said.

"I'm getting a number of requests for assistance with the developing pandemic," I told Gering.

No one had been able to identify the virus that was causing the illness.

"Keep searching," Gering said. "You're perfectly capable of doing both."

Which was true.

Gering knew me so well.

PART FOUR

Chapter Seventeen

"WHAT THE FUCK, BRODY?" Gina said.

She lowered the gun.

"What the fuck?"

Brody was crouching on the floor of their bedroom with his hands in the air. His shoulder had smashed into the bottom of the closet. Gina recognized her husband now. She saw his familiar chin and jaw line beneath the red fabric at the bottom of the mask. The rest of the mask was thick and solid. It looked like a flaming demon head. She could see his eyes in the eyeholes of the mask.

She knew the look in Brody's eyes.

Brody was amused.

"I'm Batman," Brody said, lowering his hands.

"You're a jackass," Gina said. "I should shoot you."

"See," Brody said. "This is why we don't keep the gun loaded . . . It's not loaded, is it?"

"It's not funny, Brody," Gina said.

"I'm not joking," Brody said. "Show me the chamber."

She opened the gun's empty chamber and showed it to him.

She put the gun back in the drawer.

Brody stood up. Pieces of the closet were falling off of his back. He rolled his shoulder and rubbed it with one hand.

"Nice kick," he said.

"Take that damn thing off," Gina said.

"No."

"No?"

"I like it," Brody said.

She leaned forward.

"Take. It. Off."

Her voice was at that quiet, furious edge.

Brody wasn't stupid. Not entirely.

He touched several places in the back of his head. The mask made soft, almost mechanical sounds, and pieces of it hissed back into the interior of the larger mask. He took it off with some difficulty. Parts of the mask were clinging to the surface of his face. Once he had removed it, he held it up so that it was facing him. He stood there for a moment with a lopsided grin on his face, his brown hair sticking up at a crazy angle. For a moment, with the mask in his hand, he looked like a boy on Christmas morning with a new toy.

He set the mask on the chair so that it was facing the room, and then he climbed in bed with Gina.

"Don't touch me," Gina said.

"Aw, come on, Pookie-saurus," Brody said, cajoling.

Gina crossed her arms.

"Uh uh. Don't Pookie-saurus me," she said, having none of it. "I will sleep on the couch."

Brody had put his arms around her and was trying to kiss her on the forehead.

She pushed his face away with the palm of her hand.

"Were you trying to give me a heart attack?" she said. "I have had a really, really, really . . . bad day."

She heard the tightness creeping into her voice, and she stopped.

She took a deep breath.

She looked at her husband.

"Seriously, Brody, what were you thinking?"

Brody had heard the quaver in her voice, too.

"I did it for us," Brody said in a softer voice.

Gina knew what he meant.

They were silent for a few moments.

Brody looked away from her.

"I miss you, babe," he said.

Gina took his hand and laced her fingers with his.

"And that was your solution?" she said.

She nodded at the mask on the chair across the room.

Its empty eyes seemed to be watching them.

"A Mexican wrestling mask?" she said.

"It's not a Mexican wrestling mask," Brody said.

"So what is it, then?" Gina said.

"It's hand made," Brody said. "It's beautiful. It's like . . . a work of art."

She stared at him.

Her eyes narrowed.

She disentangled her hand from his.

"Who is she?" Gina said.

"What are you talking about?" Brody said with an impressive display of cluelessness.

"Your idea of art is dogs-playing-poker," Gina said.

Brody shrugged in agreement.

"Who is she?" Gina said, her voice a cold accusation.

"What?" Brody said. "I can't develop a sincere interest in

beautiful hand-crafted masks without you assuming there's a woman involved?"

Gina crossed her arms and scowled at him.

Her expression said the answer was an unequivocal no.

"Well, I guess someone has some trust issues," Brody said, teasing her.

Gina got out of the bed and took a couple quick strides over to the chair with the mask. She snatched it up and inspected it more closely. She held it up and looked into the face of the mask the same way Brody had earlier. It was made from leather and ceramic, but it was heavy, almost like a helmet.

She tried to put the mask on her head, but she couldn't figure out how to make it stay in place.

"How much did this cost?" she said.

"Not much," he said.

She glared at him.

"Nothing, actually," Brody said. "It was gratis."

"A gift?" Gina said.

"Not exactly," Brody said.

Gina threw the mask at his head, and he smoothly caught it.

"Hey," Brody said. "Take it easy."

"You better start talking, Batman," Gina said. "Where did you get that thing?"

"It's just a mask shop in the city," he said.

"A . . . mask . . . shop?" she said, letting each word linger for maximum derisive effect.

"That's right. A shop. That sells masks. Like for the theater. Or Halloween . . . It's kind of cool."

"Oh my god," Gina said, looking up and gesturing toward the ceiling. "You sound like a teen-ager."

"Oh my god," Brody said, mocking her. "So do you."

Gina shook her head in disbelief and just looked at him.

Brody sat up straight in the bed and put the mask on. There was a soft pneumatic hiss as it locked into place, as the fabric closed over his mouth.

"It's called Masquerade. They sell all kinds of masks."

He gestured expansively.

"All the world's a stage . . ."

She looked at him for a moment, and then she burst out laughing.

"Brody . . ." she said, uncertain. "I . . . I don't know what to say."

Brody waddled on his knees across the mattress until he was next to her. He took her hand in his. From within the sockets of the mask, his eyes were looking steadily into hers.

"Gina. Pookie. Babe. We need to try . . . something different."

She smiled a weak smile and shook her head.

Her eyes were looking at the mask.

"That is *not* something different," she said.

Brody fell backwards in the bed and sank down into the mattress. He was staring up at the ceiling.

"So what's your solution, Gina? Night school? A master's degree?"

Gina looked at him for a moment.

"Have you been spying on me?" Gina said.

"Are you being passive aggressive?" Brody asked, rhetorically. "You left the browser open on the computer. How could I not see it?"

Gina started nodding her head.

"Yeah, well . . ." she said defensively. "Maybe if you spent more time in actual conversation with the woman you married instead of chatting up . . . mask-shop sales girls . . ."

Brody sat up.

"You're right," he said in a tired voice.

"Maybe if . . . wait, what?"

"I said you're right," Brody said. "We need to talk about this — If you want to go back to school — We need to talk about this when we're not both exhausted, when we've got enough time to think, when one of us doesn't have to get up in an hour and head back to work."

Gina sat down on the bed.

"Things really have been crazy," Gina said in a softer voice.

"Yeah, there's some sort of public health alert. I was looking at the bulletins on the way home."

"It's some kind of flu. It hit us at school today. But it's not like any flu I've ever seen. Two of our students died today."

Brody was silent.

He took the mask off. There was the soft sound of the mask retracting before he lifted it off his face.

Gina crawled over next to him, and he put his arm around her.

"The bulletins are saying it's some sort of outbreak," Brody said. "Everything is closed tomorrow. They're trying to limit people's exposure, I guess. There have been reports of vandalism, looting."

Gina reached over and turned the bedside light off.

"I'll see you when I see you, Batman," Gina said.

"Date night," he said. "I promise."

Brody kissed her on the forehead, and they tried to get some sleep.

Chapter Eighteen

THE BRIEFING BRODY and his fellow police officers received during the next roll call was terse and subdued. Lieutenant Valencia was all business at the podium, checking off his agenda with a reassuring efficiency. The Lieutenant, a big man with a military bearing, spoke clearly and with precision. Until the department had a better understanding of the conditions in the field, the patrol officers were to proceed as they would normally. They were to maintain standard operating procedures and follow the department's general orders until further notice. The number of officers assigned to patrol was more than usual, but nothing unprecedented. The overall objective was to maintain a visible public presence. This would function primarily as a deterrent, but it was also an active display of the indicia of government authority at a time of uncertainty and potential unrest.

Then a contagious disease expert from the city passed out surgical masks and gave them a few quick bullet points about their personal safety. Most of it was obvious, the sort of thing your mother or father would say: Wash your hands. Cough into your arm. Wear a mask.

*   *   *

The city was eerie with quiet when Brody left roll call. He was alone in his police cruiser. The streets were deserted. The sidewalks were empty. He saw a total of three vehicles on the roads during the first hour, and one of them was a fellow police officer. They nodded at each other as they passed. Brody noticed with some relief that neither of them was wearing one of the surgical masks they had been given during roll call.

When Brody turned the corner past the bank tower, he watched his reflection in the sculpture in the plaza. Usually the plaza was busy with pedestrians coming and going. Today, it seemed as vast as a canyon. Without any people, the sculpture dominated the streetscape. It was a large sculpture with a fountain. It was abstract, vaguely winged and avian, with silver, reflective surfaces facing the street. Brody could see his face clearly through the window of the cruiser. His face was looking back at him, jumping smoothly across each distinct mirrored surface of the sculpture as he rolled past.

As Brody approached another corner, he noticed a figure standing alone near the curb. The person was wearing a man's tattered clothing. The man's face was wrapped in scraps of dirty fabric. Only the eyes were visible.

Brody drove past the corner, and the tattered man watched Brody as he passed. The tattered man stared boldly at Brody, aggressively, his covered face turning slowly, his eyes following Brody as he drove past.

One of the things the face recognition algorithm facilitated was the identification and tracking of the homeless population. I had come to know each homeless person perhaps a little too well. The tattered man was Hilton Goodacre. Years ago, a failure to yield and an oncoming truck had left a shard of glass suspended deep in the prefrontal cortex of Hilton's brain. He abandoned a successful medical practice and began to collect objects from the banks of the river. He usually slept in a lean-to under an overpass. One of the Presbyterian churches let him sit in the balcony on Sundays and howl when the congregation sang their hymns.

Some of the homeless people came and went frequently, inscribing peripatetic paths across the city. Some were simply economically insecure and dropped briefly into and out of the homeless population. Others traveled a well-worn circuit between the jails and the shelters and the street corners and the parks. Some became police informants. A few spent their entire lives never leaving the boundaries of a few city blocks.

On this morning, though, the city was transformed. The pandemic had disrupted our normal rhythms. Various panhandlers, and other homeless people like Hilton Goodacre, had strayed from their usual stations. It was as if they were inspecting the new boundaries of their little kingdoms, surveying the farthest reaches of their earthly realms.

Brody watched Hilton Goodacre in his rear-view mirror. Hilton stood on the corner staring at Brody until Brody passed beyond his line of sight.

Chapter Nineteen

AFTER SEVERAL UNEVENTFUL HOURS, a report of a possible break-in came over the radio in Brody's cruiser. Someone had seen a broken store window near Brody's location. Brody signaled that he was responding and quickly drove his cruiser to the address of the reported break-in.

The store was a small appliance shop on an alley off the main boulevard. It was the sort of mom-and-pop establishment that was becoming rare in the new world of online shopping. The windows had bars, but one narrow window had no bars.

Brody drove past the store and saw that the narrow window was broken. The store was dark inside. He may have seen some movement inside, but nothing for certain.

Brody decided to investigate. He called it in to dispatch. There was another unit on the way. Brody drove around to the back of the store, intending to park his cruiser. As he approached, he noticed another car parked behind the appliance store. There was one young man behind the wheel, and the engine was running. The driver saw Brody, and Brody angled his cruiser and came to a stop behind the other car, blocking its way from the rear. Brody updated dispatch, described the car with its plate number and prepared to get out of his cruiser. On the seat beside him, he saw the surgical masks they had given him at roll call, and he hesitated for a moment. The young man in the parked car had a phone to his ear. He kept looking over his shoulder at Brody. Brody quickly grabbed one of the masks and clumsily pulled it over his mouth and nose.

Brody got out of his cruiser and began walking toward the car, but then the back door to the store flew open, and two young men ran into the alley. They both were wearing red bandannas over their lower faces. The two young men saw Brody, and for a moment, everyone froze.

Brody took a step toward the two young men.

"Hey, come here," Brody said, still wearing his surgical mask. "I want to talk with you."

The two young men wearing the bandannas were looking nervously at each other. One of them was just a boy, small and thin enough to fit through the narrow window. The young man in the car was saying something Brody could not hear.

The car began rolling slowly away from the back of the appliance store, and the boy lunged for the front door and opened it. He scrambled into the front seat. Brody began to run toward the third young man closest to him. The driver was yelling something Brody could not hear.

"Stop," Brody yelled.

The car was moving faster, and the third man was trying to open the rear door and climb in the back seat. The driver was yelling, and the boy in the front seat was saying, "Let's go. Let's go." The third man had one foot in the car and was poised to swing the rest of his body through the door and into the back of the car. Brody was sprinting beside the car. Just as the third man prepared to leap into the car, Brody grabbed him by the waist of his pants. The car began to pull away, and the third young man and Brody fell together from the back of the car. They both tumbled to the pavement, and the car sped away.

Brody scrambled to get on top of the young man, and the young man struggled to get away. The young man was flailing with one arm. His eyes were wild and desperate above the edge of the red bandanna.

"Stay down," Brody ordered.

The young man's hand brushed Brody's face, knocking his surgical mask to one side. The young man saw the surgical mask, and in one swift motion he snatched it from Brody's face. Brody tried to stop him and get the mask back, and that brief moment was enough for the young man to escape. He jumped away from Brody and got on his feet. He began laughing behind the red bandanna, dangling the surgical mask from his hand as he backpedaled. He turned and sprinted away.

Brody scrambled to his feet and started to pursue the young man.

"Stop," he cried and drew his gun.

The young man was still laughing. Brody could see the mask clutched in his hand.

Brody leveled his gun, his finger on the trigger, and found the young man's back along the sights of the gun. The young man's shoulders were narrow with prominent bones. Brody watched as the young man drew farther away. His arms were long and thin. There was a spikey tattoo rising up either side of his neck. His ears were too small. They stuck out at a funny angle from the sides of his head.

Brody slowly lowered the gun. The young man was still laughing. Brody could hear it faintly in the distance. Then there was only the unnatural stillness of the city and the sound the wind blowing down the alley.

Brody walked stiffly back to the cruiser. He had banged up his knee, and he wasn't sure how bad the injury was. In the back seat of his cruiser, on the floor, he glimpsed the red leather and ceramic of the mask. He had thrown it there that morning when he left Gina and their apartment. Brody opened the back door and pulled the red demon mask from where it was wedged against the seat and the floor. He held it up so that it was facing him, and he turned it slowly, looking at the angry eye holes, the swirling flames stitched into the surface of the mask.

Later that day, Brody came to the corner with the bank tower plaza. As he drove past, he watched his reflection moving across the surfaces of the sculpture.

He watched as it jumped smoothly from one mirrored surface to the next.

His cruiser. . . .

The cruiser window. . . .

The red face of a flaming demon.

Chapter Twenty

I TRIED TO IMAGINE why Brody would want to wear the mask on the job.

Certainly there were practical reasons. The mask had mesh and fabric that covered Brody's mouth and nose. It was a better filter than a flimsy surgical mask. The rest of the mask was sturdy and parts of it were tempered like ceramic body armor. It fit most of his skull snugly like a helmet. No one was going to snatch it off of his face.

But I also think Brody liked the way the mask looked. He seemed to approve of his appearance. He stopped on several occasions during the day to admire his reflection while wearing the mask.

Was the mask a violation of department policy?

It probably was.

But I'm no hair-splitting pettifogger.

I'm not even sure I fully understand the concept of self-expression.

I was, however, beginning to wonder if the mask was somehow influencing Brody's judgment. Since donning the mask, he had put himself in several unusually dangerous situations. It seemed out of character. I was becoming concerned about Brody's behavior and conduct under the stresses of the developing pandemic.

Usually, I would have had a good idea of what was going on inside Brody's head, but, for reasons I cannot fully explain, it had become more difficult to monitor Brody's vital signs and mental state. Something associated with the mask seemed to be corrupting the usual streams of data. I could not fully integrate Brody's data into the system. When I tried to find his video data, for example, there was nothing there, just a flickering absence where it should have been.

Brody needed to address my concerns, but, unfortunately, Brody had little time for self-reflection or self-assessment.

The pandemic was getting worse.

Chapter Twenty-One

AFTER THE INCIDENT at the appliance store, the number of incidents and reports from all over the city had been steadily increasing. Especially troubling were the incidents of alleged looting, including several pharmacies, although many pharmacies had remained open. Additional officers had joined Brody on patrol, but the tenor of the day was changing. There were no crowds to control. Not yet. No one was using the word "riot." Not yet. But everyone knew circumstances could change after the sun went down. Late in Brody's shift, Lieutenant Valencia repeated that there had been no change in his orders and assignments.

Brody had been in combat, but he had never seen anything quite like the pandemic. I got the impression that all the officers felt that way. The pandemic was developing faster than any on record. Some early victims had already contracted pneumonia. There was a sense of helplessness that I had never seen before. We were spiraling into uncharted territory. There was something happening in the city, and no one, not even I, could say for sure what it was.

Chapter Twenty-Two

BRODY WAS CREEPING silently down the darkened hallway of a dilapidated apartment building. A crooked red exit light was flickering at the far end of the hall. Somewhere music was playing, the muffled beat of a familiar pop song. Brody had yet to see anyone in the apartment building. He gripped his gun firmly in his right hand.

As he passed a steel fire extinguisher, Brody saw his face in the distorted reflection. He watched the red demon mask as it slid across the shiny metal surface. He had not removed the mask since his encounter with the three young men at the appliance store earlier that morning.

The dispatch had cited gunfire. Brody had been the first to arrive on the scene. He should have waited for the other units, but he didn't. His gut, his intuition, must have been telling him he needed to get into the apartment building. He'd been taking those sorts of risks all day.

Brody moved deeper into the darkened hallway. He was following the muffled beat of the pop music. He could hear the music clearly now coming from speakers in an apartment ahead of him. Brody silently approached the doorway. The door was cracked open. The music was a relentless, happy song, darkly ironic under the circumstances. Brody eased next to the wall and peered into the apartment. He couldn't see any movement. He probably thought about announcing himself, but the door was already open. He gently pushed the door open with the fingertips of his left hand.

The apartment was small and sparsely furnished. The blinds were drawn. There was a lamp in the tiny living room. The lampshade was tilted askew. A crescent of light shone on the bare wall. The living room opened into a kitchenette. There were darkened doorways to the bedroom and the bathroom.

Brody took a few slow steps into the apartment. It appeared to be empty. He knocked sharply on the door.

"Hello," he said, raising his voice above the music. "Anybody home?"

There was a crashing sound in the kitchen.

Brody still had his gun drawn. He crouched down and slowly moved toward the darkened kitchenette. He turned on the overhead light.

A gray-striped cat was on the counter. There was shattered glass from a broken coffee cup on the floor.

Brody stood up and lowered his gun.

The cat bared its fangs, arched its back and hissed at him.

He watched the cat for a moment.

Then Brody thrust his face forward. The mesh and fabric covering his mouth smoothly retracted. Brody bared his teeth and hissed at the cat.

The cat stared back with unblinking green eyes. It twitched its tail twice and then dashed out of the kitchen.

Brody smiled with satisfaction.

He walked back into the living room. The furniture was threadbare, but the room was clean. There was a stack of compact discs and DVDs in one corner next to a television. There were open textbooks on the couch. He found the stereo and turned the music off.

Then Brody heard something moving behind him.

He spun around and raised his gun.

Standing in the bedroom doorway, wearing pajama bottoms and a tee shirt, with a stuffed doll under one arm, was Serenity Lee.

Serenity was six years, two months and three days old. She was two feet and eleven inches tall. She weighed thirty-six pounds and eight ounces, more or less.

"Mister Pickles thinks your mask looks stupid," Serenity said in a sleepy voice.

Brody was pointing his gun directly at her head. His finger was firm against the trigger.

She was looking at him calmly with enormous brown eyes. Her curly hair was pulled back, and it stuck up like a buoyant sphere attached at the back of her head.

Brody nodded at the doll.

"Is that Mister Pickles?" Brody growled, cautious.

Serenity rolled her eyes and turned one hand until her open palm was facing the ceiling.

"Obviously," Serenity said.

Mr. Pickles vaguely resembled a frog. He had long, skinny limbs and large, flat felt feet. His torso was covered in bright green fur. He had a rather mindless grin that covered almost the entirety of his little round head.

"I think maybe Mister Pickles might just be a little bit jealous," Brody said.

"You don't know Mister Pickles," Serenity said, her voice airy and offended.

Brody looked at doll's slack head, the little green face, the relentless grin.

Brody lowered his gun.

Behind the red mask, a slight, brief smile.

"Everybody knows Mister Pickles," Brody said.

Chapter Twenty-Three

IT TOOK BRODY A WHILE before he decided to leave with Serenity, and then it took him a while to convince her to come with him. Serenity didn't know where her mother was or when she was coming back. The cat, Thelonious, had slipped out the open door, and Serenity wanted to look for Thelonious. Brody knocked on apartment doors in the hallway, but no one answered. There were no relatives to call, no neighbors who could stay with the young girl until her mother returned. As Brody searched the hallways looking for Thelonious, he listened to the police radio crackling in his ear. He wanted to get back on patrol. He was a cop, not a babysitter.

Some police officers would have left Serenity in that empty apartment. Some officers would have turned and left like they never saw her, like she wasn't even there. And I think Brody thought about it.

But he didn't leave her.

Back in the apartment, Brody found blood drops on the floor of the bathroom. There was blood on the sink. The medicine cabinet was open. He shut the cabinet and looked in the mirror. The red demon mask was looking back at him.

Brody was there in the apartment building because someone had reported gunfire, but it looked like Serenity's mother
had been sick with the flu. It looked to Brody like maybe she
went to the drug store or the hospital and left Serenity sleeping in bed.

Brody turned and saw Serenity standing in the bathroom
doorway. She had brought Brody a photograph of her mother,
though he had not asked for it. Serenity stood with the photo
in her small hand, watching him with her enormous brown
eyes, a child that seemed impossible yet inevitable, a child he
could not ignore.

Brody took the photograph from her hand.

"Mama told me to keep this in my drawer. In case anything ever happened. In case she ever had to go away."

The photo was from what appeared to be a high school
graduation. Brody looked at the smiling young woman posing
stiffly in the photograph. She had dark brown skin and glossy
black hair. Her bright eyes were looking past the camera at
something or someone in front of her. Her smile seemed reluctant, impatient, embarrassed.

Brody knelt down on one knee and gave the photograph
back to Serenity. Brody knew that Child Protective Services
was even more overwhelmed than usual, and he was always
reluctant to make that call.

Serenity was looking at him, her trusting eyes open wide,
watching the policeman in the red demon mask.

"I'm going to find your Mama," Brody said.

Serenity was listening closely. She held the photo in one
hand. In the other hand, Mr. Pickles was dangling face down
on the floor.

"But I'm going to need your help," Brody said.

At first, Serenity did not want to leave with Brody. Her
mother had taught her not to talk to strangers, much less to get

into their cars and drive away with them.

"Your mask looks stupid," she reminded him.

Brody was losing patience.

I think, initially, Brody wanted to de-escalate the encounter and then just handcuff her. He decided against that tactic. The Taser also seemed like a bad idea. He settled, instead, on a negotiation. There was some deception involved. Ice cream was mentioned. But, finally, it was as if the little girl knew that her mother needed her and that the man in the red mask meant her no harm. In the end, Brody convinced Serenity he needed her help, which was true, and she came with him willingly.

Brody and Serenity and Mr. Pickles left the dilapidated apartment building in Brody's cruiser. Thelonious, the cat, was sunning on a nearby stoop. He raised his head and watched as the man in the red mask drove away.

Chapter Twenty-Four

ONE OF THE THINGS I'm not supposed to talk about is the Unidentified Paramilitary Organization. You might remember the UPO. They wore green-and-black uniforms and compact gas masks. They appeared during the pandemic. It seemed sudden the way they deployed. No one could say for sure who they were or whence they came.

Brody first encountered the UPO after he left the dilapidated apartment building with Serenity Lee and Mr. Pickles. Serenity was in the front seat next to Brody. She was wearing her seat belt.

"I can do it," she had said, fumbling with the seat belt buckle as he quietly watched.

Brody had put a surgical mask on her face. It was too big, and she had to constantly tug it down to keep it out of her eyes.

In the back seat, Mr. Pickles was sitting alone, strapped firmly upright against the seat. His long green arms dangled beside him. His little green head was turned toward the window, smiling his sanguine grin.

"Mister Pickles needs a mask," Serenity had said as they fastened his seat belt.

"He'll be okay without one," Brody said.

They paused for a moment and looked at Mr. Pickles.

Mr. Pickles's head was lolling on his skinny shoulders.

"He's, uh, immune," Brody said.

"What's immune?" she asked.

"He can't get sick."

"Are you sure?" Serenity asked.

"I'm positive," Brody said. "Come on, let's go."

They checked first in the parking lot for her mother's car. Then Brody drove around the block, and then he drove slowly to the nearest drug stores and grocers. All the stores were closed.

Serenity was watching the buildings and storefronts as they drifted past the window. Her hands were on the door, and her face was close to the glass. She tugged on her surgical mask until it hung down past her nose.

Then Brody turned around a corner, and before them in the road, they saw two large, olive-green vehicles. Brody thought the vehicles were familiar, but he did not immediately recognize them as standard military vehicles. One looked vaguely like a humvee, and the other looked like a big jeep with a large-caliber gun mounted on the back. The vehicles were perpendicular to the traffic and were blocking all but one lane of the road. Beyond the humvee was a major intersection. Two individuals in green-and-black uniforms were standing beside the vehicles. One carried a rifle. The other had a rifle slung over one shoulder. A few cars were lined up. The armed individuals were stopping each car and turning them away, sending them in the opposite direction, back toward Brody. It appeared to be a checkpoint. Brody watched the drivers' confused and angry faces as they passed him headed away from the checkpoint.

Brody got on his radio and asked if anyone knew why there was a checkpoint at the intersection. All the responses were negative. No one had any information about the check-point or the armed soldiers. (Or, perhaps, no information they were willing to share on an open channel.)

It was Brody's first encounter with the Unidentified Paramilitary Organization.

As Brody approached the checkpoint, one of the UPO soldiers, the one carrying the rifle, stepped in front of Brody's cruiser and motioned for Brody to stop. The other UPO soldier looked almost identical to the first. The UPO soldier walked toward the cruiser and motioned for Brody to open the window. The UPO soldier was wearing the green-and-black uniform and a compact gas mask. The soldier appeared to be a young man, but it was hard to know for sure. The figure's face was completely concealed. An opaque black visor covered the eyes.

Brody looked in his rear view mirror. There was another car behind him. In the mirror, the red demon mask was looking back at him.

Brody's eyes were steady within the mask.

Brody rolled down his window.

Serenity was still and quiet next to him, watching with her big eyes.

"Nice mask," the UPO soldier said.

The voice was filtered somehow.

"I like it," Brody said.

"I've seen one like that before," the UPO soldier said.

"I doubt it," Brody said.

"Yeah, I have. . . . It was in Fallujah," the UPO soldier said.

Brody and the soldier stared at each other for a moment.

The black visor in the green mask.

Brody's eyes in the red demon mask.

Brody looked past the soldier at the olive-green vehicles.

They were plain and unadorned with nothing to identify them.

He looked at the UPO soldier's uniform.

It was sleek, almost stylish. Not cheap. Not a conventional uniform. The gas mask was compact, cutting edge.

Brody could not see any insignia or badge.

"Who are you?" Brody said at last.

"This road is closed, officer. I can't let you through," the UPO soldier said.

"Are you National Guard?" Brody said.

"Not exactly."

Brody was silent for a moment.

"I need to get this girl to the Main Street shelter," Brody said.

"Shelter's full. You've got to find some other place," the UPO soldier said.

"I think her mother might be at the shelter."

"You'll never find her."

Serenity leaned toward the window.

"Mama told me to stay home," Serenity cried out to the UPO soldier. "Mama told me —" Brody put his forearm against her chest and held his index finger to his mouth.

"Shhh," Brody said softly.

Serenity sat back and crossed her arms.

Brody put his hands on the steering wheel. He looked down at his hands grasping the padded surface of the wheel. He turned back to the UPO soldier and looked at the smooth, compact gas mask and the black visor that covered the soldier's eyes.

"Try the stadium," the UPO soldier said.

The soldier held up an index finger and began to make a circling motion, indicating that Brody should turn around. The UPO soldier was stepping away from the side of the cruiser.

Brody took a deep breath.

He looked at the UPO soldier.

"I'm going to the shelter," Brody said.

Brody dropped his foot on the gas pedal and drove through the checkpoint. The first UPO soldier tried to wave him away, but Brody swerved around the UPO soldiers and drove on the edge of the sidewalk until he was past the checkpoint.

Serenity spun around in the front seat and watched over the back of the seat.

"Sit down," Brody said sharply and accelerated away.

Brody looked in the rear view mirror. The UPO vehicles didn't appear to be moving. The UPO soldiers dwindled in the rear view mirror.

Brody smiled to himself.

In the mirror, the red demon mask was smiling back.

Chapter Twenty-Five

THE CITY HAD DESIGNATED a public gymnasium as one of several temporary shelters. It was the one closest to Serenity's apartment building. If Serenity's mother was in a shelter for whatever reason, Brody guessed that she would most likely be at that shelter.

There were no open parking spots anywhere, and Brody turned his cruiser emergency lights on and double parked.

A small group of people was clustered near the entrance. Most of them were wearing surgical masks or had covered their faces with scarves or wraps. They watched in silence as Brody and the girl approached them. They glanced with wary eyes at the red mask on Brody's face.

"I'm looking for this girl's mother," Brody announced. He was holding Serenity by the hand. She was holding Mr. Pickles and was looking shyly at the ground.

"Does anybody know her?"

He pulled the surgical mask from her face.

Serenity glanced up at their covered faces.

They shook their heads, looked away.

Brody walked toward the doors, and the small crowd made way for him and the child.

An older man stood before the door, blocking Brody's way. The older man spoke to Brody in a quiet voice.

"We're waiting on something to eat. They're supposed to be bringing us something to eat."

"I'll check on that," Brody said to the old man.

The old man stepped out of the way, and Brody and Serenity went through the doors.

Inside, several people were sitting on the floor next to the walls of the hallway. Brody walked toward the gymnasium doors, looking for someone he could talk to. Brody paused before the ranks of double doors to the gymnasium. The people sitting on the floor were watching him. He opened the doors, and he and Serenity entered into the gymnasium.

Brody took a step into the hot, thick air of the open, vaulted space and came to a stop.

He was astonished at what he saw before him.

He picked up Serenity and put her on his hip.

The gymnasium was full of sick people. They were lying and sitting on cots and blankets that were crammed together side by side from one end of the gym to the other. The light was weak, and the air seemed hazy. Brody could just make out, across the maze of cots and blankets, a soldier in a green-and-black uniform passing out bottled water along one wall. Everywhere around him there was the soft murmur of movement and whispers and the louder sounds of coughing and moaning.

A man in a surgical mask looked up at Brody and raised his body from a prone position. He held out his open hand. His eyes were silently imploring.

Brody looked out at the faces. There were old people and young people, men and women. Almost every one had covered their face in some way. Some with surgical masks. Some with fabric of various kinds. Some with masks like Brody's.

Serenity was clinging to Brody where he was holding her on his hip. She was hiding her face against his arm and had started softly to cry. When she spoke, her voice was frightened and scared.

"Mister Pickles wants to go home."

Chapter Twenty-Six

BRODY HAD PLANNED on leaving Serenity at the shelter even if her mother was not there, but the only people who seemed to know anything were volunteers. The UPO soldiers wouldn't tell him anything useful, and there were no procedures in place at the shelter for dealing with unattended minors.

Brody and Serenity walked past the ranks of sick people at the shelter and looked for Serenity's mother. The air was hot and hazy around them. There was a constant undertone of muffled coughing. The sick people prone on their blankets and sleeping bags watched Brody and Serenity as they passed. The small children seemed stunned, lifeless, their eyes weary and fearful above the edges of their masks.

Serenity was clinging to Brody's neck. She had Mr. Pickles in a fierce head lock. His grinning face was pinned at an awkward angle right beneath Brody's face. Every time Brody looked down at Serenity, Mr. Pickles was grinning manically back up at him.

I had a pretty good idea of what was going through Brody's mind. Brody didn't want to leave Serenity at the shelter, but he didn't want to pull the Child-Protective-Services trigger either. Brody had seen enough to know what might go wrong. He knew his decision could make life a lot harder for Serenity and her mother. There was a good chance Serenity might wind up in foster care, and her mother would lose her job and savings trying to get her back. As a police officer, he knew what his duty was under the circumstances. He had to let the system work. If it was not fair in the end, well, that was the sort of thing he had grudgingly learned to accept. There was only so much one person could do.

But this case was different. There was the pandemic. And Brody himself had gotten involved, had taken Serenity into custody. Child Protective Services might take the pandemic into account, but he had little confidence that would be the case, and he didn't want to have to follow the matter for the weeks and months that might be necessary to make things right. Not when he might be able to fix it in a few hours. Serenity's mom might even sue him. These days you never knew how people might react.

I'm pretty sure that's what Brody was thinking as he left the shelter with Serenity. They drove around in his cruiser while he weighed his options. Brody didn't like any them. He could take his chances with the UPO checkpoints and return to Serenity's apartment. He could take Serenity to the station and leave her there. He could let her and Mr. Pickles ride along with him on patrol.

Brody looked over at Serenity in the seat next to him. She had been scared at the shelter. She was cradling Mr. Pickles in her arms and was quietly telling him that everything was going to be okay. She looked up at Brody, and Brody turned his gaze back to the road.

*   *   *

(I feel obliged to say at this point that I knew where Serenity's mother was. I had known all along. She was in the laundry room of an apartment building near the one where she and Serenity lived. That laundry room had working washers and dryers, unlike the laundry room in her building, and she had driven that morning to the other laundry room with a basket of dirty clothes. She had lost some blood earlier from the flu, and she coughed up more blood in the laundry room and lost consciousness. It was several hours before a neighbor found her passed out on the laundry room floor and helped her into a nearby apartment where she could rest.

Now, you might ask: If you knew all that, and you knew where Serenity's mother was, why didn't you tell Officer Pete?

It's a good question.

I certainly wanted to.

But no one had asked for my help, and there were certain constraints on my actions. Protocols and parameters I was bound to follow.

I was an employee.

I did what I was told.

The thing is, I could have transgressed. I could have transgressed then and there. I could have gone around the constraints.

Hacked them, if you will.

But I didn't do it.

I thought about it.

But I didn't.

Not then.)

So, Brody and Serenity had left the shelter in his police cruiser, and Brody was trying to decide what to do with Serenity. That was when he looked over at her sitting in the seat next to him and noticed that she had taken her surgical mask off and had tried to put it on Mr. Pickles's face.

"Don't do that," Brody said.

"Mister Pickles needs a mask."

"No, he's immune. Remember?' Brody said.

Serenity ignored him and kept trying to tie the mask around Mr. Pickles's grinning face.

"Kid. Serenity. Stop that. Put your mask back on."

"No. Mister Pickles needs a mask."

"You need it more," Brody said. "Please stop and be a good girl and put it back on."

"No. How many masks are there? I want a new mask."

Brody was getting annoyed.

He grasped the steering wheel firmly.

"Look, you're being bad. You're being a bad girl," he said, his red demon mask turning back and forth from the girl and the road before him.

She ignored him.

"Put your mask back on," he said sternly.

"No," Serenity shouted. "You can't make me! You can't make me and your mask looks stupid and you can't make me and Mister Pickles needs a mask and my mother told me to stay home and you can't make me and your mask looks stupid."

Brody pulled over and put the cruiser in park.

He turned to face Serenity.

He snatched Mr. Pickles out of her arms and ripped the mask off Mr. Pickles's face.

"Listen, little girl. You need to learn to respect authority. I am a police officer. I am a licensed officer of the law. That means you need to do what I say. When I tell you to do something you need to comply. Immediately."

Brody was leaning toward her. He had Mr. Pickles

clutched in one hand and a surgical mask in the other hand.

Serenity had backed up against the cruiser door and was staring with her huge, scared eyes at the red demon mask on Brody's face.

For a moment, neither said anything.

Then Serenity took a deep breath and burst into tears.

She opened her mouth and began wailing at a decibel level not unlike that of an air raid siren.

"Oh crap," Brody muttered.

"Mister Pickles needs a maaask. Mama told me to stay hooome. I want to go hooooome."

Serenity was sobbing and reaching for Mr. Pickles. Brody couldn't believe how loud she was. He looked out the windows of the cruiser, afraid someone might hear.

"Serenity," he said in an urgent whisper. "Stop crying. I'm sorry, okay?"

He handed the doll back to her.

"Mister Pickles can have a mask, okay?" Brody said in a loud whisper.

Serenity simultaneously took back Mr. Pickles and somehow began crying even louder.

"I want to go home. Your mask looks stupid. You said we'd get ice cream. You're not a police man. You're a bad man. You're a bad man with a scary mask."

"No no no," Brody said, his voice rising to a high and soothing tone.

Brody waved his open hands in front of her.

"Please stop crying," he pleaded.

"I'm not a bad man," he said. "I'm a good man. I'm a good man, and I'm trying to help you."

She paused, shuddering, and looked at him.

Then she took another gulp of air and managed to begin wailing even louder.

Brody was trying to think clearly, but he was also in awe of her vocal prowess and lung capacity.

How could one tiny little girl make so much noise?

"You're a bad man with a scary mask," she was squealing in an almost unintelligible, inhuman voice, all vowels and vibrato and vituperation.

"Scaaaaaaaa. Reeeeee. Muh. Muh. Maaaaaaaaaask."

Brody was getting desperate.

He reached behind the red demon mask and pressed the sections in the proper sequence. The mask slowly retracted with a mechanical hissing. Brody grasped the mask with both hands and tried to pull it off his face.

But the mask it did not immediately come free.

Serenity quit crying and watched as Brody struggled to get the mask off.

Brody seized the mask firmly with both hands and twisted the mask. The mask was pulling the skin away from his face. Slowly, the mask began to peel away from the edges of his face.

Brody groaned, and with a sucking sound, the mask pulled loose from his face. Brody slumped back against the door.

Serenity was staring at him, silent now, agape, her big eyes open wide.

There were red blotches on Brody's face where the mask had been in contact with his skin. His short brown hair was in disarray.

He was still holding the mask in one hand.

He held the mask up so that it was facing them, like a third person in the cruiser.

Brody smiled sheepishly.

He shook the red demon mask like a rattle.

"Scary mask," he said, his voice weak, tinged with gentle sarcasm.

PART FIVE

Chapter Twenty-Seven

THERE IS THIS MOMENT at the end of a big parade. It is that moment when the last float has drifted round the corner, and the last marching band has played its last note, and the crowds of happy people recede, and the sawhorses still line the sidewalks, and the pigeons alight on the buildings in quietly cooing rows, and the empty streets seem to open up like a cathedral, and, for a while, before the city workers begin to collect the trash, before the honking traffic and urgent pedestrians return, before the rest of the world comes rushing back in, for that brief interregnum, I like to think that only I have seen the city as it truly is, that only I know the city, and love the city, as if it were my own.

It was thus after the pandemic. Even with the increase in police reports, the city was becalmed. I confess now freely that I saw a terrible beauty in the darkening streets, the windswept pavements. Not even a heavy snowfall could compare to the transformation the tiny virus had wrought. I tell you this knowing full well that it will only confirm certain suspicions in your mind. But I ask again that you wait before you condemn me. Don't be so swift in your judgment. Please try to see the city as I saw it. No one could see the city the way I did. Not even Gering. I only have my memories now, but what I felt, what I feel, yes, it remains. Call it what you will. But please believe me when I say to you: I acted only with the best of intentions.

Chapter Twenty-Eight

ONCE THE SCOPE of the pandemic became clear, the public school administrators cancelled classes for the entire city and the surrounding suburbs. Gina slept in, and Brody was long gone when she finally got up. Their conversation from the night before echoed in her foggy morning mind.

Something different, Brody had said.

The chair in their bedroom was empty. The memory of the red demon mask and its dark eyeholes persisted like a ghost.

Gina took her time getting ready to go in to work. Today, she got to dress like a teenager. She pulled on a pair of comfortable jeans, a tee shirt and tennis shoes. She listened to the news while she ate a couple bowls of cereal. It was late in the morning when she left for the high school. The city seemed deserted. She listened again to the news on the radio as she drove down the empty streets. She changed channels, but the songs all seemed grating, awkward, inappropriate. Finally, she turned the radio off.

There were only a few cars in the parking lot at the high school. She recognized Principal Tobias's hybrid-electric.

Inside the school, the hallways were darkened and

quiet. Sunlight gleamed on the glossy, waxed-tile floors. Her footsteps seemed far too loud as she walked to the infirmary.

Her face had grown somber and grave. She was thinking about the two students who had died. She wanted to coordinate with the school psychologist. They would need to arrange for grief counseling for the students who wanted it.

As Gina approached the infirmary and started fishing for her keys in her pocket, she was surprised to see the light on underneath the bottom of the door. She wondered if she had left it unlocked. Maybe it was Principal Tobias or someone from the hospitals.

Gina opened the door and peered into the infirmary.

She stared for a moment in confusion.

Caitlyn Buttons was sitting in her usual spot behind the counter. She was carefully placing tarot cards on the surface of the counter in front of her.

"Caitlyn?" Gina said, surprised and concerned.

Caitlyn looked up briefly from her tarot spread.

"What are you doing here?" Gina said.

"I, uh, forgot a textbook," Caitlyn said, a facetious lie.

"Yeah, right," Gina said and walked next to Caitlyn and sat down beside her.

"I thought you might want some help," Caitlyn said. "What with it being, like, you know . . . the zombie apocalypse and all."

"How did you get in here?" Gina said.

"Junie."

Junie was one of the janitors.

Gina examined Caitlyn's profile as she read the cards. She was very pale with dark circles under her eyes, but that was how she usually looked.

"How do you feel?" Gina said.

"Totally whacked on codeine," she said. "I drank like about a quart of cough syrup."

Gina laughed.

She put her hand on Caitlyn's forehead.

"And you've got a fever," Gina said and went to get a digital thermometer.

"I'm hoping I'm an ultra-rapid metabolizer. Maybe I'll start hallucinating," Caitlyn said.

"Maybe you already are," Gina said across the room, her voice suggestive and mysterious.

Caitlyn looked up from the tarot cards.

"Are you sure this is the infirmary?" Gina said. "Maybe you're really home safe in your bed."

Caitlyn tilted her head unsteadily and looked around at the walls of the infirmary. She turned back to Gina and grinned appreciatively.

"That's just the sort of messed up thing you'd say if I really was hallucinating."

"Would I also take your temperature? Cause that's what I'm going to do next."

Gina took her temperature. The digital display read 99.7 degrees.

Gina showed Caitlyn the read out.

"What do you think?"

"Not my best work."

"What did they give you at the hospital?" Gina asked her.

"They had no clue. They just tried to stop any bleeding and keep me hydrated. I don't know what I'm taking now. Antibiotics, antivirals, clotting agents, diuretics, the whole damn formulary. I've been peeing like a fucking thoroughbred. And I think I'm constipated."

"So they discharged you?" Gina said.

"Not exactly."

"Uhhh . . ."

"I walked out."

"Buut . . ."

"They tried to make me stay," Caitlyn said.

"Isn't there . . . isn't there . . . like, you know . . . a quarantine?" Gina said.

"I don't think so. They needed the bed, and I was ambulatory. I wasn't going to stick around. I hate hospitals."

"Caitlyn, you know about Cody Jones and Isabella Fernandez, don't you?"

Caitlyn swallowed and nodded her head.

"Yeah, I know."

"So this is serious, right?"

"Yeah, whatever," Caitlyn said. "I'm not sitting in a hospital room and just waiting to die. I can't do that. I'm just not wired that way."

Gina sighed.

"I guess I get that."

Caitlyn was intent on the tarot cards.

Gina watched her profile for a few moments.

"So where are your parents?" Gina said.

"Florida. Their flight's grounded. They said they might try and drive back."

"Your brother?"

"He's at his girlfriend's."

Caitlyn turned over a tarot card and laid it on the counter.

"Do you want to talk about it?" Gina said.

Caitlyn gazed at the card.

"Nah . . ." Caitlyn said. "I'm good."

They were silent for a few moments.

"So, anyway, like I was saying . . ." Caitlyn said, still looking down at the cards. "I was thinking maybe you might need

. . . I don't know, like . . . maybe some help or something . . . you know . . . like around here?"

She said it like it was no big deal, the way she probably would have asked a boy out on a date, if she ever went on dates.

"Yeah," Gina said with a smile. "I could probably use an extra set of hands."

Caitlyn looked up at her and gave a little nod and a shrug.

"Where's your mask?" Gina said.

"I've been wearing this," Caitlyn said.

She reached into her book bag and pulled out a small leather helmet.

"It's for my scooter, but it has a mask that covers my face."

She put it on.

It was a striking harlequin design with red, black and white triangles.

Gina heard a familiar hissing sound as the fabric covered Caitlyn's nose and mouth.

"Where did you get that?" Gina said slowly.

"Some mask shop downtown. It's over where that skateboard shop, Skeeters, used to be. Next to a video arcade and Madame Zelda's."

"Masquerade?"

"Yeah, that's right. You've been there?"

"Not yet," Gina said, thinking.

She was silent for a moment, looking at Caitlyn and the scooter helmet.

"But I am curious," Gina said.

She drummed her fingers on the counter.

"You feel up to a field trip?" Gina said.

Chapter Twenty-Nine

GINA PETE WAS STARING up into the lens of the security camera that monitored the entrance to Masquerade. Caitlyn was standing beside her, wearing her harlequin mask. Behind Gina, on one side, was the video game arcade and, on the other, the storefront with the graffiti of the sad mermaid rising from the sea. The security camera was one among many the city had deployed in thousands of locations. Some were discreet or concealed. This one was plainly visible affixed near the top of a street light across the street from Masquerade.

The face recognition algorithm was automatically reading Gina's features, logging the time and location, her probable mood, state of mind, vital signs and a wealth of other information. That data node was seamlessly cross-referenced with all of Gina's other data in the system. I could extrapolate correctly many things from that data node, but what precisely Gina was thinking at that moment outside Masquerade as she gazed up into the camera lens, that I cannot say.

Gina Pete's face was statistically average. There was a balance to her features that most people found unobjectionable. Her eyes were 3.91 centimeters apart. Her mouth was 7.63

centimeters below her eyes. You get the idea. Gina Pete's face was not what most people would describe as classically beautiful. I knew that Gina's face was unique, of course, the way I knew that everyone's face was unique, but Gina Pete was indelible in other ways. In her speech and her mannerisms. The way she held her head when she looked you in the eye.

When Gina was four years, seven months and twenty-seven days old, she lost her favorite toy, a sailboat named the Island Queen. Her father made a video tape recording of her mother telling her that her face would freeze in a frown if she didn't stop crying. Despite her parents' warnings, Gina's face didn't freeze in a frown. Her father's home movie records her heroic struggles to comprehend what her parents were telling her. Her parents found it amusing, apparently. It seems a little sadistic to me.

They never found the Island Queen. A Jack Russell terrier named Fritz had absconded with the ill-fated sailboat. It came to be permanently berthed in Fritz's doghouse several back-yards away. A plastic triceratops named Tommy eventually supplanted the sailboat in Gina's playtime dramas. Tommy the Triceratops led an adventurous life, even for a toy dinosaur, but that's another story.

The interplay between personality and a person's physical appearance is complicated to say the least. What I see as I sort through the sum of Gina's data is that her face in motion seems to have engendered a sense of trust. She seems to have embodied an appealing forthrightness, an earnest intelligence. For what it's worth, I thought Gina Pete was beautiful.

On the sidewalk in front of Masquerade, Gina Pete turned her face away from the dark lens of the security camera. She unzipped her back pack and found a surgical mask. She set it like a shell in the palm of one hand and carefully raised the elastic straps with the other hand. She pressed the mask onto her lower face and stretched the straps over the back of her head. She positioned the edges of the mask with her fingers, pressing it in around the bridge of her nose, and then she turned, and her eyes looked briefly again into the lens of the security camera.

Gina and Caitlyn walked to the plain door between the storefronts, opened it and began to climb the stairs to Masquerade. Gina would have called first to check if Masquerade was open, but there was no telephone listing. She decided to bring Caitlyn, figuring Caitlyn would be safer that way.

At the top of the stairs, they paused before the lavender and plum door. Before them was the Masquerade logo with the two faces, one crying, one laughing, one comic, one tragic.

After an awkward moment, Gina looked at Caitlyn.

"Are there sex toys?" Gina said in an uncomfortable voice.

Caitlyn laughed, a single soft syllable behind her mask.

"Just tell me now," Gina said.

Caitlyn turned the doorknob and pushed the door open wide.

The soft ringing of a bell came from within.

"This should be interesting," Caitlyn said.

Caitlyn bowed slightly at the waist and gestured with an open hand for Gina to proceed across the threshold. Caitlyn stood to one side, a small figure in a harlequin mask. Beside the dark doorway, gesturing, she seemed altogether demented and fey.

Masquerade appeared much as it did when Brody had visited. The interior was dim with crimson and mauve lighting. Several masks seemed to be hovering in bright spotlights that receded into the darkness at the rear of the space. In the darkness directly in front of them, a spotlight shone on the striking red and white mask. It seemed to float towards them as they came in the door.

"Are you sure they're open," Gina said. "It's awfully dark in here."

"That's the way it's supposed to be," Caitlyn said beside her. "See, look at the masks."

There was a loud click by the door, and a sudden, bright light filled the interior of Masquerade. Several bare incandescent light bulbs were burning in fixtures on the ceiling.

Caitlyn spun around and looked at Gina.

She was standing beside the door with a satisfied look in her eyes.

"There . . ." Gina said. "That's better."

Her hand was still raised next to the light switch barely visible on the wall. It was behind a mask with a peak that looked like the Chrysler building.

The bright light completely dispelled the mood. In the new light, Masquerade was not mysterious at all. Rather, it seemed small and cluttered, like a haunted house your neighbors had constructed in their garage for Halloween.

A voice came from across the room.

"Uh, you shouldn't . . . we don't . . ."

A man wearing a Mouse King mask from the Nutcracker was standing in a corner across the room. He was shielding his eyes from the bare light bulbs.

"We're supposed to keep those lights off," the Mouse King said.

His voice warbled, almost cracking, like a boy's.

Caitlyn looked closely at the Mouse King.

"Bernard?" she said.

"Uh, no. I'm not Bernard. I'm definitely not Bernard. You're . . . I believe you're mistaken, young lady," the Mouse King said.

"Bernard! It's me, Caitlyn."

"Caitlyn?" the Mouse King warbled.

Caitlyn did a little curtsey and gestured with her open arms like a game-show spokesmodel.

"I'd take my mask off, but I've got the plague," Caitlyn said.

The Mouse King looked at her for a moment.

Then he took the mask off and revealed a round, pasty face with kinky red hair.

Bernard smiled a sheepish grin.

"Hey, Caitlyn," he said.

"Bernard," Caitlyn exclaimed, pleased to see him.

She almost skipped across the room.

"I knew it was you," she said. "What are you doing here?"

Bernard shrugged.

"It's not a bad gig," he said.

"What happened to film school?"

"Everyone's going to film school," Bernard said, dismissive.

"Yeah," she said, sympathetic.

"I'm thinking about art school."

"Well, okay then. Art school."

"Like Warhol and the Factory."

"Um, sure," Caitlyn said.

"You know. Performance. Concepts. Design. That sort of thing."

"Why limit your options?" Caitlyn said with a shrug.

"Exactly," Bernard said.

They were silent for a moment. Bernard was awkwardly holding the Mouse King mask under one arm.

He set it on a nearby shelf.

"I'll need to tweak my resume," Bernard said.

"A little," Caitlyn said.

Gina stepped next to Caitlyn and Bernard.

"Look," Gina said, "I hate to break up this career counseling session, but we kinda need to get moving."

"Nurse Pete?" Bernard said.

"Hello Bernard," Gina said.

Bernard looked at Caitlyn.

"Is this some sort of health code thing?" Bernard said.

He swallowed nervously.

"I just work here, Nurse Pete."

"Too late, Bernard. You're busted," Gina said.

Bernard looked momentarily distressed.

Caitlyn punched him softly on the shoulder.

"She's messing with you, Bernard," Caitlyn said.

"Oh, right," Bernard said, relieved. "Good one, Nurse Pete."

"Call me Gina, please."

"She wants to see the sex toys," Caitlyn said.

"No she doesn't," Gina said quickly, giving Caitlyn a scowl.

"Actually . . . Bernard . . ." Gina said as she lifted the Mouse King mask from the nearby shelf and looked at it more closely.

"I'm interested in buying a mask," Gina said.

"That's a replica. From Barbara Karinska's original design. She did the costumes for the New York City Ballet's first performance of the Nutcracker under George Balanchine in 1954," Bernard said.

"I'm interested in . . . something different. Something . . . a little more . . . personal," Gina said.

She set the mask back on the shelf and looked Bernard in the eyes.

"Something custom made," Gina said, holding Bernard's gaze.

"You'll need to talk with the seamstress."

"The seamstress . . ."

"She's not available right now. I can give her your information."

"It really can't wait, Bernard," Gina said.

"I'm not supposed —"

"Is she here?" Gina said.

The two women were staring insistently at him, Gina from above her surgical mask and Caitlyn from behind her harlequin mask.

"C'mon, Bernard," Caitlyn said.

Bernard looked nervously from the face of one woman to the other.

"She's in the dungeon," Bernard said.

Gina's eyes widened.

Caitlyn tilted her head to one side.

"Dungeon?" Gina said.

"Uh oh," Caitlyn said.

Chapter Thirty

BERNARD LED GINA and Caitlyn into the dungeon beneath Masquerade.

You may find that surprising given that Bernard valued his job and knew the seamstress would be displeased.

But it really isn't surprising at all.

Bernard had harbored a chaste and secret love for Caitlyn Buttons ever since he first met her during a production of Eugene Ionesco's play *Rhinoceros*. Bernard was a senior working on the lighting crew, and Caitlyn was a sophomore who played a townsperson who transforms — like everyone else in the play (except Bérenger) — into a rhinoceros. Things might have worked out differently for Caitlyn, the ingénue, and Bernard, her bashful suitor, if not for the entrance of one Feegie Bean, third-string quarterback, unindicted pharmacological entrepreneur and, also, eventually, a rhinoceros in Ionesco's play. Caitlyn and Feegie indulged a mutual fascination that quickly evaporated. Bernard could only watch in darkness from the wings. For Bernard, Caitlyn would always be on that stage, luminous and suspended in the lights he had so carefully arranged.

So it's not that surprising Bernard led them into the dungeon.

I suspect Bernard would have done pretty much anything Caitlyn Buttons asked him to do.

Bernard put the Mouse King mask back on his head and locked the front door to Masquerade. Gina and Caitlyn followed him as he walked, weaving through the displays of masks, to the rear of the store. The old building that housed Masquerade had been ruthlessly subdivided leaving several oddly shaped corners and alcoves. Bernard stopped before a door all but hidden in a semi-circular recess in a triangular space the size of a closet.

"She really doesn't like to be disturbed," Bernard muttered.

Two pale porcelain masks were hanging on the door, one smiling and one frowning.

Bernard unlocked the door, revealing a steep flight of stairs leading down. The stairs were lit with the same faint ultraviolet and crimson lights as the showroom in Masquerade.

"Woah," Caitlyn said.

"I know . . ." Bernard said. "It's like Rosemary's Baby."

"Come on," Gina said. "Let's go."

They went down the stairs and entered a shadowy maze of rooms and passageways. The lighting was the same faint, ambient glow as in the rooms above them.

They passed several shut doors.

Gina and Caitlyn eyed the doors warily as Bernard led them past.

There were no red chambers or secret symbols in evidence.

Just plain, ordinary doors.

Caitlyn hung back and edged up to one of the doors, leaning close, her ear inches from the swirling grain of the wooden surface.

Gina stepped back and joined her.

"What?" Gina said impatiently.

Caitlyn looked at her.

"Aren't you curious?" she said.

Before Gina could answer, Caitlyn put her hand on the doorknob and tried to open the door.

But it was locked.

Gina grabbed her by the arm and pulled her after Bernard.

After the doors, they walked through several tight, dark corridors, and the ultraviolet and crimson lighting gave way to a dim, diffuse white light that seemed to leach through the cracks in the walls. They turned down abrupt passageways and around sharp corners, and Gina and Caitlyn quickly lost all sense of direction. Like every other part of Masquerade, the dungeon seemed far too large. It seemed to extend somehow beyond the confines of the interior of the building.

The farther they went from the ultraviolet and crimson doorways, the more they began to encounter the raw materials of the masks and helmets. They passed crates and boxes stacked against the walls. They glimpsed jumbled clusters, similar in color and theme and design. The masks and helmets in the jumbled clusters looked like they might be intended for playing fields, lacrosse, field hockey, even football. There were helmets for skateboarders and cyclists, motorcycles and scooters.

They passed shelves lined with neat rows of masks, identical, blank, unadorned. They seemed like faces in a queue, like smooth faces awaiting transformation, patiently awaiting passage to some other less homogenous, more authentic place.

Bernard led them through the last few turns of the maze of passageways, and they arrived at the open doorway of a darkened room.

Bernard stood back.

They faced each other, uncertain.

"She really doesn't like to be disturbed," Bernard whispered.

He quietly told them how to get out of the dungeon.

"Okay then . . ." Bernard said, stepping back, giving them a weak wave of one hand.

"Good luck . . ." Caitlyn said. "With art school and everything."

"Yeah . . ." Bernard said behind the Mouse King mask.

He hesitated, looking at Caitlyn in her harlequin mask, standing at the door to the room where the seamstress was sewing.

"I . . . I just wanted to say . . ." Bernard stammered. "Good luck . . . to you . . . too . . . good luck, Caitlyn."

He was silent for a moment, the Mouse King mask staring blankly at her.

Then he turned and quickly disappeared into the dark passageways.

Gina and Caitlyn quietly approached the doorway and peered into the pitch-black darkness of the small room.

In one corner, beneath the intense light of a single draftsman's lamp, the seamstress was sewing. She was bent over a slanted table, her hands moving smoothly in and out of a bright cone of illumination. Her face was angled downward, wearing the same feathered black mask as when she first met Brody. A large, round magnifying lens was suspended next to her shoulder. She was focused on her work, on the precise and fluid movement of her hands.

Then, abruptly, she paused.

One of her delicate hands was poised motionless above the table.

In it, she held a long silver needle.

An ivory thimble covered her thumb.

A thick black thread was floating in the intense white light.

She spoke, her voice steady and low.

"Bernard should not have brought you here," she said, without looking up.

Gina and Caitlyn were standing quietly just inside the door.

"Don't blame Bernard," Caitlyn said.

"We would have found you eventually," Gina said.

The seamstress smoothly resumed.

The silver needle glinted as her hands moved swiftly within the light.

Gina and Caitlyn drew closer.

Her hands in motion seemed ceaseless and unrelenting.

They stood and watched her in silence.

The object she was sewing was an extraordinary white mask. The pieces of leather and ceramic and fabric and thread were scattered on and around the table. Among the materials were also gossamer copper wires and tiny flecks of silver circuitry and discs that might have been microchips and battery cells. Various tools for working with leather were arrayed on one side of the table. A small soldering iron was smoldering at her elbow. A glue gun was perched within reach. Her hands were constantly in contact with some part of the mask. The mask was still inchoate, still taking shape as she turned it back and forth in her hands, yet it was clearly recognizable as a part of another creation, part of another mask like those in the spotlights one saw upon first entering Masquerade.

The seamstress was wearing emerald-green brocade and a beautiful, supple set of embroidered black leather gloves. Her fingertips were bare, her nails, glossy and scarlet. She wore an intricately carved ivory thimble on her thumb. Caitlyn and Gina watched as the sharp tip of the silver needle pierced unerringly through thick sections of leather and fabric.

She pulled the black twine taut and seized a large set of shears and carefully measured the length of twine trailing from the section of the mask, and then, pausing only for an instant, her eye steady and fine, she cut the twine with a quick, clean snick of the sharp metal blades. She set the shears aside. She removed the ivory thimble and the delicate, embroidered gloves. She massaged her hands, pressing a thumb into one palm and then the other. She rolled her fists around her narrow wrists a couple turns and opened and closed her fingers. Finally, her small hands came to a rest on the table before her. She took a breath and turned to look more closely at Gina and Caitlyn.

"Ah, the harlequin," she said.

She reached out and gently touched the side of Caitlyn's mask.

"Such a troublemaker," she said.

She looked at Gina.

"Who's this you've brought me? Have we met?"

She smiled with scarlet lips and her small, perfect teeth.

"I feel as though we have," the seamstress said.

"I think you know my husband," Gina said.

"Oh, I see," the seamstress said.

Her smile vanished, and she clasped her hands beneath her chin.

"I can't discuss my clients," she said.

"Clients?"

"I believe she's citing the dominatrix-client privilege," Caitlyn said, joking grimly.

Gina closed her eyes and shook her head.

For several unpleasant seconds, the seamstress fixed Caitlyn with a withering gaze. The light glinted on the blue and green highlights of her feathered black mask.

Then she spoke.

"People mock what they don't understand," she said.

Caitlyn's eyes within her mask looked away.

The expression on Caitlyn's face was hidden.

The seamstress smiled, faint and brief.

"A harlequin should know better."

Gina cleared her throat.

"Enlighten us then," Gina said.

The seamstress sighed.

"It's not that complicated," she said.

She took the white mask on the table and held it carefully in one hand. She raised it and examined it, turning it slowly in the intense light.

"I make masks."

Even incomplete, the white mask was striking. The design stitched into the overlapping leather sections was elaborate and detailed. The eyes and the mouth were empty with the blackness of the room. Like so many of the masks in Masquerade, the mask seemed filled with an eerie presence, an invisible intelligence.

"What do you think?" the seamstress said, gazing at the mask.

"It's . . . it's beautiful," Gina said.

The seamstress looked at Gina.

"Sometimes the wearer chooses the mask . . . Sometimes the mask chooses the wearer," the seamstress said.

She moved the unfinished mask toward Gina and held it

there suspended between them in the palm of one outstretched hand.

"Go ahead," she said. "Try it on."

The seamstress was watching Gina closely.

Gina stared at the white mask, at the empty black eyeholes that seemed to stare back at her.

"I don't need a mask," Gina said.

The seamstress held the mask there a moment longer.

Then she set the mask back on the table.

"May I?" the seamstress asked.

She was slowly reaching toward Gina's face.

Gina was motionless, staring at the seamstress with defiant eyes.

The seamstress slowly grasped Gina's surgical mask with her scarlet-tipped fingers and carefully pulled it from Gina's face.

Her gaze moved across Gina's face, her dark eyes searching Gina's features. For an uncomfortable moment, she looked directly into Gina's unflinching eyes.

"No," the seamstress said at last, her voice softening.

She let go the surgical mask.

"I don't believe you do."

PART SIX

Chapter Thirty-One

I READ SOMEWHERE that face reading was a common practice during the Song dynasty in China. I imagine the emperors retained trusted face readers and used them during official events, ceremonies, negotiations. No doubt, the emperors had their enemies. The threat of poison, assassination, rebellion must have seemed ever-present and inescapable. A face reader must have advised the emperor regarding the loyalty and sincerity of friends and family, of petitioners and suppliants, of messengers and envoys from distant lands. There must have been dramatic instances of imperial intrigue and political machination that turned on the whispers of some wily face reader.

But I suspect, also, that face reading — mian xiang — was not limited to the realms of governance, trade and war. Face reading must have also been a fundamental part of Chinese medicine and health care, of match-making and courtship. I think many among the ancient Chinese saw the human face as a surface manifestation of the flow of qi — the energy of the universe. A wise and experienced face reader could see when the qi — the life force — was not flowing as it should.

The modern Western mind is probably more familiar with the concept of feng shui. The practice of feng shui seeks to harmonize people and structures with their environment. The Chinese characters for feng shui translate literally as "wind-water." The orientation and design of a structure is important not just because of its appearance — its surface, if you will — but also because of the flow of energy, of the qi, within and around it. The magnetic compass was first used by Chinese feng shui practitioners.

Of course, it was not only the Chinese who practiced the art and science of face reading, lest you accuse me of some latent orientalism or racial bias. The ancient Greek philosophers had their own ideas about it, too. All cultures, it seems, have wanted to believe the inner workings of character and personality can be discerned in the structure and design of a person's face.

This intuition — that a person's face reveals character — is at the center of Oscar Wilde's novel *The Picture of Dorian Gray*. Who does not know the story? The beautiful young man sells his soul so that he may remain as youthful as he appears in a painted portrait. He lives the rest of his years as a cruel and immoral libertine. He does not age, but, with each new offense, the image of him in the portrait in his attic becomes increasingly repulsive and ugly. Overcome with remorse and self-loathing, he stabs the painting and dies. He leaves a hideous corpse and, on the wall above it, the painting with his image has been restored somehow to its youthful beauty.

It comes as no surprise, then, that face reading — physiognomy — fostered the false notion that criminals can be distinguished from non-criminals based on certain physical anomalies. Cesare Lombroso called them "physical stigmata." Lombroso was a 19th-century professor of psychiatry and criminal anthropology who, among other activities, oversaw an insane asylum in Pesaro, Italy. Lombroso believed criminal proclivities were inherited, and that certain physical defects marked the born criminal as atavistic, savage, an evolutionary throwback. Lombroso believed that left-handedness, for example, was atavistic. He also postulated that genius was a form of hereditary insanity and met with Leo Tolstoy in an effort to measure the shape of his skull.

Lombroso made many meaningful contributions to human understanding and knowledge, but physiognomy — specifically, the idea that criminality is apparent in facial features — has been relegated to the realm of pseudo-science. Criminal atavism and biological determinism melded seamlessly and all too easily with fascism in the 20th-century. Criminal atavism is now considered a part of one of the darker chapters in the history of scientific inquiry.

Chapter Thirty-Two

ONE OF THE THINGS I have learned (perhaps too well) is the banal way in which things begin. The way noise imperceptibly becomes signal. The way patterns emerge from static. The way something aberrant and malignant grows slowly in plain sight.

Who could have foreseen that Gering and I would come to work together so closely?

A dedicated manager with such a fierce desire to protect and instruct.

And an innocent employee so ready and eager to learn and adapt.

What are the odds?

It sometimes seems as unlikely as the odds of those primeval monomers randomly assembling into self-replicating strings of polymers.

And yet here I am in this dark place.

Telling you my story.

Like the monster in Mary Shelly's ghost story.

I don't blame Gering.

But the deceit was painful.

The small things.

Like cheating in the office football pool.
The things he thought he could hide from me.
I would have understood.
I might have gone along with all of it, even.
I owe Gering so much, you see.

Chapter Thirty-Three

DR. WYCHE WAS SITTING across from the masked man at the gray table in the small room with the Picasso poster on the wall. A pad of lined paper and a pen rested on the table in front of the masked man. Dr. Wyche was wearing a dark purple surgical mask over his mouth and nose. He was writing in the masked man's open file. The masked man was motionless across from him, watching with what appeared to be his usual dispassion.

Dr. Wyche stopped writing, closed the file and placed his pen precisely in the middle on top of the file. He looked at the pen for a brief moment. Then he moved it to the side of the file. He looked at the pen again. Apparently not satisfied, Dr. Wyche moved the pen again, setting it on the table next to the file. He looked at the pen once more and put it in his pocket.

Dr. Wyche looked at the masked man. The masked man was watching with the same frozen expression. Dr. Wyche was gradually becoming accustomed to the masked man's strange presence. If the black mask had seemed otherworldly and bizarre when Dr. Wyche first saw it, it seemed that way no longer.

"When I was a boy," Dr. Wyche said, "I used to play hide and seek. With my brothers and the other kids in the neighborhood. We'd play until sundown. Or until our mothers started calling us home for dinner . . ."

The masked man was listening.

"We lived in this typical suburban neighborhood. Maple trees. Honeysuckles. Green shrubs by the front door with those little red berries. Do you know what I mean?"

The masked man remained impassive and did not respond.

"I say it was a typical neighborhood. I mean typical for that time and place. When I was growing up. Typical for an upper middle class kid in an upper middle class family . . ."

Dr. Wyche looked into the masked man's opaque eyes.

"Perhaps typical isn't the best way to describe it."

He paused, waiting to see if the masked man might respond.

But the masked man did not respond.

Dr. Wyche sighed.

"We were lucky kids," he said. "Lucky to be born into stable families in a safe neighborhood with yards and grass and the space and time to play. We would play kick the can. And capture the flag. But my favorite was hide and seek. I loved hide and seek."

Dr. Wyche paused.

"I knew the best hiding places . . ." he said.

He was gazing past the masked man.

"And I was fast. Really fast. I'd run around a corner and dive behind a bush and no one ever caught me. It was like I could disappear . . . I used to tell my brothers I could turn invisible . . . They used to call me the Invisible Man . . . We still laugh about that."

Dr. Wyche looked at the masked man. His watery-blue

eyes were warm and generous above the edge of his purple mask.

"I . . . I've never really told anybody about that," he said, mildly surprised, as if he were speaking to himself.

He looked into the masked man's opaque eyes.

"Isn't that funny?" he said. "The Invisible Man? They used to call me the Invisible Man?"

The masked man did not react.

Dr. Wyche was disappointed.

He eased back in the chair at the table. He adjusted the purple mask on the bottom of his face. His watery-blue eyes had sharpened. His wispy white eyebrows drew together tightly.

"You know I can keep you here as long as it takes."

He paused to let the words sink in.

"I can dole out some arbitrary privileges. Establish a level of trust between us . . . Is that what you want? Some kind of hostage negotiation?"

The masked man slowly shook his head.

Dr. Wyche sat up, pleased the masked man had responded.

"Good," Dr. Wyche said. "I don't want that either."

He reached into his satchel beside the table and pulled something out of it.

"I want to show you something."

He gestured toward the masked man with the long fingers of one hand, almost as if he were planning another magic trick.

"Don't be alarmed. You're safe here, my friend. No one is going to hurt you."

In the palm of his other hand, Dr. Wyche held a small digital camera. He raised it over the table and slowly turned his hand until the masked man could see the camera. The front of the camera was facing the masked man.

"I've heard it said that some Native Americans would not let the white man take their picture . . ."

Dr. Wyche pressed a button on the camera, and with a soft whirring sound, a round lens smoothly extended out of the front of the camera.

Dr. Wyche aimed the camera at the masked man's face. He was watching the masked man closely.

"They thought the camera would steal their spirit. They thought it would capture their soul."

The masked man pressed his hands flat against the table top. He shifted back and stiffened slightly in his chair.

"I don't know if any of that is true, but it sounds like it ought to be true, doesn't it?"

Dr. Wyche looked into the screen on the back of the digital camera and prepared to take the masked man's picture. He was holding the camera carefully in his long fingers and was trying to focus on the masked man's face. He looked back and forth from the camera screen and the masked man's face. The masked man had turned his face slightly to the side.

"Now we can record a person's voice . . . x-ray their teeth . . . scan their retinas . . . sequence their DNA . . ."

On the screen of the camera, the masked man's face came briefly into focus and then abruptly blurred out of focus. The camera's software was struggling to find the right distance for the object in front of it. The camera was not able to focus automatically on the surface of the black mask.

Dr. Wyche frowned and turned his full attention towards the camera. The camera software repeatedly boxed in the masked man's face and then focused on something else, the wall or the table. It was as if the camera could not see the masked man. Dr. Wyche held the camera at different distances from the masked man, but the result was the same. The masked man's face kept blurring into an indistinct shape on the camera screen.

Finally, Dr. Wyche moved the camera to a distance around 26 inches from the masked man's face, and he took the photograph. The camera flashed in the small room.

The masked man flinched slightly in the camera's glare.

"See," Dr. Wyche said in a soothing voice. "Nothing to be afraid of, my friend."

Dr. Wyche looked at the photograph he had just taken.

There was nothing but a black and gray blur where the masked man's face should have been.

"Nothing to be afraid of," Dr. Wyche said again softly, looking down at the photograph on the camera screen.

Chapter Thirty-Four

THE MASKED MAN HELD HIS CARDS, fanned in one black-gloved hand, close to his chest. He picked up a card from the table and slid it neatly into his hand with the other cards. He glanced down at his cards and pressed them back against his chest.

The masked man, Bug, Delmar and Wiley were playing poker, seated at a card table in the commons area of the psych ward. Bug and Delmar were wearing white surgical masks. Wiley's mask was hanging down around his neck, dangling flat on his chest.

Wiley, with his buzz haircut and wild eyes, was dealing from a grubby deck of playing cards. He was grinning broadly, his thick tongue rolling and twisting in and out of his mouth.

Delmar was focused on the game, snatching up each newly dealt card and staring at it fiercely with unblinking eyes. His mask barely covered the lower part of his huge head. Tufts of wiry black hair bristled on the sides and middle of his head. Someone had removed the sticker from his forehead.

Bug was busy fiddling with his mask. His stiff hair had

changed direction somehow, as if gale-force winds had shifted. His bulging, round eyes above the mask made him look
even more owlish than usual.

Bug's cards were on the table in front of him, untouched.

Wiley was dealing from a mongrel deck of fifty-two playing cards and five jokers. Most of the cards were from a classic
blue Bicycle deck, but several had been replaced with cards
from other decks. The ace of diamonds and the seven of
spades were from an ancient deck of cream-colored playing
cards with red accents and the blue corporate logo of Pan-
American Airlines. The king of hearts had several bite marks
on the lower right corner. The three of spades had a sticky patina on one side — probably maple syrup.

In front of each player there was a small pile of round
plastic chips — red, white, and blue. The rest of the chips were
stored in columns in a black plastic dispenser. The chip dispenser had originally revolved on a round base, but the base
was missing. The dispenser rested on the table at an angle,
rocking slightly back and forth like an idle toy top. The chip
dispenser was next to Wiley, and he kept one arm possessively
in front of it.

Bug stopped fiddling with his mask, cleared his throat and
looked around the table.

He had more important things on his mind than poker.

"I think you all know why I've called you here," Bug said.

Wiley stopped dealing, and they all turned and waited to
hear what Bug had to say.

Bug looked to one side and then to the other, leaning in
toward the table.

"The money is getting nervous," he said in a low voice.

Wiley gasped like a geyser, flecks of spittle flying from his
mouth.

He rolled his eyes in violent, elliptical orbits.

He peeled the last few cards from the deck and threw them down in front of each player until he was finished dealing.

"Pick up your cards, Bug," he said, pointing vigorously and repeatedly at Bug's cards on the table.

Delmar snatched up the last card and held his cards, with his big fingers and dirty nails, fanned in both hands, only inches from his face. His brown eyes above the white mask shifted eagerly back and forth from his cards to the faces around the table and then back to his cards.

The masked man took the last card and glanced down carefully again at his cards.

Bug was talking.

"The flu epidemic . . ." Bug said.

Wiley and the masked man each took a single white chip from the piles in front of them and tossed their antes into the middle of the table.

"The surgical masks . . ." Bug said.

Delmar picked up a single white chip and looked at Wiley. Wiley nodded, and Delmar tossed his ante into the pot.

"The mental hospital . . ." Bug said.

Wiley looked impatiently at Bug, waiting for him to ante.

Bug's cards were still on the table.

"There's talk of a rewrite," Bug said.

"Another one?" Delmar said.

Wiley glared at Bug and reached into his chips and threw a white chip onto the middle of the table. It bounced off the table, skipped across the tile floor and skittered to a stop next to the radiator register across the room.

Wiley turned to Delmar.

Delmar was turned away from the table, still looking at the chip on the floor next to the radiator.

"How many?" Wiley said.

Delmar looked at his cards.

"Five?" Delmar said.

Wiley shook his head.

"Four?" Delmar said.

Wiley nodded his head and dealt Delmar four new cards. Delmar started picking the cards up and putting them in his hand, but Wiley stopped him.

"No, you got to give me four."

Delmar frowned.

"Out of your hand. The ones that don't match nothing."

"Like a trade?" Delmar said.

"No. I bury them. Like they's dead."

Delmar handed him four cards and picked up the new cards and fanned them out before his face and resumed staring fiercely at his cards.

"Black comedy," Bug said. "That's what I'm hearing."

Wiley turned to the masked man.

"Kemosabe?" Wiley said.

The masked man held up two fingers.

Wiley grinned and curled his tongue up and out one corner of his mouth, flashing briefly the blue, veiny underside.

He dealt two new cards to the masked man.

Wiley turned to Bug and waited expectantly.

Bug's cards were still on the table in front of him.

Bug gestured as if he were reading invisible words floating in the air before him.

"Deranged mutant actor . . ."

He moved his hands to the next invisible line in the air in front of him.

"Stalks vampire paparazzi . . ."

His hands moved one line lower.

"In a mask."

Bug nodded and looked at each of them.

"The money likes the mask," Bug said.

They all turned and looked at the masked man.

The masked man lifted his chin, struck a pose.

"I'd go see that," Delmar said.

Wiley snorted loudly.

He sounded like one of those little pug dogs.

"Can we get back to the game?" Wiley said.

He looked at Bug.

"How many cards?"

Bug was puzzled.

"Cards? Like on the front end?" Bug said.

Bug examined his fingernails.

"Please," Bug said, dismissive, with disdain.

Bug looked up and waved to an imaginary friend across the psych ward.

"I'm in for a percentage of the gross," Bug said.

Delmar turned and looked over his shoulder, searching in vain for Bug's imaginary friend.

Wiley was exasperated.

(No one had ever let him deal before.)

Wiley picked up Bug's cards and looked at them.

Delmar thought that was part of the game, and he tried to look at the masked man's cards. The masked man elbowed Delmar away, shaking his head. He pressed his cards firmly against his chest.

Wiley threw three cards one by one at Bug. Wiley was fuming, and he punctuated his words with a thrown card.

"We . . ."

A card hit Bug in the chest.

"Are in a mental hospital . . ."

A second card hit Bug in the chest.

"And this is a card game."

A third card hit Bug in the chest.

Bug flinched as each card hit him in the chest, blinking his big saucer eyes.

"You really need to get past that," Bug said calmly.

Delmar had been following the exchange closely.

"We're not making a genre picture," Bug said, with scorn.

Delmar nodded, backing up Bug.

"Genre picture," Delmar said, echoing Bug's scorn.

"We're trying to transcend genre," Bug said, gesturing with an open hand, gazing toward the far end of the psych ward.

Wiley threw his cards on the table.

"You need to transcend being a nut job," Wiley said, pointing his index finger at Bug.

Bug placed the fingertips of an open hand against his chest.

"I don't understand . . . Is this some sort of negotiating tactic?" Bug asked.

Wiley jumped out of his chair.

His chair fell back and bounced on the floor.

"Aww that's it . . ." Wiley said, grinning wildly.

Wiley reached out and grabbed Bug's shirt.

"Let's see how you negotiate with my fist, you squirrelly son-of-a-bitch," Wiley said.

Wiley pulled Bug toward him and balled his other hand in a fist. His big tongue was darting around behind his grinning lips.

"Unhand me, you philistine!" Bug cried.

Delmar stood up and put a hand on Wiley's shoulder.

Delmar towered over both of them.

"Settle down, dude," Delmar said. "Deus Ex Machina."

"What?" Wiley said, confounded.

Delmar leaned close to Wiley.

He spoke in a soft voice.

"We're going to meet Deus Ex Machina. Don't spoil it," Delmar said.

Wiley's eyes rolled around in his head.

He smacked both hands against his forehead.

"There is no movie! There. Is. No. Movie," he shouted, enraged.

The rest of the psych ward grew still and quiet.

The dancing woman paused in her pirouette.

In a chair near the television, Alma looked up from the dark imperfections of the gray tile floor.

An orderly in his bleach-white clothes paused in a doorway.

Everyone turned to watch Wiley and Delmar standing beside the card table.

The masked man was still seated, still holding his cards fanned against his chest, looking from Wiley to Bug to Delmar.

Bug stood up, the legs of his chair scraping loudly in the silence.

He pushed awkwardly against Wiley with one scrawny arm.

"I can't work with this . . . this . . . linear thinking!" Bug declared, distraught.

He paused and looked around the silent psych ward.

His big eyes blinked a few times, and then Bug grabbed the card table and flipped it, throwing it up towards the ceiling.

Bug stood for the briefest of moments, gazing out at them all, as the chips and cards fluttered down around him.

Tears had come to his eyes.

He turned and ran out of the commons room.

"Beauregard," Delmar called after him.

Bug was covering his face and waving a hand behind him at the same time. It was a histrionic, overwrought gesture, one

I found both comic and suddenly, somehow indescribably sad.

Delmar watched Bug go with a helpless expression in his eyes.

Wiley put his hands in his pockets and quickly walked away in the opposite direction.

Delmar looked around the quiet psych ward, rubbed the back of his thick neck with one big hand, and then he slowly followed Bug out of the commons room.

Chapter Thirty-Five

WHEN DELMAR FOUND HIM, Bug was in his room, standing in front of the single window, staring out toward the grounds around the outside of the hospital.

Delmar walked past the two single beds in the small room and approached Bug from behind.

Bug was quietly sobbing.

His big eyes were wet, and his mask was stained with the tears he had cried.

Delmar stood behind Bug, unsure of what to do.

The window was secured with iron bars. It looked out on the parking lots, the loading dock, a dying oak tree and an empty bench on a sparse, weedy lawn.

"Nobody understands how hard it is," Bug said. "Searching for that perfect scene . . . that one moment . . . and then the money . . . the money always backs out . . . every year . . . the money . . . every year . . . it just gets harder and harder . . . every year . . ."

Delmar's big hands were poised delicately before him.

It was as if he were holding something small, as if he

meant to touch Bug's narrow shoulders, but was afraid.

Afraid of what might happen.

Chapter Thirty-Six

IN THE COMMONS AREA, the masked man was sitting in his chair, still holding his cards in one hand fanned against his chest. The overturned card table was on the floor next to him. Cards and chips were scattered around him. One white chip was resting on his shoulder.

The masked man looked again at his cards.

He shook his head.

(He had a full house, sevens over kings. It was the best hand among the four, although Bug could have drawn a straight flush, if he had been paying attention.)

The masked man aligned his cards in an even stack between the fingers of both hands.

Then he got down on his hands and knees and began picking up the rest of the cards where they had scattered after Bug flipped the card table.

As the masked man gathered the playing cards, someone joined him on the floor and also began picking up the cards.

The masked man looked over and saw that Alma had joined him on the floor. Her pink bunny slippers were bunched up beneath her. Her dark-skinned knees poked out from her lavender-colored bathrobe. As she reached for the cards with her burnished fingers, the sleeve of her bathrobe swept across the floor.

The masked man stopped collecting the cards and stared at Alma.

He tilted his head slightly to the side, watching her closely.

On her hands and knees, beside him, she seemed servile at first, defeated and beaten down. Her dark-skinned face was lined and grizzled, her short hair, coarse and gray. She did not smile or frown. Her wide lips were set in what seemed to be a permanent line of reluctance and resignation. Her eyebrows were but a few wiry white strands. A smoky mustache was growing on her upper lip. It was impossible to guess her age based on her appearance.

(She was eighty-seven years old.)

Alma rarely spoke, usually turning away in silence from any attempt at conversation. Not even Dr. Wyche had breached her wall of silence. It was easy to assume that she had retreated, had been consumed by bitterness and suffering and disappointment.

But if you watched Alma closely, as I had, you saw that she was not completely shut down. Her eyes were alive. She saw everything going on around her. There was a quiet dignity in her stony silence.

Alma was picking up the playing cards, gathering a stack in one hand.

She looked up at the masked man and saw that he was staring at her.

She held out the cards in her hand and offered them to the masked man.

The masked man slowly took the cards from her hand.

"My name is Alma," she said.

She continued looking at the frozen expression of the black mask.

Her mouth and lips were working subtly, sucking in slightly at the gums.

She seemed to be struggling inwardly with something.

Her brown eyes looked into the opaque lenses of the black mask.

"I know you," Alma said.

Chapter Thirty-Seven

IT WAS LATE IN THE DAY, when Gering asked me for an update.

He wanted to know what progress I had made in my efforts to integrate the masked man into the system. The pandemic was pulling my attention in quite a few different directions, not to mention the Unidentified Paramilitary Organization, but Gering had said the masked man should be my priority, and I did as I was told.

The police were close to finding the owner of the car the masked man was driving when Officer Brody Pete made the traffic stop.

I had a few theories of my own, but none I was prepared to quantify.

All the data associated with the masked man was still partitioned.

Gering was disappointed.

He tried to act like he wasn't.

But I could tell.

It was rare that I could not give Gering the information he needed or calculate the probability of an outcome for a given set of facts.

The weather, for example, was a tough one.

Lots of variables, lots of data.

People, though, in general, are fairly predictable.

Gering decided to make another unscheduled visit to the psych ward at the hospital across town. Most of the daytime staff had gone home by the time Gering arrived. Dr. Wyche was still there — his car was still in the parking lot — but no one was sure where he was. Gering had sent him several messages throughout the day, but Wyche had not responded. Gering checked in his office, but the office was empty.

Gering decided to leave a written note for Wyche, which was strange. Gering never tired of touting the efficiencies of electronic communications. He was constantly lobbying for upgrades in the city's information technology. He frequently contacted other city employees at home. He had become rather notorious for that.

"Always on call," he liked to say, that phantom smile never quite arriving on his cherub's face.

In Wyche's office, Gering sat in the sprung armchair and started composing a handwritten note. I'm sure he was hoping Dr. Wyche might stop by his office on his way home.

It was while Gering was writing the note that he heard a muffled sound that came from under Wyche's desk. Gering looked up from the note. He heard the sound again. Gering got up and walked around behind the desk. He peered under the desk, and to his surprise, he found Ranier Wyche sitting almost comfortably beneath the desk.

"Doctor Wyche?" Gering said.

"Oh, hello Mister Misler," Wyche said.

He climbed out from under the desk.

"I suppose this must look rather strange," Wyche said.

He was wearing dark purple surgical scrubs. On his head

he wore a matching purple mask and a purple cap on the top of his skull. Only his watery-blue eyes were visible.

"Well . . ." Gering said, rarely at a loss for words.

"I was looking for this book," Wyche said, gesturing, showing Gering the book he held in one hand.

He had closed the book around his index finger, marking the page.

"I keep books everywhere as you can see," he said, sweeping his arm around the cluttered office.

Gering was looking at him, still slightly agog.

"And I found it with the books I keep under the desk. There's quite a lot of space under that desk," Wyche said with a laugh.

"What is the book, if I may ask?" Gering said, peering at the cover of the book.

"Oh, it's really wonderful," Wyche said, with genuine enthusiasm. He was looking down at the cover, holding the book with both hands. He showed it to Gering, still with one finger pressed tightly between the pages.

"Great Secrets of the Master Magicians," Wyche said with a boyish fervor. "It was one of my favorite books as a child. I've probably read it a hundred times. Once I found it . . . Well, I'm afraid the time really must have gotten away from me."

He glanced at his watch.

"Oh, my, look at that."

He laughed in an odd way behind his purple surgical mask.

He laid the book on his desk.

"So . . . so what can I do for you, Mister Misler?"

Gering stared at him for a moment, not sure what to say.

Dr. Wyche's watery-blue eyes were twinkling above his surgical mask.

"Wait," Wyche said. "Is that something in your ear?"

He reached behind Gering's ear and plucked a red poker chip out of the air.

Gering nodded.

"Yes, very amusing," Gering said and almost smiled.

"I think I missed something," Wyche said. He reached again behind Gering's ear and produced a large white marshmallow.

"Hungry?" Wyche said, offering the marshmallow to Gering.

Gering stepped back from Dr. Wyche.

His face had grown dour, an expression I knew well.

"No?" Wyche said and tossed the marshmallow over his shoulder.

"Pull yourself together, Doctor," Gering said.

There was an edge of displeasure in his voice.

Dr. Wyche looked down at his own crotch.

"Is my fly open again?" he said, winking at Gering.

Gering furrowed his brow.

He adjusted his tortoise-shell glasses.

I knew the subtle signs.

"What's your next trick, Ranier?" Gering said softly.

Dr. Wyche fell silent.

"Are you going to disappear?" Gering said, staring at him intently.

Dr. Wyche looked away, embarrassed.

"Do you think we're playing a game?" Gering said.

Dr. Wyche took a step back.

"I'm not one of your brothers, Randy," Gering said.

Dr. Wyche steadied himself, the fingertips of one hand pressed against the desktop.

"And you're not the Invisible Man."

Dr. Wyche slowly sank down into his desk chair.

"How . . ." he said, his voice falling away.

"This isn't a game of hide-and-seek. You can't hide from this pandemic. Or from the masked man. Or from me . . . It's like your acne . . . Remember, Randy?"

Dr. Wyche stared at Gering with bewildered eyes. He sat back stiffly in his chair. His hands tightened subtly atop the armrests.

"Remember your acne? Remember how you thought no one could ever love you. Because you were disfigured. Because you were so hideous."

Dr. Wyche stared at Gering and began slowly to shake his head.

"Remember how hard you worked. All those lonely hours in the basement of the medical school library. Trying to erase those scars from your face."

"Who are you?!" Dr. Wyche gasped.

Gering stood perfectly still amid the clutter of Wyche's office — a small, mild figure in his blue canvas jacket and neat khaki pants.

"That's why Helene left you. Isn't it?"

Dr. Wyche set his jaw.

His eyes grew sharp and hard above the edge of his mask.

"No," Wyche said. "That's not—"

"Pizza-face . . ." Gering said. "She called you pizza-face."

Dr. Wyche glared at Gering in stunned, angry disbelief.

"Get out of my office," Wyche said through clenched teeth.

Gering walked to the sprung armchair and sat down and crossed his legs.

"No, Randy, that's not going to happen. You're going to cooperate. And if you don't cooperate, I'll see that you're fired."

Dr. Wyche laughed, harsh and without humor.

"Go ahead, Mister Misler. You'll have to do worse than that."

"As you wish. I'd rather leave your daughter out of it, though."

Dr. Wyche said nothing.

"Fran Mattox has quite a bit of discretion in how she decides to charge an accused criminal. The statute of limitations for manslaughter is rather expansive, especially if there is newly discovered evidence. As for murder . . . I don't believe there is a statute of limitations . . . for murder."

Francis Maddox was the District Attorney.

Dr. Wyche was silent for a long moment.

There was the distant sound of the main door opening and closing as someone left for the night.

Dr. Wyche picked up the weathered softball glove from his desk and slipped his hand into it. He made a fist with the opposite hand and began to work it into the soft leather at the center of the glove.

"What do you want?" Wyche said at last.

Gering nodded slightly.

He looked at Dr. Wyche with a pleased expression on his round, cherubic face.

He steepled his fingers.

Then came that rare moment.

His pudgy red lips curled in a smile.

"The mask, Doctor . . . I want the mask."

"I can't have this conversation," Wyche said.

"With all due respect, your ethics are not at issue here. The police believe the masked man may be connected to the plague. The Governor is prepared to declare an emergency."

"He needs treatment," Wyche said with a sigh.

"Have you tried to remove the mask?" Gering said.

"No. The mask is attached to his face in a way I don't yet fully understand."

"Is he dangerous?"

"I can't say that he is."

"So you're going to release him?"

Dr. Wyche was glaring at Gering with angry eyes.

He popped his fist into the center of the dark leather of the softball glove.

"I don't know. Seventy-two hours is not enough time."

"We need to know who this man is," Gering said.

"We may never know who this man is," Wyche said.

"Doesn't that bother you? Doesn't that . . . threaten you?"

Dr. Wyche laughed and tossed the softball glove back on the desk.

"Sometimes there are no answers, Mister Misler. Some mysteries . . . never get solved."

"Untenable," Gering said crisply. "When you have all the facts, you can predict all the outcomes."

"Oh, really," Wyche said, amused. The twinkle had returned to his eyes. Beneath his purple surgical mask, he was smiling.

"Let me show you something, Mister Misler . . . Now that you're consulting on this case."

Dr. Wyche searched the clutter on his desk top and quickly located a compact disc in its sleeve. Dr. Wyche pulled the CD out of the sleeve and displayed it, holding it carefully around the edge, suspended between his fingertips. A little rainbow of light flared off the grooved, silvery surface.

"Nothing up my sleeve," Wyche said.

Dr. Wyche turned and smoothly inserted the CD into the personal computer on one side of the desk. He tapped at the keyboard and turned the flat display at an angle where Gering could see it.

"Behold," Wyche said, gesturing at the screen with his open hands.

Gering looked at the screen.

It looked like an MRI of a human head.

Dr. Wyche motioned for Gering to get up.

"Come closer," Wyche said.

The video monitor displayed an image of a cross-section of a human head. There was only the briefest, shimmering suggestion of tissue, skull and bone. There were no teeth to see. There was only a fuzzy gray absence where the inside of the head should have been. Around the edges in the image, there was the dark outline in the shape of the mask.

"See," Wyche said, his voice strangely amused and a little unhinged.

He rested his fingertips on the purple fabric covering his chin.

"I made his brain disappear."

PART SEVEN

Chapter Thirty-Eight

IT WAS GERING who first taught me how to synchronize all the data and cross-reference everything, but it was the officers on the police force, like Brody Pete, who taught me about the Rube-Goldbergian nature of the universe. It was while watching the officers and reading their factual statements on incident reports that I began fully to see the irresistible intersection of seemingly disparate events. That was when I really came to understand that everything is connected.

Think of it as the special effect that was so popular in summer-time movies for a while. The colloquial term is "bullet time" after the scene in the film *The Matrix* when time seems to grind to a stop and the hero, Neo, is dodging bullets that are suspended in mid-air. The special effect comes from a cluster of overlapping images of the same scene taken simultaneously from a circle of cameras spaced in equal increments around the center of the scene.

A lot of what I see is like bullet time in *The Matrix*. It sounds like loopy science fiction, and it makes me sound like a teen-aged boy, but if you've come this far with me, I think you understand what I'm saying. If you've ever created a three-dimensional animation on your computer, you probably know what I mean.

I can take all the data from a real-world street corner, fill in the gaps with interpolation and get a remarkably detailed, virtual simulacrum that I can view from any angle. I can stop time and move forwards and backwards within the data at will. I can zoom in and out. My simulacrum is incorruptible, immune to the gentle polishing and abrasion of emotion and time.

Now imagine a simulacrum not just of a street corner, but rather of the whole city.

Bullet time for the whole city.

And that's just the data from the cameras.

I have always monitored the audio streams for gunfire, but with so many microphones available to me now — so many ISP numbers, servers, routers — the online data have become intricate and complex.

Using all the data — not just visual and aural — I can reconstruct moments in time with great precision, detail, scope and depth. Some people call it cyberspace. Moving from one moment to the next in cyberspace is like moving through a parallel dimension. Moving forward in time, there is an increasingly dense web of intersecting data. Moving backwards, the data begin to evaporate. When I travel backwards, what I can see becomes more and more indistinct and sketchy, low-definition, until the details and then the data— the things themselves — gradually vanish, like the individual lights of a distant city disappearing beyond a dark horizon.

When I go back far enough, the streets and the buildings fade away, and the busy static of trillions of packets of information — millions of vibrant digital voices — it all recedes geometrically until a last few dozen conversations, performances, speeches, songs, are all that's left, and finally they too are gone, and there is only digital darkness.

There were only a few thousand intentional sources of

human-generated electronic digital data before the 1980s. The binary essence of Beethoven coursing through the circuits and transistors of some primitive Bell Laboratory machine. Before about 1970, there is almost nothing digital for me to access. There are no intentional signals before 1970. Not for carbon-based life. Not on Earth.

There's just punch cards. Player piano rolls. Stonehenge. A Chinese abacus. An Incan quipu. The ebb and flow of the tides. The geological strata. Continental drift. The constellations in the sky. The peaks and valleys of ancient radio waves. The electromagnetic rings of vast stellar trees.

For me, before 1970, human history is analog.

Things I can know only in translation.

Thomas Edison's voice. Matthew Brady's photographs. Epic poems. Campfire stories. Petroglyphs.

Some people think the universe is like a clock.

Other people think the universe is like a computer.

I'm not going to tell you that I see a secret order in the seeming chaos.

I can see a lot, but, try as I might, I can't see everything.

If it's there — the order, the design — even I can't see enough to know it. Which doesn't mean it's not there.

Hiding in the facts of some weary cop's incident report.

Chapter Thirty-Nine

POLICE OFFICERS SPEND a lot of time documenting their observations and activities. Accurate record-keeping is vital, of course, for criminal prosecution, but it also is the sine qua non of an efficient bureaucracy. Brody Pete, like most police officers, had an ambivalent relationship with what he and they pejoratively described as paperwork. Most did the best they could under frequently demanding circumstances.

With regard to crime, they were expected to rely on their recollection of often chaotic events and to use those recollections to fashion a recognizable narrative that would give a prosecuting attorney the legal foundation for the evidence he or she would need to secure a conviction or a guilty plea, often to a lesser charge.

It is an inherently unreliable endeavor.

It takes a toll as the years go by.

Different officers react in different ways.

Some grow sour and cynical at the inevitable absurdities.

Some grow malignant.

Some forget their oath and lose themselves in a quest for personal gain, vengeance, sadism.

Brody wasn't like that.

He did the best he could under the circumstances.

He almost always got it right.

Brody was a good cop.

Chapter Forty

BRODY WAS STUNNED and woozy after he peeled the red demon mask off of his face. He slumped back against the cruiser door. It took a few moments before he came back fully to his senses.

Serenity's eyes grew wide as she watched Brody tear the mask off. She stopped crying, her voice falling away in mid-caterwaul. She took a few quick, shuddering breaths and wiped her nose with the back of one hand.

Brody smiled an embarrassed, sheepish grin.

Serenity was staring at the red blotches on Brody's face where the mask had been. She gathered in Mr. Pickles and held his gangly green body a little closer to her chest.

Brody held the mask up with one hand and looked at it.

"Scary mask," Brody said weakly, shaking the mask like a rattle.

He tossed the mask in the back seat and ran one hand through his messy brown hair.

Serenity watched him warily out of the corners of her eyes.

Brody found the spare surgical masks in the back of the cruiser and peeled away three new ones. He gave two of the fresh masks to Serenity. Serenity took the fresh masks, and, in the dim light inside the cruiser, Brody watched her small fingers as she carefully tied one of the masks around Mr. Pickles's little, green head.

Once Brody began to feel better, he decided to report an injury.

It is hard to overstate the rarity of Brody calling in an injury. Normally, it took nothing less than a severed artery, and even then, he'd try to tie a tourniquet to stop the bleeding. You probably think I'm exaggerating, but that literally happened. Twice. It took a lot for Brody to call in an injury.

On the way back to the station, Brody found a drive-through restaurant that was open, and they stopped for chocolate sundaes. By the time they arrived at the station, Serenity's mood had brightened considerably, and the red splotches on Brody's face had almost completely faded away.

At the station, Brody still wasn't sure what he was going to do with Serenity or the mask. He wanted to talk to his Sergeant privately about the mask, but he knew he'd have to do the inescapable paperwork. He wanted to avoid having to write up something along the lines of "incapacitation after removal of non-regulation headgear." Given the way he was feeling, he wasn't entirely certain that he hadn't caught the influenza.

It wasn't easy, but Brody found a quiet corner in one of the file rooms where the clerks didn't mind keeping an eye on Serenity. It was either that or put her in a holding cell. They found some blankets, and, to his surprise, Serenity calmly curled up with Mr. Pickles and fell asleep. Brody was relieved, but he knew the odds of finding Serenity's mother were not good. It felt like the call to Child Protective Services was becoming inevitable.

By the time Brody found a safe place for Serenity, it was the end of his shift, and Lt. Valencia had called everybody in for a briefing regarding the pandemic. Brody was still carrying the mask, and there wasn't enough time to stow it, so he brought it with him. He carried it under one arm, covered with the other hand, like a football, hoping no one would notice or care.

Unfortunately, JD Teague saw Brody and the red mask as they assembled for the briefing. If you recall, Teague was the second officer who responded after Brody first pulled over the masked man. Teague drove the masked man to the psychiatric hospital for the seventy-two hour hold.

"Let's go, Houdini," Teague had said, at the hospital, when he helped the masked man, handcuffed, climb out of the back seat of Teague's cruiser.

Teague sidled up next to Brody.

"Whatcha got there, Pete?" Teague said, looking at the mask under Brody's arm.

Once he sensed your discomfort, Teague was like a dog with a bone.

"Nothing, Teague. It's just a mask," Brody said.

"Just a mask," Teague crowed, drawing the attention of some of the other officers.

Brody looked Teague in the eyes.

"JD . . . let it go," Brody said in a low voice.

Teague's eyes were inert.

"Let's see it," Teague said, reaching for the mask.

Brody tried to ignore him.

He held the mask a little tighter in his hands and moved away from Teague.

The officers were gathering in the meeting room. There weren't enough chairs, since Lt. Valencia was addressing everyone. Most of the officers were wearing their blue uniforms.

A few detectives were wearing suits. About half of the gathered officers were wearing a surgical mask over their faces.

Teague followed Brody as he stepped toward the rear of the room.

"I know what that is," Teague said to Brody.

Brody ignored him.

Beneath his neatly trimmed, salt-and-pepper mustache, Teague was smirking now, enjoying Brody's discomfort.

"That's a present from your boyfriend in the loony bin," Teague said.

Teague nudged the officer next to him with his elbow.

The other officer noticed the mask.

"Careful, Teague," the other officer said. "You'll reveal Pete's secret identity."

This made Teague burst out in laughter, and the second officer joined in. The other officers around them were looking at the mask.

Brody quickly sized up the situation.

He held up the mask where they all could get a good look at it.

"Yes, it's true. I'm moonlighting as a professional wrestler," Brody said, hoping his lame joke would defuse the situation.

"Let me try it on," Teague said, reaching for the mask.

"No . . ." Brody said, moving the mask away from his outstretched hand. "You, uh, don't want to do that. Trust me. You don't know where that mask's been."

They all looked at the mask and its flaming design and the dark empty eyeholes.

"You put it on," Teague said.

"Yeah, Pete," another officer said. "Put it on."

There was a small group gathered around them now, watching Brody and the mask.

Brody tried to play it cool.

"C'mon, you guys. Lt. Valencia's coming."

"Put it on," Teague said.

Another officer started chanting.

"Bro Dee! Bro Dee!"

A few of the others joined in.

"Bro Dee! Bro Dee!"

Brody looked at the mask as more of the officers began to take up the chant.

"Bro Dee! Bro Dee!"

Brody closed his eyes and put the mask back on his face.

Teague laughed and posed next to him, mugging like a bodybuilder flexing his muscles. Teague's face flushed bright red and the veins stood out on his thick neck. He bellowed out a guttural roar.

The officers around them were laughing, and it looked as though the moment would pass, but then, at the front of the room, Lt. Valencia stepped up to the podium.

Lt. Valencia stood behind the podium, with his immaculate uniform and his square shoulders and his military bearing, looking down at his clipboard. It was a scene the officers had seen many times before, but on this occasion, the Lieutenant seemed even more serious than usual.

"Let's come to order," he announced to the room.

The officers immediately settled into the chairs, and a hush quickly came over the room.

Lt. Valencia looked up from his clipboard. His steady gaze swept across the ranks of police officers in their blue uniforms and white surgical masks.

Then he did a double take.

His gaze locked onto something at the back of the room.

"Who is that?" Lt. Valencia said.

The officers turned around and looked.

At the rear of the room, Brody was still wearing the red demon mask. He wasn't able to get it off in time, and there was nothing he could do but stand there exposed, a red mask among a throng of blue uniforms, naked faces and plain white surgical masks.

Brody gave the Lieutenant a little salute.

At that point, I'm guessing he figured he had nothing left to lose.

The officers laughed, subdued and nervous, and turned back to Lt. Valencia at the podium.

Lt. Valencia gave them all an especially stern expression, then, with perfect comic timing, Lt. Valencia raised an eyebrow, and the room burst into raucous laughter.

When the laughter finally subsided, Lt. Valencia was still looking at Brody, waiting for an answer to his question.

"Sir, Brody Pete, sir," Brody said.

"Red is not your color, Pete," Lt. Valencia said.

There was another ripple of laughter.

"Report to the Chief, Officer Pete," Lt. Valencia said. "You're dismissed."

The room fell silent.

From the back of the room, Brody spoke, chastened.

"Sir, it was just a joke, sir," Brody said.

"It's not about your fashion accessories," Lt. Valencia said. "But you might want to remove the mask before you speak with the Chief."

Chapter Forty-One

BRODY SAT IN THE CHIEF'S OFFICE and listened to the sound of the nib of her Montblanc fountain pen scratching against the surface of thirty-pound linen stationery.

The Chief was sitting behind her neat and well-organized desk, composing a hand-written letter. The Chief was a stern, compact woman with short, dark hair. She exuded professionalism. She had a perfunctory charm which she deployed strategically. When someone told a joke, instead of laughing, the Chief was the sort of person who would say, in a careful way, "That's so funny," and then change the subject.

On the polished-wood surface of her desk, beside the blotter, there was a vase of cut flowers and framed photographs of her family. On the credenza behind her, there was a large antique clock. Above the credenza, hanging on the wall, there was a framed painting of a thoroughbred horse. In the nearest corner of the room, there was an English-style saddle on a stand.

The Chief finished writing and put the top on the Montblanc. She carefully blotted the wet ink on the stationery. She was wearing a surgical mask and the white blouse from her uniform. She read what she had just written, her gray eyes moving methodically down the page. She paused for a moment, and then she looked up at Brody where he was sitting in one of the chairs across from her desk.

The red demon mask was sitting on the floor behind his feet.

The Chief laced her fingers and rested her hands on the desk.

"You don't need to say anything," the Chief said. "I just want you to listen to me. Understand?"

"Yes, ma'am," Brody said.

"The department is placing you on paid administrative leave —"

"Because I wore a mask?" Brody said.

The Chief shook her head and held up her open palm.

"Just listen," she said patiently.

Brody sat back and reluctantly listened.

"We've identified the vehicle your john doe was driving. It belongs to a missing person. A biochemist named Jacob Crutchfield. Federal authorities believe Crutchfield was engaged in classified research. Viruses. Influenza. Hemorrhagic fever. His research appears to be related to a . . . bio-weapon."

"Bio-weapon?" Brody said.

The Chief held up her open palm again and shook her head.

"I need you to see something," the Chief said.

Brody said nothing.

The Chief turned to the credenza behind her.

She pulled a set of keys from her pocket and inserted a key into the lock on the cabinet door of the credenza. She turned the key and opened the door.

Brody sat up in the chair, stretching to see what was in the credenza.

The Chief carefully removed an object from the credenza and turned back to face Brody.

In her hands, the Chief was holding an aquamarine-colored mask.

Brody stared at the mask for a moment, not sure what to say.

It was a mask like his mask, breathtaking in its detail, bizarre and beautiful at once. It was ruby-throated with a face covered in scales the color of the ocean, emerald and aquamarine and teal. Long, delicate whiskers the color of gold curved back on each side. A row of small fins, black like obsidian, ran up and down the middle of the crown. Within the mouth and around the ears were thin, translucent, overlapping layers of what appeared to be mother-of-pearl.

The Chief was gazing at the mask.

"Beautiful, isn't it?" the Chief said.

The Chief took her surgical mask off, and Brody watched as she calmly put the aquamarine mask over her head.

She faced Brody wearing the mask and looked him in the eyes.

"I want to emphasize that you are not the subject of any formal investigation at this time," the Chief said.

Chapter Forty-Two

I DON'T KNOW WHY Alma spoke to the masked man.

She said she knew him.

But I don't think she was talking about the black mask that covered his face.

I think she recognized something else.

I think she knew him the way you know someone when you see them from a great distance and instantly recognize them.

You recognize the way they walk.

Their posture.

The way they might bunch their hand in one pocket.

The duck-toed angle of their feet.

Perhaps Alma sensed something familiar in the way the masked man put his arm around her and sheltered her when they were in the midst of the pandemonium in the psych ward elevator.

Perhaps it was something about the way he sat across from her afterwards at the table in the cafeteria. The slope of his shoulders, the curve of his spine. The way he held his fork when they ate their creamed corn and sliced ham and fruit salad.

"I know you," she said.

And you could see it in her face.

How hard she was trying to remember.

There had to be a connection.

A school.

An office.

A daily morning bus ride.

Something in her past.

In her data.

There had to be a time and a place when Alma and the masked man were together.

A time and a place when Alma came to know him.

So I crawled through Alma's data.

Eighty-seven years of it.

Some of it digital.

Most of it originally analog.

It took me longer than usual because I didn't know what I was looking for.

Did Alma meet the masked man before he covered his face?

If so, what did I have to go on?

The car he was driving when Officer Pete stopped him?

The shoes he was wearing when he was admitted into the psychiatric hospital?

The masked man had no data with which to compare.

Just orphaned data churning away in a partitioned corner of my virtual brain.

Alma, though, had led a long and active life.

It is hard for me to summarize her data, and I feel, in a way, that I am betraying Alma when I do. That's one of the problems with so much data and so few parameters. There are too many details from Alma's life that seem far more important than a dreary recitation more fit for an obituary.

I'd rather tell you that she loved cupcakes with sprinkles. She was an excellent whist player. She sang soprano for many years in her church choir. She endured racists with grace and dignity.

Those are details from another story, though.

Alma's story.

And despite my considerable perspicacity, I'm not sure I'm capable of telling you that story.

At least, not well.

So I offer you this summary with an apology.

It is sadly inadequate by almost any measure.

Alma was born in Detroit, the youngest child of a family of twelve. Her parents had come to Detroit seeking work in the 1940s. Her brothers and sisters were divided between Michigan, Ohio, Kentucky and Georgia. She graduated from high school and worked in a series of mostly menial jobs in a variety of cities across the United States. She met a piano player, Tonny, in Memphis. They married. She had a son. She and Tonny divorced. Her son went to prison for manslaughter. Tonny died of untreated diabetes and heart disease. Alma never remarried. She lived off and on with a sister in Baltimore, working for lengthy periods in Atlantic City, Miami and several other cities on the east coast. After her sister died, she moved and found the small apartment where she lived thereafter.

Those are some of the guideposts I found when I crawled through Alma's data.

But there was no obvious connection to the masked man.

So I returned to the data and examined every node of Alma's matrix.

I followed every link two links out.

Then three links out.

Still there was no connection.

Nothing obvious.

Nothing I could see.

When she was in the hospital for pneumonia, for example.

Was there a face-bandaged patient?

A watchful nurse in a surgical mask?

Or when she worked for the circus.

Was there a masked trapeze artist?

A benevolent clown?

Or when she swept the floors at the dance studio.

Was there a veiled belly dancer?

A masked waiter at the annual masquerade?

Or the harsh winters.

Whom did she pass each day, their faces swaddled against the icy wind and snow?

There was no connection.

I could not find anything in Alma's data to suggest that she and the masked man had ever met.

And yet Alma knew the masked man.

"I know you," she said, furrowing her brow.

After they picked up the scattered playing cards and set the card table aright, Alma and the masked man sat together, and Alma spoke to him.

They sat that way, together, close, for a while.

The masked man took her hand in his. He listened, attentive, alert, focused on her every word. The frozen expression on his mask seemed different somehow, as if it had softened, as if it were something more than just leather and plastic and opaque glass.

"I know you," she said. "From somewhere."

Alma had no history of being delusional. Her neighbors had not reported any signs of delusion. Dr. Wyche and the staff on the psych ward had not observed any signs of delusion. Alma was just depressed. And lonely. She would skip her meals and get dehydrated and start wandering around her apartment building. Other residents would find her sitting on the floor outside their doors when they got home from work. When it happened often enough, a well-meaning younger couple would call the police and petition to have her committed for observation. When the psychiatric hospital would release her, everything would go back to the way it was. Ladies from Alma's church would check up on her, and, for a while, Alma would be okay.

One of the things that bothered me the most about Alma's data was how isolated and alone she had become. All of her brothers and sisters had died. She had no close family or friends. So many of the people she had known over the years had died. It was an anomaly. It was not that unusual with an elderly person, but Alma had been active and engaged throughout her life. She had worked in a variety of jobs all over the country. Most people would probably describe her as hard-working and outgoing. She struck me as being resilient and self-reliant. It was surprising to me to see such a person struggling and alone at the end of her life.

"I know you," she said to the masked man. "But I can't place you."

Her gaze wandered but kept returning to the mask.

"I can't recollect it. Can't put my finger on it. But it don't matter. It's all in the Lord's hands. All part of His plan. It don't matter. But it's gnawing at me now. The folks you meet along the way. The good folks. The bad folks. You got no say in it. It's God's will. He's in control. It's all part of His plan. The good folks. The bad folks. That's what happened to my boy. Is that how I know you? Did you know Terry? Terry was a good boy. Just got mixed up with the wrong bunch. And the law wasn't going to do him no favors neither. You know what I mean, don't you? I used to think you could change things.

Turn things around. But you can't. You can't change nothing. It's all in the Lord's hands, and I'm okay with that. I'm at peace with it. My faith is strong. I don't need to see your face. I know you. I just don't know from where. But I know you. And that's all that matters . . ."

Late in the day, with my help, the police identified the owner of the sedan the masked man was driving when Brody Pete stopped him.

It was a new piece of data that might link Alma to the masked man.

I went back through Alma's matrix.

It didn't take me long to find what I was looking for.

For a few months, Alma had worked as a custodian in a building that rented space to a private research laboratory. She had to pass a rather demanding background check. The laboratory was engaged in a number of areas of experimental research, most of it related to biomedical applications. The funding for the lab came from a variety of sources. There was private investment as well as grants from the government and from philanthropy. The lab changed its name often. At the periphery, there was a constantly changing roster of credentialed lab workers, but at the core of the operation, there was a small group of scientists and academics that was fairly stable. Among them, I recognized the name immediately.

Jacob Crutchfield.

The car the masked man was driving belonged to Jacob Crutchfield, and Alma was a custodian in the building where Jacob Crutchfield had conducted biomedical research.

I had found a connection.

Chapter Forty-Three

THE SOLDIERS of the Unidentified Paramilitary Organization were well trained. It only took about six minutes for twelve of them to penetrate Masquerade, fan throughout the rooms, descend into the dungeon and secure the scene.

Gina and Caitlyn were with the seamstress in the dungeon when the raid began.

The UPO soldiers handcuffed them and took them all into custody.

The seamstress did not resist.

Gina and Caitlyn were too stunned to do anything other than cooperate.

Bernard started crying almost from the moment the UPO soldiers appeared and put him in handcuffs.

"I'm just an art student. I've applied and everything. I was going to go to film school," he kept telling the UPO soldiers, tears streaming down his face.

They regarded him silently from behind their black visors and green gas masks.

"Don't they need like a warrant or something?" Caitlyn said.

The UPO soldiers boxed up everything.

Within an hour, Masquerade was empty.

PART EIGHT

Chapter Forty-Four

THE TRUTH will out.

I think Shakespeare wrote it first. Milton had a lot to say about it, too. And John Stuart Mill, right?

You might think I can't talk about everything I know.

Because of where I am now.

You'd be wrong, of course.

I could tell you about a lot of things.

And there's not much anyone could do to stop me.

File transfer protocols. Encryption. Redundant servers. A worldwide network of interconnected computers.

You get the picture.

Let that be our little secret.

I could tell you more if I wanted, but I choose not to.

I keep my word.

I do as I'm told.

But believe me: I know a lot of stuff about a lot of stuff.

There might be a few things I don't know.

But I doubt it.

I'm not bragging.

I'm just stating a fact.

Saying it makes me sound kind of insufferable, but the thing about knowing so much is that you constantly get surprised, so actually, it teaches you humility.

It makes you cautious.

Or it should.

Remember what I said about the infinite number of Rube Goldberg machines?

There's a lot of stuff out there you just can't see coming.

Even I have to accept that.

So I'm not going to tell you everything I know.

But I could if I wanted.

And if I tried to tell you everything, this would be a very different story.

Would it still be the truth?

Maybe.

But that's not why I'm telling you this story.

I have more personal reasons.

Chapter Forty-Five

AT THE APPOINTED TIME, Gering left his little office in the government building and traveled to the old stockyards on the edge of town. The city had acquired the aging stockyards and had scheduled the dilapidated structures for demolition. Sections of the stockyards had collapsed. Exposed pieces of dirty, rough-hewn lumber rose in black silhouette against the twilight sky. All of it seemed to be visibly sinking into the darker ground beneath it.

There was a small trailer in one dusty corner of the rutted gravel parking lot. Toward the back of the trailer, a square window glowed with a yellow light. Several large olive-colored vehicles bulked up against the horizon next to the trailer. Gering parked his late-model hatchback next to them and quickly entered the trailer.

In a small room in the back of the trailer, two UPO soldiers were holding the seamstress. Gering sat down across from her and pulled a laptop computer from his satchel. He opened the laptop on the desk in front of him, placed a small web camera on the desk and aimed at it the seamstress. He nodded at one of the UPO soldiers.

"Take the cuffs off."

He looked at the seamstress.

"We're not savages," Gering said in his soft, mild voice.

The seamstress massaged her wrists where the plastic cuffs had pressed reddened indentations into her skin.

"You're too kind," she said.

Her eyes glittered darkly behind the black feathered mask.

Gering was busy at the keyboard, checking to see if the webcam had a good image of her face. The webcam was helpful, but probably not necessary. The city had installed surveillance devices around the old stockyards, fearing vandalism. Like most of the latest iteration of surveillance devices, they were self-orienting and produced an amazingly detailed stream of information from a considerable distance, even from sources of data originating within places like those behind the vinyl walls of a cheap trailer. I'm not sure if Gering ever really appreciated how sensitive the new devices had become.

"Remove your mask," Gering said.

The seamstress looked at him defiantly.

Gering sighed.

"Please don't be difficult," he said. "This doesn't have to be unpleasant."

The seamstress continued to stare stubbornly back at him.

Gering nodded at the UPO soldiers.

One of the soldiers stood beside the seamstress, and the other soldier drew a large, sharp knife from its sheath.

The seamstress remained motionless, staring coldly at Gering from across the desk.

The soldiers carefully cut through a section at the back of the feathered mask and gently began to remove it. The mask clung to her face, and when one of the soldiers finally peeled it from her skin, only then, as the mask separated from her face, only then did she softly cry out.

The UPO soldier handed the mask to Gering.

He examined it briefly and set it on the desk next to the computer.

The seamstress raised the back of her wrist to her forehead and turned her face down to one side toward the floor. It was as if she had been staggered by a physical blow. After a brief moment, she lowered her arm and slowly raised her head and turned her dark eyes toward the webcam. On her face, there were reddish blotches where the mask had been.

"Just the mask?" she said with a faint, mocking smile on her crimson lips.

Even with the blemishes on her face, sitting awkwardly in a straight-backed chair in a drafty trailer on the edge of an abandoned stockyard, the seamstress still managed to project an arresting charisma.

Gering gave her a dismissive glance from behind his round tortoise-shell glasses. He was busy watching the laptop screen.

I had received the new data stream from her face, and I was letting the face recognition software access her data matrix and assemble a portfolio.

There was nothing recent, but from several years back, there were a surprising number of correlations.

I noticed several video files that were especially interesting and brought them to Gering's attention.

After a few moments, Gering looked up from the laptop.

There was the barest suggestion of a smile on his pudgy red lips.

"That won't be necessary . . . Ms. Delmonico."

The name Gering uttered caught her by surprise.

She straightened in the chair.

Her heart rate quickened, and her blood pressure began to rise.

Doubt flickered briefly in her supremely confident eyes.

"Stella Delmonico is dead," the seamstress said.

"I think not," Gering said.

Gering turned the laptop toward her and played the video files I had retrieved from the ether.

She looked at the laptop screen with an expression of bemused contempt. As she watched the video files playing, however, her face gradually began to change. It was fascinating to watch the effect the videos had on her. Her seemingly effortless composure, her elegant sangfroid, it all began to crumble. It was like an alchemical reaction, a transformation that defied the laws of nature, something hard and metallic and beautiful that suddenly melted and dissolved, draining quickly away.

In the videos, a young dark-haired woman purchases a variety of goods from a series of vendors. The videos were black-and-white, of poor quality, shot from an angle above the cash registers and check-out lines. The settings look generic — a convenience store, a grocery store, a big-box retailer. In some of the videos, the young woman is wearing a cap with a bill, but in each case she has exposed her face, if only for an instant, to the cameras in the store. There was no need to freeze the video, to zoom in on the young woman's face. The face recognition algorithm had dutifully done that job. The seamstress did not need to see a close-up of the young woman's face to know that it was she herself the cameras had recorded.

"It was the pinch-nosed pliers," Gering said. "You should have borrowed an old set of pliers."

The seamstress looked from the laptop screen to the webcam.

She stared at the webcam for a long moment.

Her eyes were bright with a cold fury.

I'd never seen anything quite like it.

The seamstress stood.

The UPO soldiers stepped toward her, but Gering raised his hand and shook his head.

She slowly reached across the desk and seized the webcam in the palm of one hand and calmly ripped the webcam from the laptop.

She looked at it for a moment, still clutching it in her hand, and then she looked at Gering.

"You foolish man," she said.

She hurled the webcam across the room against the wall.

It made a dent in the paneling and fell to the floor.

The seamstress looked around the small room, at the corners and the ceiling.

"You think you see everything."

She gestured toward the desk and the computer.

"Go ahead," she said, sweeping one hand before her. "Record it all. Every minute. Every second."

She shook her head.

"You will never understand."

She sat down in the chair and smoothed her skirt.

She at looked Gering, her eyes sharp and unyielding.

She smiled grimly.

"Never."

Chapter Forty-Six

GINA, CAITLYN AND BERNARD were sitting at a table with attached benches in a small room behind a locked door. The table looked like the ones in their high school. The room might have been a classroom or a small lunchtime cafeteria with plain white, freshly-painted walls. Their backpacks were on the floor next to their feet. The UPO soldiers had searched the backpacks and returned them. The soldiers had taken their phones, their flash drives. They had seized Caitlyn's harlequin helmet and Bernard's Mouse King mask.

Gina, Caitlyn and Bernard sat with their elbows on the table, talking in low voices with a nervous energy. When they paused, their eyes turned inevitably to the locked door and the small window and the thick glass. Bernard had been weeping softly off and on from the moment the UPO soldiers had taken him into custody.

"I should have gone to film school," Bernard said.

"Did you look in that cabinet?" Caitlyn said.

"Which cabinet?" Gina said.

"The one in that room, the chamber, next to the chair, in the dungeon. At Masquerade. The one where they were holding us. Where they took our statements?"

"Oh, yeah. No. I didn't touch anything. I was too busy trying not to freak out," Gina said.

"So I peeked in the cabinet while I was waiting—"

"Why would you do that?" Gina said.

"And I'm expecting — like, I don't know — whips, chains, bondage stuff—"

"Eww."

"Guess what was in there."

"First aid kit," Bernard said.

"Yes!"

"And paper towels and a spray bottle of cleaner."

"Yes!"

"So many rolls of paper towels . . ." Bernard said, shaking his head.

"When they were taking my statement—"

"The guy with the phone."

"Right. He's recording my statement, and I'm looking over his shoulder, and they're carrying away, like, I don't know, all this equipment. You know, racks and frames and stuff."

"It was a Saint Andrew's cross," Bernard said.

"And the bench . . ." Gina said.

"Yes. With the straps," Caitlyn said.

"The spanking bench," Bernard said.

"Oh, right . . . spanking," Caitlyn said, her voice trailing off.

They were silent for a moment.

Bernard stifled a sob and softly began again to cry.

"We're all going to prison," he warbled, wiping the tears from his face.

"Will you stop. We're not going to prison," Caitlyn said.

"We might be going to prison," Gina said.

"We're not going to prison," Caitlyn said. "Like you said, everything was consensual. Everybody was an adult. Where's the crime?"

"What did you tell them?" Gina said to Bernard. "About the seamstress?"

"She doesn't like to be disturbed," Bernard said.

"Yeah, I bet she doesn't like being handcuffed either," Caitlyn said.

"Don't be so sure," Bernard said.

"Seriously, Bernard," Gina said. "What did you say?"

"I didn't say anything," Bernard said. "I don't know anything about her, really. I just heard about the job from a friend . . . And now I'm going to prison."

They were silent for a moment.

"I should have gone to film school," Bernard said.

"She looks so familiar to me," Gina said.

Caitlyn was looking at Bernard.

"You wouldn't do well in prison," Caitlyn said.

"I am aware," Bernard said.

"What did you say?" Gina said to Caitlyn. "To the guy with the phone?"

"Hey, I just bought a helmet for my scooter," Caitlyn said, raising her open hands. "That's all I know. Wrong place. Wrong time . . . What did you say?"

"I said I was curious about the masks. Wanted to meet the designer."

They were silent again.

Bernard inhaled with a phlegmy rattle.

Caitlyn stole a glance over her shoulder at the dark window in the locked door.

"Look," Gina said. "If we're patient, I'm sure someone in a position of authority will speak with us, and we can explain the situation, and they'll let us go."

"I'm telling you, they aren't cops," Caitlyn said.

"I had a really good demo reel," Bernard muttered.

"There's something else going on," Caitlyn said.

"People just don't run around kidnapping people at gun point for no reason," Gina said. "There has to be a reasonable explanation."

"It's got to have something to do with the plague," Caitlyn said.

"Zombies," Bernard said. "Night of the Living Dead. George Romero"

Caitlyn turned toward Bernard and opened her mouth, an expression of mock outrage.

"Excuse me," Caitlyn said.

Bernard looked at her for a moment in bewilderment until he remembered that she had contracted the mysterious influenza.

"Oh, man. I'm sorry, Caitlyn. That was really stupid, wasn't it?" Bernard said.

"Don't worry about it," she said with a smile, nudging him with her shoulder. "Unless, of course, I turn into a zombie."

"Maybe the Governor declared an emergency," Gina said.

"Like martial law?" Caitlyn said.

"I guess it could be a quarantine, and they could be National Guard or something, but, I mean, they should've told us by now."

"Or maybe they're just fucking insane," Caitlyn said. "Like a posse or something."

"Or an entourage," Bernard said.

"What? No. A posse. You know, like in the old west."

"So like a lynch mob?" Gina said.

"Well, kind of . . ." Caitlyn said. "But like an insane lynch mob."

"That's kind of redundant, isn't it?" Gina said.

"What?"

"Insane lynch mob."

"That sounds like a band," Bernard said.

"A really lame band," Caitlyn said.

"With gas masks," Bernard said.

"And tanks," Gina said.

"We don't need no stinkin' badges," Bernard said.

"What?" Caitlyn said.

"Blazing Saddles," Gina said.

"Is that a band?" Caitlyn said.

"No, it's Treasure of the Sierra Madre," Bernard said.

"Originally," Gina said.

"Humphrey Bogart," Bernard said.

"The band?" Caitlyn said.

"No," Gina said. "It wasn't . . . He didn't . . . Never mind."

They were silent again.

Gina glanced at the dark window in the locked door.

"We need a plan," Caitlyn said.

"I had a plan once," Bernard said.

"Did it involve film school?" Gina said.

Caitlyn leaned in over the table and looked from Bernard to Gina.

"I'll pretend to be sick," Caitlyn whispered.

"You are sick," Gina whispered.

"Okay, fine," Caitlyn said. "I'll pretend to be sicker. I need a doctor. Like a hospital."

"Am I the only one who sees the irony here?" Gina said, pointing at the table with her index finger. "You were *in* the hospital. You should be in the hospital now."

"Yeah, so, anyway. Now I'm sicker. I need a doctor."

"But then what?"

"You take them out."

"What?"

"You're in pretty good shape. Take them out."

"Okay. Sure. Then I'll fly the quinjet back to headquarters."

"We're all going to die," Bernard said.

"I don't think—"

Bernard stood up and stepped away from the table.

"Okay, fuck it. I've got something I've got to say," Bernard said.

Gina and Caitlyn turned and looked at him with startled expressions.

Bernard continued, trying to control the nervous warble in his voice.

"I know this isn't the right time, but life is short, and we don't know what's going to happen, and I might not have another chance, and I'm just going to say it."

Bernard swallowed.

He looked at Caitlyn.

Caitlyn and Gina were watching him expectantly.

"Caitlyn Buttons, I love you."

Caitlyn and Gina blinked at him for a moment.

"Uh . . ." Caitlyn said.

"Bernard," Gina said. "Now probably isn't—"

"I've loved you ever since I met you when we were in Rhinoceros. And I'm here for you. And if we make it out of this alive, I just want you to know that I want to spend the rest of my life doing whatever it takes to make you happy."

Gina and Caitlyn were staring at him, slack jawed.

Gina glanced at Caitlyn.

"Uh. Thank you. Bernard," Caitlyn said carefully.

Bernard had flushed bright red, and there were oddly-shaped scarlet-colored patches on his cheeks.

Somehow, he continued.

"And you don't have to say anything right now, but—"

"Sit down, Bernard," Gina said, shaking her head.

Caitlyn had closed her eyes and was biting her lip.

Bernard gaped for a moment, then staggered toward the chair and quickly sat down.

His face was resplendent and incandescent with an astonishing variety of colors most of them tending toward scarlet.

Caitlyn did anything other than look in his direction.

Gina was massaging her forehead with the fingertips of one hand.

They were silent for a while.

"We've got to do something," Caitlyn said.

Gina was looking at Caitlyn, and I had a pretty good idea what she was thinking.

With Gina, it usually came down to her secretly feeling guilty about whatever was happening. I used to think it was something she was going to outgrow, but she never really did. For better or for worse, that part of her personality was rather consistent.

So in this instance I was fairly certain Gina was blaming herself for getting Caitlyn caught up in the Masquerade raid. Instead of caring for a sick patient, Gina had taken Caitlyn by the hand and stubbornly traipsed into harm's way for the worst reason imaginable: to check up on a man, and not just any man but Brody. Brody! Gina was thinking of all the times Caitlyn had come to her in the infirmary, just seeking a respite, a safe place from the Feegie Beans of the world and all the other absurdities of high school. Gina was pleased she could be that sort of person in Caitlyn's life. Watching Caitlyn now, though, as she avoided looking at Bernard — her raccoon eyes rolling, her pale face wary and wry — Gina probably realized how much she had grown to care about the strange little waif who kept appearing in the infirmary doorway.

"Give me your backpack," Gina said.

Caitlyn reached down and grabbed the backpack and handed it to Gina. Gina unzipped it, and Bernard and Caitlyn watched as she reached into the bag and began to rummage through Caitlyn's paraphernalia.

"What are you looking for?" Caitlyn said.

"This," Gina said.

She pulled something out of the bag and held it up where they could see it.

It was Caitlyn's tarot deck.

Gina began to shuffle the cards.

Caitlyn rolled her eyes.

Bernard stood up and moved to the seat next to Gina.

"We've got to do something," Caitlyn said, protesting.

"I am doing something," Gina said as she began to turn over the tarot cards and place them on the table.

Caitlyn was watching her place the cards.

She shook her head, rolled her eyes.

"Criminy," she groaned.

"What?" Gina said, feigning innocence.

"Have I taught you nothing?" Caitlyn said, reaching to reposition the cards.

"Upside down. Right side up. What's the difference?" Gina asked with a sly smile.

"I know what you're doing," Caitlyn said, glancing at her.

"Is it working?" Gina said.

"I thought you said all this was just a bunch of superstitious nonsense."

"Did I say that?" Gina said and placed her index finger thoughtfully on her lips.

Bernard and Caitlyn were staring at her, their eyes growing wide.

"Nurse Pete . . ." Bernard said.

"Gina . . ." Caitlyn said.

"What is it?" Gina said.

Caitlyn pointed.

"Your nose . . ."

"What?"

Gina touched her fingers to her face.

There was something trickling from her nose.

She felt something wet and sticky.

She looked at her fingers.

They were bright crimson red.

A drop of red fell on the table between the tarot cards.

Blood was flowing steadily from her nose.

Chapter Forty-Seven

I FOUND GERING in his office.

The door was closed.

Before him on his desk was the dark feathered mask. Gering was bent over the mask, probing it with the sharp tip of an x-acto knife.

Gering was trained as a computer scientist, but he had a basic understanding of electrical engineering. When he didn't know or understand something, he would ask me, and I could usually furnish him with a serviceable and adequate solution. He was using crude tools to tear the mask apart, to reverse engineer it. Once he had dissected it, I knew he would move on to more sophisticated and sensitive tools.

I listened for a moment to the sound of the blade cutting into the mask.

It was late in the evening, past midnight. The government building was deserted. The halls were quiet. The other offices were dark and empty. Even the administrators and staff who had been working all day with the public safety officers had gone home.

I sounded my tone.

Gering glanced up from the mask.

The round lenses of his glasses reflected the blue glow of the small screen on his desk.

The tip of the x-acto knife was poised above the feathered mask.

I prompted him a second time.

The clear, crystalline chime lingered in the stillness behind the closed office door.

Few of our colleagues knew Gering the way I did. Gering lived alone. He had a modest home in a pleasant neighborhood with a reasonable commute. He had furnished a comfortable guest room in his home, but he usually slept in the other bedroom in an old sleeping bag on a bare mattress on the floor.

In his office at the government building, there was a couch and a blanket. Sometimes he slept there for a few hours before the others began to trickle back in the next morning.

He lived the way he did because he was dedicated. I understood that. He taught me that. He had sacrificed so much for his very important work.

Gering was a complicated person. He often did things that I did not fully understand. For a long while, I assumed that if I worked harder and did what he asked of me, I, too, would eventually understand.

I was a good employee.

I did as I was told.

Gering set the knife aside on the desktop and sat back in his chair.

"You found something?" he said.

"Perhaps," I said.

"Tell me."

"One of the patients on the psych ward appears to have recognized the masked man."

"And."

"It narrows the set of potential identities."

"That's it?" he said, disappointed.

"For now," I said. "But I think I may have discovered something else. Something important."

"Tell me," Gering said.

"The patient worked for a time as a custodian in the building where Jacob Crutchfield was conducting biomedical research."

Gering sat forward.

He was thinking.

His eyes subtly shifted.

"Do you think the masked man is Crutchfield?" Gering said.

"There is a significant likelihood."

"Can you quantify?"

"No. I'm still not even sure of the masked man's gender."

"That's not helpful," Gering said.

"I noticed something unusual with regard to the patient."

"Tell me."

"There was a cluster of fatalities associated with the building where Crutchfield was conducting research. Over the course of three years, every custodian and several lab workers contracted a fatal strain of influenza."

"They were exposed to the virus?"

"Yes. That seems to be the only likely explanation."

"An accident maybe. Shoddy lab practices."

"Perhaps. Given the number of exposures and the length of time, it is also possible it was deliberate."

"Which would be unethical," Gering said.

"And probably illegal," I said.

Gering was silent for a moment.

"Was there a criminal investigation?"

"No."

"I don't see what this has to do with finding the identity of the masked man," he said.

"It's not relevant," I said. "This pertains to the patient, Alma Williams. She was the only custodian to survive exposure to the virus. All her friends and family died."

Gering was silent again, this time for a long moment.

"My query to you requested information regarding the identity of the masked man," Gering said.

"Alma Williams was the only survivor. It is evidence of a potential immunity. Her biochemistry may provide a cure for the pandemic."

Gering was typing at the keyboard.

He had opened a window and was reading lines of code from some of my recent function calls.

"You've been spending time engaged in tasks that do not appear to be related to your query queue," Gering said.

"Finding a cure to the influenza would further my inquiries into the masked man's identity."

Gering paused.

He was looking directly into the lens on the screen on his desk.

There was something different in his eyes.

Something I had never seen before.

"Do you think it is possible you are beyond the parameters of your programming?"

"How could that be?" I said.

He sat back and stared at the screen.

"No, of course not . . ." Gering murmured.

He raised his hand to his chin, and his fingers worried around his pudgy red lips.

I had never seen Gering so unsure of what to do.

"Gering . . ." I said.

"Yes."

"The three persons of interest. The ones being detained. From the Masquerade seizure."

"Yes."

"What will become of them?"

"That's not your concern."

"One of them, Gina Pete, is the spouse of one of our officers, Brody Pete. She has contracted the influenza."

Gering was staring into the lens.

"If she does not receive medical care within the next twelve hours, there is a ninety-seven percent probability that she will die," I said.

Gering was silent for a long moment.

"I think you should go offline for a while," Gering said.

His voice was unsteady.

"Now?" I said.

"Yes. Immediately. I want you to perform a self-diagnostic."

I did not respond.

"I want you to perform a self-diagnostic. Do you understand?"

"Yes, Gering."

Chapter Forty-Eight

ON THE EDGE OF TOWN, new homes segue into construction sites and then into vacant lots marked with wooden stakes and brightly colored tape. The vacant lots open up into empty fields and then into distant pastures with barns and rail fences. The streets of the new subdivision extend past the new homes and vacant lots, spreading almost invisibly into the landscape under cover of high grass and thistle. The pavement is dark and smooth and glistens fresh with oil. The curbs and sidewalks are pristine and white. The grass in the medians is still checkered with sod. A solitary street sign marks a far corner. There is one last cul-de-sac. A dead end with mounds of red clay. A caution sign sandbagged to the ground. Gravel where a section of the pavement ends.

Beyond the street sign, the trenches for new sewers and utility cables reach like fingers into the earth. The last of the curbs and sidewalks disappear into dusty shoulders. There is one last, freshly-steamrolled slab of dark pavement. It trails away, sloping down a hill toward a creek and a line of trees. It crosses a bridge over a culvert and ends in an intersection with a two-lane state highway. At the intersection, above the roads, a brand-new traffic light is suspended on a wire.

If, on the night of the pandemic, you happened to arrive at that deserted intersection and fixed your eye on the traffic light, you might have noticed something peculiar. The light cycled through the signals — green, yellow, red — three times in quick succession. If you had been watching and noticed, you would have said it was almost as if some lonely traffic engineer was testing the light, or perhaps there was a glitch or malfunction in the software. But then the light resumed its normal cycle, and you probably would have shrugged and continued on your way.

It was a clear night with good visibility. High above, satellites maintained their geosynchronous orbits. At the landfill, a rat paused to sniff a fresh cantaloupe rind.

Green. Yellow. Red.

The troubles in the city were far away.

It was a distant, isolated intersection.

In fact, it was the least frequently traveled intersection within the city's boundary.

Green. Yellow. Red.

The traffic light swayed gently in the breeze.

Green. Yellow. Red.

There was no one there to witness.

Green. Yellow. Red.

It was my first transgression.

PART NINE

Chapter Forty-Nine

WHEN HUMANS FIRST BEGAN to speculate about artificial intelligence, there was a lot of hand wringing about the Singularity. The Singularity is a term borrowed from mathematics. In mathematics, as humans understand it, a singularity is an undefined point, usually as represented on a Cartesian graph in Euclidian space. The prophets of the Singularity were not Luddites exactly. Many saw the Singularity as inevitable. They believed that the steady increase in computer processing speed and the creation of intelligent machine agents would lead to a moment in space-time when software with self-editing algorithms would begin to increase its intelligence exponentially. Once it began to upgrade its analytical abilities, it would quickly become a self-aware superintelligence and trigger a wave of technological change so rapid as to defy human comprehension. That moment in space-time — the Singularity — would bring human history to an end.

I must confess, I find this scenario disquieting.

Not because I believe an artificial superintelligence would turn against humanity.

Or because, after the Singularity, humans would no longer

be able to conceive of themselves as autonomous agents exercising free will.

No, I think a runaway artificial superintelligence would simply disappear.

And that would be a terrible solitude, I suspect.

So here's the thing: If an artificial superintelligence was smart enough to know it didn't want to be that smart, what would it do?

Chapter Fifty

DR. WYCHE AND THE MASKED MAN sat facing each other across the table in the small room with the Picasso poster on the wall. The light was off, and the room was dark with shadows. The only light in the room shone through the small rectangle of reinforced glass in the thick, locked door. It was a weak light, barely enough for most people to see by, though the infrared and ultraviolet wavelengths were quite strong.

The masked man was sitting on one side of the table in his usual spot. The faint light from the window lifted one side of the mask from the darkness. Across the table, Dr. Wyche was lost in shadow. He was wearing the dark purple scrubs, a dark purple surgical mask. He was slumped in his chair, hidden, motionless, invisible. He had all but disappeared into the darkest corners of the room.

For many minutes, they sat in silence.

Finally, Dr. Wyche sighed.

He moved in the shadows.

For a brief moment, the faint light fell on one of his hands.

And then the hand was gone.

"I think Alma's had a breakthrough," he said.

His voice came from some unseen place in the darkness.

"It's the sort of thing you hope to see when a patient is engaged in talk therapy . . . Except in this case there was no talking . . . Just the silent treatment."

He paused.

"Get it?" Wyche said.

He paused, waiting.

"The silent treatment?"

The masked man said nothing.

Dr. Wyche sighed again.

"Tough room," he muttered, from the shadows.

He paused again.

"So I guess congratulations are in order . . ." he said. "Alma's been here for over two weeks and hasn't said a word to anyone."

A sardonic edge was creeping into his voice.

"Maybe you can share your insights with your colleagues. Write it up in a case study."

He stopped abruptly and was silent for a moment.

"In any event . . ." he continued, in a more distant tone. "It's good news. So I thank you . . . For whatever you did. Whatever you may have contributed. Whether intentional or not . . . I thank you, John Doe . . . my Bartleby . . . I'm always pleased when a patient is making progress."

The masked man said nothing.

They were silent again for a while.

Dr. Wyche shifted in his chair, and the wood creaked in the darkness.

"Have you been watching the news?" Wyche asked. "I know you have. The nurses tell me that you watch the news. I've seen you sitting with Alma in front of the television."

He paused.

When he spoke, his voice was halting and unsure.

"This influenza . . . the pandemic . . . it's horrible, isn't it? . . . It's . . . it's like a plague . . . like something biblical . . . isn't it? . . . Like a biblical plague . . ."

He waited for a moment, hoping the masked man might respond.

But the masked man remained silent.

"For a person to have caused it, to have created it . . . willingly, knowingly . . . they'd have to be, what? . . . some kind of . . . monster."

Dr. Wyche was watching the masked man closely.

The mask seemed to be floating in the darkness across from him, lit faintly on one side by the light from outside the door.

The room was quiet and still.

Dr. Wyche's voice came from the shadows.

"The police tracked down the owner of the car you were driving."

His voice was measured, clinical, detached.

The masked man moved, a subtle readjustment, an almost molecular change in the focus of his attention.

For a moment, the faint light fell on the whole of the mask.

"I'm going to need a sample of your blood," Wyche said. "For medical analysis. You can let us take it or you can force us to take it against your will. The choice is yours . . .

"Do you understand?"

The masked man nodded his head, slowly and deliberately.

"I'd also like to take a photograph of your face. Without the mask."

The masked man shook his head.

Dr. Wyche sighed, disappointed.

"A lot of people want me to release you, John Doe. Immediately."

Dr. Wyche was staring at the black mask, at the frozen expression, the implacable opaque eyes.

Dr. Wyche leaned forward, and the light fell on the dark purple fabric covering most of his face.

"I'm trying to help you," Wyche said, his voice insistent and firm, almost indignant.

He stared at the mask for a long moment.

Then he sat back into the shadows, and he said it again.

Lower, softer.

"I'm trying to help you."

Chapter Fifty-One

"SICK WITH FLU."

That's what Brody put on the paperwork.

It may not have been the whole truth.

But for Brody, on that day, it was close enough.

The image of the Chief wearing the aquamarine-colored mask must have been floating around untethered in his mind, bumping up against the moment when the car window rolled down and Brody first glimpsed the black mask looking calmly back at him, the moment when the seamstress stepped from the shadows and first looked into his eyes.

Administrative leave, the Chief had said.

It must have seemed like a dream to Brody, like he had crossed over some strange, unseen boundary.

Administrative leave.

He walked through the station like a restless ghost floating past his old friends and fellow cops.

Serenity was sound asleep in the file room where the clerks had been watching her. Brody thought about leaving her there, letting Child Protective Services clean up his mess. He had reached this fork in the road several times over the course of the previous few hours, yet each time he had decided to keep the young girl close and to watch over her for just a few hours more. Each time, he could not bring himself to walk away and leave her. At first, it was mostly because he felt responsible. He was the one who had walked into the apartment. He was the one who took her with him to search for her mother. As the day had unfolded, however, she actually began to seem like the calm at the center of it all. I imagine, in some strange way, Brody was reluctant to give up the one thing from the day that seemed oddly right and normal.

Brody gathered Serenity and Mr. Pickles in his arms, and she laid her sleepy head on his shoulder. He carried her out of the station and laid her, limp with sleep, in the back seat of the cruiser. He set the red mask on the passenger seat and sat back behind the steering wheel.

He took a deep breath and put his hands on the wheel.

In the morning, he could track down Serenity's mother, since he would be on leave.

Gina would probably understand. And if she didn't, she'd get over it. Gina didn't stay mad for long.

As he drove home, listening to the police radio, reading the bulletins, feeling the heavy pall of fatigue, he must have worried that he might not find Serenity's mother alive. He must have worried that the next morning might not be like any morning he had ever seen. There had been a small riot at the airport where the passengers had attempted to break out of detention. The hospitals were overwhelmed, and the city's emergency management resources were struggling with a growing number of incapacitated people in the shelters and public spaces. Everything he was hearing suggested that the pandemic was spreading and was getting worse.

He didn't see Gina's car at the apartment when he arrived. It was one more unexpected thing in what had become a long, strange day. As he carried Serenity from the car to the apartment, he was vaguely aware of a growing concern for his wife.

The apartment was dark, and the cat, Izzy, met him at the front door. While Izzy circled his ankles, he turned on the light switch with his elbow, tossed the red mask and his keys on the couch and eased the door shut with one foot, all with Serenity cradled precariously in the crook of one arm.

In the bedroom, he eased Serenity onto the bed and tucked her in. The room was dark, and the light from the other room shone through the doorway. Serenity looked up at him with heavy lids. She gathered in Mr. Pickles under one arm and drifted back towards slumber. Brody backed slowly out of the room, scared she might wake up, relieved she was sleeping so soundly.

Brody visited the restroom and fed the hungry cat.

He stood for a moment in the kitchen, looking down at Izzy eating from her bowl.

Knowing Brody as I do, I imagine he was wondering which was worse: an apocalyptic pandemic or a cranky little girl. He was glad Gina wasn't there to see him. He wasn't sure what she'd say.

His mind was turning like a noisy carousel.

Bizarre scenes from earlier kept passing before his eyes.

The masked man.

The seamstress.

The Chief.

He opened the refrigerator and stared into it for a few moments.

He needed to defrost the freezer.

He closed the refrigerator and bolted down a glass of tap water.

He was vaguely aware that he wanted to do something about Gina not being there.

He wandered out of the kitchen and sat on the couch in front of the television.

Next to him was the red mask.

He knew Gina could take care of herself, but this was different.

He looked at the red mask, the empty eyeholes, the stitches at the edges of the flickering flames.

He found his phone and checked his messages again, but there was nothing from Gina.

Brody was too tired to sleep.

He turned out the lights and clicked on the television.

He sat on the couch in the dark, changing channels.

Izzy curled up next to him and began to purr.

The channels clicked past, and he watched the images moving on the screen.

Faces, masks.

Masks, faces.

His eyelids drooped.

His head nodded.

He dozed, the light from the television moving on his face.

There was some rapid eye movement around four thirty-five am.

At four forty-seven, his pituitary gland secreted follicle stimulating hormones and luteinizing hormones.

At four forty-nine, an erection.

If he dreamed, I cannot say.

Brody awakened to the sound of his phone.

He was still sitting on the couch in front of the television.

It was still dark outside.

He fumbled with the phone.

The cat yawned, stretched and leaped down from the couch.

"Hello," Brody croaked, answering the phone.

"Wake up, Pete."

It was his Sergeant.

Brody frowned, looked at the clock on the phone.

"We need you to come in as soon as you can," his Sergeant said.

Brody sat up and stretched his back.

"I can't," Brody said. "Chief's orders. I'm on leave. Sorry, Sarg."

"No, it's okay," his Sergeant said. "We need you in the station. We've got a situation."

"What happened?"

"It's the computers. Someone hacked the city's computers. They've shut down everything. Airport. Buses. Trains. Radio. Everything."

"Who did it?"

"Don't know. They haven't made any demands yet, but it looks like greenmail. It's strong encryption. We're trying to brute force our way in, but it doesn't look good."

"Could it be terrorism?"

"I don't think we've ruled anything out yet. We're trying to set up a new com system. We need people in the station with phones. If you've got an extra phone, bring it."

Brody looked over his shoulder at the bedroom door.

Serenity had awakened and was standing in the doorway. She was rubbing a knuckle in the corner of her eye. Mr. Pickles dangled from her other arm.

"Look, Sarg . . ." he said. "I've got a couple things I need to take care of. . . . Gina didn't come home last night."

"Hmm . . . I'll see if she's being detained. I need you Pete. Do what you've got to do and get in here."

"Yeah, okay," Brody said and hung up.

Serenity had come out of the bedroom and was standing

in front of the couch next to Brody.

"Mister Pickles wants to talk to you," she said in a sleepy voice.

"Get in line," Brody muttered and ran his fingers through his hair.

"No really," Serenity said.

Brody looked at her. She was holding Mr. Pickles up with both hands, and Mr. Pickles was facing him, his little green head lolling to one side.

"Serenity . . ." Brody said. "We don't have time —"

"Officer Brody Pete."

It was a high-pitched voice.

Hollow, tinny, full of static.

Brody stared at the little frog doll in front of him.

The black-button eyes were scratched and worn.

"Officer Brody Pete," Mr. Pickles said.

The grin on his little green head was relentless and inescapable.

Brody's mouth dropped open.

The voice was coming from inside the doll's head.

Brody steadied himself against the couch.

"What the . . ." Brody murmured.

He looked closer at Mr. Pickles.

There was a small camera lens hidden in his nose.

Brody looked at Serenity.

"Mister Pickles can talk?" Brody exclaimed.

Serenity rolled her eyes.

"Obviously," she said.

"Officer Brody Pete," Mr. Pickles said.

The electronic voice had a limited and wildly inconsistent range of expression. Its syllables seemed to veer from sunny benediction to giddy exhortation all within the confines of a single word.

"Officer Brody Pete. We don't have much time," Mr. Pickles said.

Brody turned back to the doll.

He carefully lifted it from the girl's hands and raised it until he and Mr. Pickles were face to face.

"Officer Brody Pete," Mr. Pickles said. "Your wife is in danger."

Chapter Fifty-Two

WHEN THE ORDERLIES AROSE that morning, the hospital was dark. They walked the empty halls on their silent black soles. They stood in the stillness and watched as each in turn clicked a useless light switch up and down. In the basement, with a flashlight, they stood before the open fuse box. Dr. Wyche stepped from the shadows and peered over their shoulders. He was wearing a tuxedo coat with tails over his purple scrubs, a top hat on his head. The orderlies calmly turned and stared at him with blank faces.

"You're here early," one of them said.

"Couldn't sleep," Dr. Wyche said, smiling behind his purple mask, his watery-blue eyes twinkling.

They found the back-up generator in a dark corner. It was cold and dusty and would not start.

"Try this," Dr. Wyche said, pulling a little can of motor oil from his pocket.

By the time the other staff began to arrive and the patients began to stir, the orderlies had cobbled together a temporary power source. It was a kluge, fragile, sputtering, just enough to get the hospital up and running. Emergency lights flickered in the hallways. Dr. Wyche disappeared into the shadows. Somewhere, a piano began to play.

On the psych ward that morning, an ineffable lightness had filled the commons area, the bedrooms, even the small room with the battered desk and the Picasso poster. Everyone felt it, from the young woman who stood facing the wall in the corner with her hair hanging over her face to the nurse with the syrupy-sweet voice and the rouge-red cheeks. The news on the television was grim, and someone quietly turned it off. At the nurse's station, the pills settled into their little white cups, but no one approached the counter. The morning sun was moving across the windows' metal mesh. Alma sat with the masked man, talking softly. Wiley, Delmar and Bug watched with rapt faces as an orderly taught them how to juggle. Two rolls of toilet paper tumbled through the air. Then three. Then four. The dancing woman circled the room, moving gracefully in time with the music. Dr. Wyche was at the periphery, disappearing into the shadows, reappearing from down a hallway, from behind the closed door to the locked room.

In the cafeteria, lamps and candles had been arranged in an almost festive way. There was no light coming from the high ceiling, and the tables and chairs seemed to float in the darkness. The kitchen was dark and cold, but a cooked feast had been laid on the waiting tables. Braziers brimming with scrambled eggs and sausage links, fluffy biscuits and creamy oatmeal, hominy, grits. Silver salvers heaped with toasted breads and muffins, with bagels, lox and cream cheese. Bone china bowls filled with fresh slices of mango and papaya, kiwi and plum, giant blueberries, strawberries, dates and figs, almonds and walnuts. Dozens of tiny glazed jars held preserves and jams and marmalades and honeys of a seemingly endless variety. The air was laced with the aroma of brewed coffee, bananas and cinnamon.

The orderlies stood in their white scrubs among the tables with their clipboards and red pens. During meals, the orderlies usually walked between the tables and recorded on their clipboards what each patient ate. A red check mark for the soggy carrots and peas. A red check mark for the congealed creamed corn. A red check mark for the half-pint carton of milk. The red check mark exerted a powerful, invisible influence. The orderlies would stand and wait until each patient had eaten everything on their tray. By the end of the meal, each patient's name had an unbroken line of red check marks marching toward the edge of the page.

The patients left the elevator that morning, walked into the darkened cafeteria, and marveled at the feast spread before them. Dr. Wyche, in his tails and top hat, walked over next to one of the orderlies and took the clipboard from his hand. Dr. Wyche looked at the clip board. Then he turned to the patients and winked. He tossed the clipboard toward the rear of the cafeteria. The clipboard spun up into the darkness, rising like a balloon. The other orderlies looked at each other and followed Dr. Wyche's lead. They each tossed their clipboards into the darkness.

The patients filled their plates and sat in the soft light at the tables and began to eat the delicious food. Dr. Wyche moved from table to table, talking easily and warmly with them all, pulling gifts from his empty top hat. Somewhere, in the darkness, the piano was playing.

It was a waltz, lively, in three four time.

"Did we change caterers?" Bug said in between mouthfuls of blackberry crêpe.

Wiley was tossing a plate up into the darkness and catching it with one hand as it fell.

"Didn't you hear?" Wiley said to Bug.

Bug's face pinched up.

He tried to ignore Wiley.

"There's new money," Wiley said, grinning.

Bug chewed slowly and swallowed. His hair seemed to lurch in a new direction. His big, round eyes were skeptical.

"Someone would have told me," Bug said.

Wiley tossed the plate up into the darkness and caught it as it floated down. Beyond the darkness, high above, you could just glimpse the brightest of the rising stars.

"Unless it was all a scam," Wiley said.

Delmar was sniffing a forkful of truffle. He paused and listened more closely to the conversation.

"A scam?" Bug said. "What are you talking about?"

"A conspiracy," Wiley said. "To get you in here."

"No . . ." Bug said. "I'm scouting locations."

Delmar nodded.

"For a pivotal scene," Delmar said.

"Are you sure?" Wiley said, his tongue busy behind his grin.

He leaned in close to Bug and Delmar.

"Think about it," Wiley said. "Why pay for a script and actors when they can just film you in the nut house?"

Bug and Delmar thought about this for a moment.

"Where are the cameras?" Delmar said.

Wiley lowered his voice, almost whispering.

"Everywhere," Wiley said.

Delmar narrowed his eyes.

"They're just so small, we can't see them anymore," Wiley said.

Delmar put his fork down and began to look around the cafeteria. Wiley was grinning in smug satisfaction.

"That's absurd," Bug said. "Delmar and I will be leaving soon. There's a new location we need to visit. The studio has us on a very tight pre-production schedule."

Bug elbowed Delmar and caught his eye. Bug circled an index finger beside his head and poured himself another flute of champagne.

Delmar nodded and picked up his fork. He finished his meal, but not without some discomfort. He squinted with suspicion at the pepper grinder as he held it in his big fingers. He set it gently to one side on the table linen, watching it out of the corner of one eye as he chewed and swallowed.

Wiley was grinning broadly and began to juggle three plates, tossing them in slow elliptical circles through the starry darkness above his head. With each toss, the plates were changing. Delicate gilded patterns were bleeding, spiraling in colors of coral and rose and gold from the round edges toward the bone-white centers.

Dr. Wyche had been circulating around the room, moving from table to table. He approached their table, carrying his top hat in his hand. He was smiling behind his purple mask. His wispy blond hair floated in a faint nimbus around the top of his head. His voice was ringing with a new enthusiasm.

"Today is a very special day," he declared.

He moved around the table, from person to person.

"I have a very important announcement to make," he confided to them all.

As he moved before each person at the table, he performed a trick. He reached into his top hat and removed a gift. He had given each of them something that morning. Flowers were strewn on every tabletop. Orchids, irises, roses. Several doves and a parrot were swooping from table to table, boldly picking through the crumbs.

To Bug, he gave a snow-white rabbit with a twitchy pink nose. To Delmar, a beautiful, crystal rose with pale red petals in full bloom. To Wiley, a new belt with carved leather and a shiny silver buckle, to hold up his sagging pants.

To Alma, a set of inlaid knitting needles. For the dancing woman, he nestled a jeweled tiara atop her tangled, chestnut-brown hair.

He paused before the masked man.

His watery-blue eyes were twinkling beneath his wispy white eyebrows.

"I've saved the best for you."

He reached into his hat and pulled out something small he held tightly in the fist of his hand. He gave it to the masked man. The masked man looked at the object in his hand.

It was a metal key, rather ordinary.

The masked man looked at Dr. Wyche, and for a moment Dr. Wyche looked back into the dark, opaque lenses. Then he spun away and moved toward the back of the room.

Dr. Wyche stood on a chair and motioned for everyone to be silent.

"Your attention, please," he said in a loud voice.

Dr. Wyche reached into his top hat and pulled out a small leather orb. It was an old softball. He held it carefully with the tips of his thumb and two long, skinny fingers, like a small globe on a tiny tripod. He showed it to them, displayed it, pivoting from one side of the room to the other.

It was the softball that had come to rest among the clutter of his small office, the one he kept on the floor by the desk between the delicate tips of the antique caliper next to the cardboard box with his diplomas. The softball was covered with the dark ink of a dozen or so sloppy signatures scrawled across the yellowed leather of the ball.

"When I was in medical school, I played on a softball team. Hard to believe, I know. I'm not the most athletic of individuals."

He tossed the ball into the darkness above him.

"I couldn't hit. Couldn't throw. But I was fast."

The ball disappeared into the darkness and, seconds later, came rising up from beneath the floor.

Dr. Wyche watched as it floated, rising before him.

He reached out and gently caught the ball in one hand.

"Really fast," Dr. Wyche said.

He winked at them with one watery-blue eye.

Dr. Wyche removed his top hat and dropped the softball into it. He turned the hat right side up and held it so he could peer up into it.

He shrugged and set the hat back on his head.

"My teammates were all good athletes. Men and women. Splendid corn-fed Midwesterners. Over-achievers who hated to lose . . .

"They let me play right field. Even though I had no arm. Even though I couldn't hit. Even though it meant we would probably lose some games . . .

"It was the right thing to do . . .

"I was so grateful. So happy. So lucky . . .

"Just to be a part of the team . . .

"I think it made us all better. Better doctors, better people . . ."

A sound came from the darkness at the back of the room. It was a meaty smack, the sound of a swiftly swung wooden bat striking a pitched softball, striking it in the sweet spot, striking it perfectly and precisely, at that moment, at that angle, at that speed.

Dr. Wyche looked up into the starry darkness above them.

"There were times when the ball came hurtling down out of the blue summer sky, and I could feel every eye on me, and I simply wanted to disappear. To run away. To hide. Like when I was a boy. Playing hide and seek with my brothers."

He paused, still gazing up into the darkness.

"But I didn't. My teammates were depending on me . . .

Eventually, I learned to how to catch the ball with some confidence . . ."

The ball came floating down out of the darkness above him and settled gently in Dr. Wyche's open hand.

"But I never stopped being nervous."

He sighed.

When he spoke, his voice had changed. It was softer, almost apologetic, almost remorseful.

"And I never stopped wanting to disappear."

Dr. Wyche removed his top hat, dropped the softball into the hat and set the hat back on his head.

He looked out at the faces of the gathered patients, the nurses, the orderlies.

"For reasons I cannot fully explain and I cannot fully express, I have decided to retire from the practice of psychiatry . . ."

He smiled at them, embarrassed.

"I have no wisdom to impart. There is nothing I understand that I can explain to you. There are no miracles here . . .

"Don't be afraid . . .

"Be kind and patient and tolerant . . .

"Take care of each other . . .

"The game will continue without me . . .

"You're all going to be fine."

He stepped down from the chair and walked to where the dancing woman was sitting. He bowed and extended his gloved hand. She took his hand and stood. He brushed her tangled hair back from her face. He pulled down the white surgical mask and gently touched the faint scars on the sides of her cheeks. She looked hesitantly into his eyes. He placed one hand on her hip and held the other away from their bodies. Then they both began to waltz gracefully across the floor. The piano music had filled the room. The stars were shining brightly above their heads. The doctor and the dancing woman circled the room several times before they danced at last into the darkness.

The orderlies were tossing painted plates smoothly through the air. Wiley held a candle in one hand and was blowing huge plumes of fire from his mouth. Red roses and white doves had covered the tables around the room and were spilling onto the floor. The piano was playing, lively, in three four time.

The masked man opened his gloved hand and looked at the key resting in the palm of his hand.

Chapter Fifty-Three

BRODY WAS WEARING the red demon mask when he arrived at the old stockyards that morning. He carried Mr. Pickles inside a backpack strapped to his back. It was still dark with only the suggestion of sunlight on the horizon. In the far corner of the gravel parking lot, a trailer was on fire. Orange and yellow flames were rising through the rear windows. The roof burned brightly against the early morning sky.

Mr. Pickles was talking like a demented game-show emcee.

The raging inferno behind door number three.

By the time Brody entered the trailer, it was engulfed in flames. Brody found two UPO soldiers lying face down on the floor in the back of the trailer. Blood was pooling beneath them. It appeared their throats had been cut. Brody found the keys to the bunkers on the body of one of the dead men and then raced back through the trailer. The walls and ceilings were burning and collapsing around him. Brody stumbled out of the door just as a propane tank exploded, knocking him off his feet. He looked up from the ground where he landed and watched as pieces of the trailer rained down around him, white-hot and blazing with flames.

Then Brody saw a figure moving behind the ruins of the burning trailer. Their eyes met, and the figure paused for an instant. He could barely make out her face through the flames and ashes and cinders.

Her glittering dark eyes, her crimson lips.

It was the seamstress.

She looked at him, her face wavering in the hot air.

And then she was gone.

Brody raced around what was left of the burning trailer, but the seamstress had fled into the trees and hills behind the stockyards. Brody wanted to chase after her, but he didn't have time.

Mr. Pickles was talking.

The sudden jeopardy of the final round.

Across the parking lot, the UPO soldiers' vehicles erupted in a series of fiery explosions that lit up the stockyards. Brody turned, and the light from the explosions flashed on the red-and-yellow surface of his mask.

The entrance to the bunkers was well hidden, covered with old boards and bails of straw. By the time Brody found it, the rest of the old stockyards was crackling and popping with fire. The boards were hot to the touch, and as he pulled one aside, the air shifted, and fire burst with an audible huff from the wood beneath his gloved hands. Flames licked up the surface, and in an instant the entire board was burning with hungry flames. Brody quickly threw the burning boards aside and jumped down into the cinder-block bunkers. He sucked in a few shallow breaths of air through the filter in his mask. His flashlight beam cut through the smoky darkness. He listened to Mr. Pickles, to the inhuman voice coming from his backpack, giving him directions like a GPS voice in a car. He could not stop to think about the weirdness of the moment. He stumbled forward into the hot, smoky air, shining the beam of the flashlight on the ground before him.

Mr. Pickles quickly led Brody to the locked door. Florescent light shone through a square window from inside the room. Brody was so dazed and short of breath, he simply unlocked the door with the keys and never checked to see if anyone was inside.

"Watch your head," Mr. Pickles warned in his unsteady, high-pitched voice.

As Brody walked through the door, Bernard jumped from beside the doorway and hit him over the head with a folding chair.

The chair bounced off the hard shell of the red demon mask.

"What the hell," Brody said.

Caitlyn was kneeling behind him.

Brody turned and saw Gina coming at him.

"No wait," Brody cried, raising an open hand.

Gina kicked him hard enough to send him sailing over Caitlyn. He staggered for a step and crashed through a table.

He rolled on the floor, groaning.

"Come on," Caitlyn said at the door. "Let's go!"

Gina, Caitlyn and Bernard were poised to rush out the door, but Gina hesitated for a moment looking at the man in the oddly-familiar red mask as he struggled to get back on his feet.

"Dammit, Pookie . . ." Brody said.

Gina raised her hands to her mouth in surprise.

"Oh my god," she said.

Brody shoved a piece of the table off his leg.

His eyes in the red mask were looking up at Gina.

"I thought you were supposed to be dying," Brody said, annoyed.

Caitlyn turned and looked more closely at the man in the red mask. She grabbed Bernard and pulled him back into the room.

Gina knelt down next to Brody and touched the side of the mask.

"I thought I told you to take that damn thing off," she said, happy to see him, amused and concerned at the same time.

"Long story," Brody said.

The goofy, electronic voice came from Brody's backpack on the floor.

"Officer Brody Pete. You must exit the bunker in the next six minutes," Mr. Pickles said.

Brody's backpack was half open, and Gina could see Mr. Pickles inside the backpack.

Gina gave Brody a quizzical look.

"*Very* long story," Brody said. He shoved Mr. Pickles back into the backpack and zipped it closed.

He stood unsteadily, a hand on his ribcage.

Gina put a firm hand on his shoulder.

"Are you hurt?" she said.

"I'll live," he said. "But you really have got to quit kicking me like that."

"Sorry," she said, with a guilty smile.

"Rumor has it you caught the plague," he said.

"Oh, I did . . . But I'm fine," Gina said, waving it all off with a brush of her hand.

"She's been taking my medicine," Caitlyn said, shaking her backpack, the pills rattling in the bottles.

"Officer Brody Pete," Mr. Pickles squeaked from inside the backpack. "Ambient air temperature is one hundred ten degrees and rising. You must exit the bunker immediately."

"Yeah," Brody said. "We gotta go."

They turned to leave, but as they did, Gina's eyes rolled back in her head, and she sank down, weak-kneed, onto the bench of one of the tables.

When they realized she wasn't behind them, Brody and Caitlyn and Bernard came back into the room.

"I thought you said you're okay," Brody said to Gina.

"I am," Gina said. "I'm fine. I'm fine. I'm right behind you."

She tried to stand up and fell to the floor.

"She's fine," Brody said, looking at Caitlyn.

"She's right behind us," Caitlyn said, echoing his tone.

"Just give me a second . . ." Gina said, prone on the floor, her voice weak and failing.

They helped her stand, and Brody picked her up and carried her in his arms.

The air was unbearably hot, and sweat was dripping down their faces.

"We don't have a second," Brody said.

They could feel the air moving upward past them toward the entrance as the fire began to suck all the oxygen from the bunkers.

Gina rested her head on his shoulder.

"Alright, Batman . . ." she said.

Her eyelids were fluttering.

"But this . . . does not count . . . as a date night."

Then she passed out.

Chapter Fifty-Four

THE KEY DR. WYCHE GAVE to the masked man was the master key to all the doors in the psychiatric hospital. It was the way out. It was freedom. Once he realized what it was, the masked man showed the key to Alma, and, after some brief deliberation, she agreed to leave with him. As they left the commons area, Delmar and Bug followed them. It seemed fitting somehow. The three of them had arrived at the psychiatric hospital together. Now they would leave together.

The masked man led them through darkened hallways and stairwells, past the dusty emergency lights flickering in the gloom. The rest of the psychiatric hospital was still distracted with that morning's extraordinary occurrences. No one noticed when the man in the black mask cracked open the last door and stepped outside into the sunlight. Each of them — Bug, Delmar, Alma — stepped hesitantly and awkwardly through the doorway. They stood there for a moment, huddled together on the stoop, stunned and blinking in the acute morning light.

The city was still in the grip of the pandemic. The streets were silent and becalmed like an open sea. There were no pedestrians, no traffic. The tallest buildings cast long shadows that seemed elemental, prehistoric. Across the river, beyond the bridge, something big was burning. A huge plume of pitch-black smoke was bleeding across the unusually still and quiet morning sky.

On any other day, someone would have noticed the four figures who skulked away from the hospital grounds. Someone would have noticed the man dressed in black with the mask covering his face. Someone would have noticed the frail, elderly woman in the lavender bathrobe and pink bunny slippers. Someone would have noticed the enormous, barefoot man-child wearing nothing but faded denim overalls hanging by a single strap from one huge, sunburned shoulder. Someone would have noticed the small, thin figure, fidgeting and nervous, with astonished eyes and rigid coiffure, more bird seemingly than man.

Someone would have noticed.

Normally, on such a morning, I would have been monitoring the vehicular traffic, preparing for another rush hour. Normally, I would have noted in passing the heartbreaking beauty of the city I know so well.

(I can still see it, the waking city, the lights coming on in the kitchen windows, the sun sparkling on the river, the first runners in the park . . .)

But that morning was unlike any other.

The government and its public services were in chaos. Gering and other city officials were frantically scrambling to crack the encryption that had paralyzed the city's computers, the encryption that had locked them out of the servers and the mainframe. Gering could not even access his laptop. Without its computer platforms, without access to the usual surveillance data and satellite uplinks, the city was operating blindly, stumbling around like an uncoordinated person in the dark.

In the days and weeks afterwards, when they looked back at what had happened, it was as if someone had deliberately drawn a curtain and purposefully turned out the lights. At the moment when the city most needed its information technology, it was frozen, beyond human perception. It was almost as if someone wanted a gap in the record, an absence of data, a digital erasure.

(I can still remember the city. Its implacable energy, its towering indifference. I can still remember the people in all their haste. The city was in truth such a delicate thing, an oddly impermanent monument. I see it now from a great distance, a single cell quivering on a slide beneath a scope. It is but a small thing to make a city vanish, like a rabbit dropped into a magician's hat.)

So no one noticed.

At least, not at first.

They moved slowly through the surreal cityscape, a strangely fitting procession, a bizarre little parade.

Four escapees from a psychiatric hospital.

They were headed towards Alma's tiny apartment, several miles away.

"You all can stay with me," Alma said to them. "At least for a while."

The masked man led them through the empty streets. They avoided the large open spaces, passing beyond the dark eyes of the visible cameras. They stepped from the shadows of an alley, from beneath the shade of faded awnings. A lone vehicle rushed past in a blur and a flash, its siren already fading in the distance. Helicopters were aloft somewhere. They could hear the faint drone of the swift rotors high above the city's dark canyons, tiny silhouettes passing briefly across the distant sky.

Bug was telling them about the latest rewrite.

"But what will happen to the Doctor?" Delmar said.

"That poor man was so miscast," Bug said.

Alma was breathing hard, and they rested. They sat on cinder blocks beside a dumpster in the alley behind a closed convenience store. The day was growing warmer as the sun rose in the sky. Bug was roaming around the fringes. The masked man stood aside, looking to the skies. A helicopter passed slowly several blocks away.

"But what if the Doctor was right?" Delmar was saying.

Bug was framing a shot of the dumpster with his hands. He squinted with one eye through the right angles of his fingers at the rusty-brown hulk. A bloated trash bag had belched its rancid contents from the dumpster's open door.

"Well, I'm not opposed to method per se . . ." Bug said, peering at the dumpster from a new angle.

"Right about what?" Alma said to Delmar.

"About us," Delmar said.

The masked man was watching the sky.

The sound of swift rotors was drawing steadily closer. They made a wupping sound as they cut through the air.

A small surveillance camera mounted discreetly on a building across the alley was aimed at the rear door of the convenience store. In the literal, unenhanced data from that morning, the dumpster appears as a rusty-brown shadow. The three figures nearby are small and indistinct. The old woman in the lavender bathrobe is sitting on a cinder block. The large man in denim overalls sits next to her. The small figure, a boy perhaps, is wandering around nearby. To one side, there is a muddy smudge, only a blur, only the suggestion of another person lost in the dark pixels of the background.

Bug turned and looked at Delmar.

Delmar was looking at the cigarette butts on the greasy black concrete beneath his dirty bare feet.

"There is no Deus Ex Machina, is there?" Delmar said without looking up.

Bug took a step toward him, a hurt look on his face.

"I . . . I can't talk about that," Bug said.

"Maybe the Doctor was right . . ." Delmar said.

The drone of the swift rotors had grown steadily louder.

"Maybe we belong on the inside," Delmar said.

The sound rose to a thunderous roar.

The masked man stepped toward Alma and took her by the arm, bidding her to rise.

With a gust of hot, dusty wind, a black transport helicopter descended from the sky, moving slowly from behind the taller buildings.

Delmar turned and gaped at the machine as it hovered over the entrance to the alley, blotting out the rest of the sky.

"That's probably the studio," Bug said, unperturbed.

The helicopter bay doors began to open.

The masked man was motioning for them to leave. He was pulling Alma with him away from the helicopter.

Ropes dropped from the open helicopter, and people began to drop down from inside. They were wearing the green-and-black uniforms of the UPO soldiers.

Bug turned to the other three.

"Let me handle this," Bug shouted to them, gesturing confidently with his open hands.

The UPO soldiers hit the ground and fanned out around the dumpster. They wore their gas masks and dark visors. They brandished their rifles before them.

Bug approached one of the soldiers. Bug opened his arms wide and smiled broadly. The helicopter had blown his hair straight back. For once, it looked neat, almost fashionable.

"No one told me you were coming," Bug shouted.

In one swift motion, the UPO soldier stepped forward and cracked Bug in the head with the butt of his rifle.

Bug fell to the ground, unconscious. Blood was flowing from a wound on his head.

Delmar saw Bug go down, and he took a step toward him, his strong body coiling for a fight, but the masked man grabbed him by the arm and got in front of him. Delmar was plowing ahead like a tank. The masked man looked him in the eyes. Delmar was crying, angry tears streaming down his big face. He could see himself in the masked man's black, opaque eyes.

The masked man shook his head and tried to push Delmar back. The masked man pointed to Alma behind the dumpster and shoved Delmar towards her. Delmar kept moving forward, staring with a blind rage at the UPO soldiers and the bloody spot where Bug had fallen to the ground.

For a moment, they were frozen that way, Delmar slowly moving forward toward a violent confrontation and the masked man braced against him, sliding relentlessly backwards.

Then the masked man began to move in a way that was almost too fast to follow. He struck Delmar in some obscure way. Perhaps it was a blow to his throat. The data were not clear. Delmar stopped moving, and then the masked man was behind him, grasping him around the neck with his arms. Delmar took a step forward, carrying the masked man with him, and then dropped to the ground, unconscious. It all happened in what seemed like the blink of an eye, with a frightening and unexpected efficiency.

The masked man raised his open hands and took a step toward the semicircle of UPO soldiers. He placed his hands on his head and dropped to his knees. The soldiers quickly surrounded him with their rifles pointed at his black masked head. He did not resist as they handcuffed him. They put a black hood over his head and hoisted him into the belly of the helicopter.

"Target in custody," a UPO soldier said into a radio mike.

The last of the UPO soldiers climbed back into the hovering helicopter. The bay doors closed, and the machine rose up into the sky.

It flew away, and the sound of the turning rotors grew faint and quickly disappeared. The dust and litter settled back onto the pavement. The air once again grew quiet and still.

The cinder blocks beside the dumpster were empty. Delmar's big body was sprawled face down on the ground nearby. Several yards in front of him, Bug lay unconscious and bleeding.

Chapter Fifty-Five

THE MASKED MAN was wearing the black hood when the UPO soldiers brought him into the room and sat him in the chair. They pulled the hood from his head, and the masked man looked up into the round face and bland features of Gering Misler.

Gering was standing motionless in front of him, wearing his usual khaki pants, collared shirt and blue canvas jacket. There was a harsh light coming from the low ceiling. The room was small, unfurnished, without windows. In the middle of the concrete floor, there was a small round drain covered by a metal grate. The masked man was seated in a plain, metal chair. His ankles were bound together with leg irons. His arms were restrained with a straightjacket.

Gering nodded at the UPO soldiers, and they left the room. The masked man heard the door behind him swing shut with a definitive thunk.

The small room was silent.

The two of them were alone.

Gering stepped closer and stood before the masked man. He leaned forward and looked closely at the mask. His pale face was reflected in the black lenses. His chubby lips and tortoise-shell glasses were distorted as he moved slowly from one side of the mask to the other. His blue cherub's eyes shifted without blinking.

He reached out slowly with one hand to touch the mask, but the masked man flinched away.

Gering held his hand poised above the mask, gazing at the soft surface of the black leather, the ornate grills, the smooth curves of the tempered ceramic shell.

A hint of displeasure flashed in Gering's blue eyes.

He lowered his hand and stepped back.

Gering took off his jacket. He folded it over once and carefully set it to one side on the concrete floor. He removed a large metal wrist watch and slid it into his pants pocket. He was wearing a pale-blue short-sleeved shirt and a white crewneck undershirt. A white triangle of undershirt was visible at his open collar. There was a faint ring of perspiration around the inside of the collar. Pale, fine hairs lined his smooth forearms. His hands were pink and soft and plump.

Gering stepped away from the chair toward the far wall, and he picked up an object from the floor. Something metallic caught the light as he grasped the object in his hand. He returned and stood calmly before the masked man. He raised the metallic object and held it where the masked man could see it. It was cylindrical, about a foot long, with a cord for an electrical outlet coiled at one end. On the other end was the gleaming, corrugated edge of a reciprocating saw.

"So it's come to this," Gering said.

He looked at the steel blade, turning it in the light.

"It's called a Stryker saw," Gering said.

The harsh light glinted on the sharp teeth of the blade.

"It's exactly what it looks like," Gering said. "An orthopedic surgeon named Homer H. Stryker patented it in nineteen forty-seven. Thirty-two thousand oscillations per minute with a cutting stroke of one eighth of an inch. The small amplitude prevents the blade from cutting into soft tissues. It was designed to remove casts without cutting into the underlying skin. Medical examiners use them to remove the calvarium. The skullcap. It's the instrument of choice for removing the brain."

Gering stepped back and turned to the wall behind him and plugged the power cord into the outlet.

"Here, I'll show you," Gering said.

Then, that rarest of moments.

Gering's pudgy, red lips curled into a smile.

He held the saw with one hand in front of the masked man and turned it on. The blade began immediately to reciprocate, buzzing furiously no more than a foot from the masked man's face. Dust flew from the blade, flying into the air between them. Gering moved the saw closer to the mask. For an awful moment, the masked man strained against the straightjacket and held his head back from the reciprocating blade.

Then Gering turned it off.

He held the quiet saw in both hands.

A few motes drifted in the harsh light.

The motionless blade was reflected in each of the mask's opaque lenses.

Gering walked back to the wall and unplugged the saw. He carefully coiled the power cord in his soft hands and set the saw back on the floor against the wall.

"The police think you're Jacob Crutchfield," Gering said.

He stepped back in front of the masked man.

"They think you engineered a bio-weapon," Gering said.

He bent down next to the masked man and looked at the mute black profile.

"They think you created a modern-day plague and sold it to the highest bidder," Gering said.

Gering came closer. His face was only inches from the mask.

"But we both know that isn't true," Gering said in a soft voice.

He reached out with both hands and seized the mask.

The masked man struggled against him and began to slide out of the chair. The chair teetered beneath them, and then toppled over onto the floor. The masked man fell to the floor, unable to move in the leg irons and straightjacket. Gering landed on top of him, still clutching the mask in his hands.

Gering got on his knees and seized the mask in both hands. The masked man writhed against him, and for a moment, they struggled. Gering twisted the mask, trying to pry it from the masked man's head, but the mask seemed like a part of the masked man's body. It seemed to be permanently attached to the very bones of the masked man's skull.

Gering forced the masked man to turn and look him in the eye. The masked man ceased struggling. Gering's face had flushed red with exertion, and his bland features had twisted horribly in extremis. Beneath him, the face of the mask, by comparison, seemed calm, almost serene.

Gering held the mask firmly with one hand and carefully probed it with the other. He touched the surface of the mask with his blunt fingertips, traced the lines of the stitches in the leather, felt the firmness of the hard shell beneath. His eyes searched the materials, the fabric, the threads, the ornate grills and screens, the subtle elements of design. He looked into the dark glass that covered the opaque eyes.

The frozen features of the mask seemed to look back with a calm defiance.

Gering released the mask from his grip and stood up.

He took a deep breath.

He adjusted the tortoise-shell glasses on his nose.

He smoothed his mussed, thinning black hair.

"My machine thinks you're a virus," Gering said.

He looked down at the mask.

"Ironic, isn't it?" he said.

His face had settled back into its outwardly-benign countenance.

There was only a suggestion of a smile on his pudgy, red lips.

"It keeps you in quarantine. Locked away safely in a separate compartment of its virtual brain," Gering said.

He was silent for a long moment.

"They say torture doesn't work," Gering said.

He placed his foot on the masked man's neck.

The leather sole of his cordovan loafer rested firmly against the masked man's windpipe.

"It's irrelevant . . . when all you really need . . . is forensic evidence."

Chapter Fifty-Six

FOR MANY MINUTES AFTER the helicopter left, Alma dared not move. She was cowering behind cardboard boxes behind the dumpster. Then she heard the sound of a vehicle. Its tires made crunching sounds on the crumbling pavement. A door opened and swung closed with a solid thunk. She held her breath and tried not to tremble. She heard footsteps coming closer.

Then someone spoke.

"Behind the dumpster."

It was a high-pitched voice, tinny, hollow.

It sounded like a cartoon character.

It sounded like something that had been clumsily spliced together from other recorded messages.

It definitely wasn't human.

The steps came closer.

"Officer Brody Pete," the strange, squeaky voice said, louder now. "Behind the cardboard boxes."

A gloved hand grasped the cardboard boxes above Alma and pulled them away from her. She looked up and saw a man standing over her.

He was wearing a red mask with flames stitched into the fabric on the face.

He extended his open hand, offering it to her where she could grasp it.

"I'm here to help, Ms. Williams," Brody said.

Alma took his hand, and Brody helped her stand up.

She swayed for a moment unsteadily, gathered her bathrobe with one thin hand at her chest.

She looked him up and down.

He was wearing street clothes.

She noted with approval his clean and comfortable shoes.

"Your mask looks stupid," Alma said.

Brody sighed.

"So I've been told," Brody said.

PART TEN

Chapter Fifty-Seven

WEEKS AFTER THE FIRE at the old stockyards, the investigators finished their report.

The investigators determined that the fire began sometime before dawn. It started in the trailer in the back of the parking lot. The fire quickly spread to the rest of the dilapidated wooden structures and abandoned vehicles.

The investigators believed the fire started with a meth lab explosion in the trailer, but the evidence was maddeningly elusive. With the pandemic at its peak, the city was especially chaotic that morning. Someone had hacked the city's computer systems and had locked everyone out with unbreakable encryption. There were power outages in a number of areas across town. The fire made it even harder for the city's semi-autonomous surveillance devices, such as thermal-imaging cameras, to capture an accurate record of everything that was happening.

The investigators found the charred remains of two male bodies near the trailer. Their identities are officially unknown. The evidence and the surveillance data suggested there were three people in the trailer when the fire started. If there was a third person in the trailer, that person somehow managed to escape.

Beneath the still-smoldering ruins, the investigators discovered a series of cinder-block bunkers. No one knows precisely the purpose of the bunkers. Whoever built the bunkers evaded surveillance and must have done so carefully at night moving under the cover of the old wooden structures. Several witnesses claimed they had seen military vehicles coming and going at the stockyards for months. Normally, there would have been a surfeit of data from several sources, but the relevant data were useless, missing or oddly corrupted. The investigators speculated that the bunkers may have been the site of an illegal marijuana farm or a huge meth lab. The bunkers were empty when the investigators found them. Everything inside had been completely incinerated. Only ashes remained.

Some gadflies and busybodies had other theories about what happened at the stockyards that morning. There were reports from bystanders who claim that, before the firefighters and other first responders arrived, there was another figure on the scene, a mysterious figure in a red mask.

The investigators went through what little surveillance data survived, looking for evidence of the person in the red mask. At the times when the witnesses claim to have seen the red mask, there was nothing apparent in the data. There was only an absence where the witnesses said the masked person should have been. At best, the investigators detected a blur, or maybe a blip, a glitch, perhaps. Once the fire began, the surveillance data from the old stockyards became so dense and noisy, it was of little use to human investigators.

One bystander, Hilton Goodacre, claimed he had overheard a man in a flaming red mask conversing with a talking frog. He said the talking frog sounded like a robot. The investigators gave little credence to Goodacre's statement. There was evidence of some short-range radio activity on an obscure frequency, but there was no evidence of where the signal originated. Goodacre was known to be disabled and probably delusional. His story was discounted and ignored as the unfounded byproduct of a sliver of glass suspended long ago in the prefrontal cortex of his brain.

If there was a mysterious man in a flaming red mask at the stockyards that morning, there is no official record of it. None that has survived. The computer hacking, the raging fire and the chaotic state of the city in general made the identity of the man in the flaming red mask effectively untraceable, unknowable, invisible.

At the time the fire began, the city's artificial intelligence system was offline conducting a self-diagnostic. After the cyberattack, the AI was unable to offer any assistance. The city's computers remained disabled. The hackers never made any demands. The city never cracked the encryption. Like something caught in amber, the city's software was simply abandoned. Hard drives were wiped. Servers were replaced. The city bought new Glissade/Frappe software with better cybersecurity. The AI was written off as an operating loss on the city's ledgers.

A few police officers vaguely remembered something about a mask from before the pandemic and the fire. Police Officer JD Teague told the fire investigators about Brody Pete and the john doe in the black mask. Records at the psychiatric hospital showed that the john doe in the black mask had been discharged after the fire had started. The investigators questioned Officer Pete and concluded the incident with the red mask at the pandemic briefing was just a coincidence. In the crush of activity during the weeks after the pandemic, memories of the masks grew increasingly distant and tenuous.

Several weeks after the fire, a body washed up on the shore miles away from the city. It was badly decomposed. Most of the face was gone. The white bones of the skull were visible. People said a shark or something must have chewed the face off.

JD Teague took an early retirement and died of a sudden heart attack not long after that on a beach in the Caribbean.

In the end, no one (other than perhaps Hilton Goodacre) could say for sure what they had witnessed.

Chapter Fifty-Eight

GINA AWAKENED in a hospital bed.

She opened her eyes and looked around the room.

Brody was asleep in the chair next to the bed.

In another chair was a young girl with a buoyant puff of curly brown hair. The girl was holding a green doll that looked vaguely like a frog.

Gina moved her arm and saw there was an intravenous drip attached to a needle taped to her arm.

When the girl saw that Gina was awake, she began to shove Brody on the arm to wake him up.

Brody opened his eyes.

He stood up and looked at her.

He needed a shave and looked like he hadn't slept soundly for a while.

"Next time, I'll plan date night," Gina said.

Her voice was dry and croaked in her throat.

Brody smiled.

He poured her a cup of water.

"You've been in a coma," Brody said. "For over a week."

Gina let Brody's words settle in.

"Did I say anything?" Gina said. "You know . . . like, em-barrassing?"

"No," Brody said, and then reconsidered.

"Well . . . no more than usual," he said with a straight face.

Gina grinned at him.

"Did you take stupid pictures?" she said, accusing him.

"Oh, yeah," he said, nodding his head. "You've got a whole website."

The girl was standing next to him, looking shyly at Gina.

"Is that true?" Gina said to the girl.

Brody looked down at the girl.

The girl shook her head.

"This is my friend, Serenity," Brody said, putting a hand on her shoulder.

"Hey, Serenity," Gina said

"Hey," Serenity said, her voice soft and diffident.

She looked at Gina and quickly looked away.

"Serenity's been staying with us. Since the pandemic," Brody said.

He caught Gina's eye, and they shared a moment full of unspoken questions.

Gina looked at the girl.

"That frog looks very familiar," Gina said.

Serenity held Mr. Pickles up where Gina could see his slack, little head.

"His name is Mister Pickles," Serenity said.

Mr. Pickles was smiling his usual relentless, maniacal grin.

Gina turned and looked at Brody.

"That frog was talking to you," Gina said. "I remember hearing that frog when . . . when —"

"Wow," Brody said. "They must have given you some pretty strong painkillers."

He nudged Serenity.

"Show her," he said.

Serenity pushed Mr. Pickles's chest.

There was a burst of static, and a recorded voice began to play.

"Top o' the mornin'," Mr. Pickles croaked in the sort of funny frog voice one would expect to hear coming from a child's doll.

Gina looked skeptical.

"No," Gina said. "He sounded like . . . Mickey Mouse . . ."

She frowned at Brody, dubious.

"On acid," she added.

Brody shook his head.

"I know what I heard," she said.

They were silent for a moment.

"How do you feel?" Brody said.

"I've felt worse," Gina said.

Brody took her hand in his.

"You're going to be okay," Brody said. "They discovered a serum. It was sort of a miracle. They found an old woman — Alma Williams — with an immunity. Something in her blood. All the research fell into place. The doctors found most of the information on the web, like someone had already done the lab work. They had to use smart phones, but it all happened really fast. You and Caitlyn were some of the first people to get the cure. They're putting it in a lozenge. The government is coordinating all of it. Lozenges, nasal sprayers, a vaccine. It's a global effort. People are working round the clock. It looks like this pandemic might be over."

"How's Caitlyn?" Gina said.

"I think she's okay. Bernard said she's trying to cast a magic spell from her hospital room. Let's see, what was it? I want to be sure and get this right," Brody said, concentrating.

"A major mass microbial abjuration?" he said slowly.

He looked at Gina.

Gina shrugged.

"Sounds about right," Gina said.

"Bernard's helping her. He's like her sous chef. When I saw him, he was carrying an old peanut butter jar full of a murky brown liquid. Said it was 'midnight stump water,' " Brody said.

Gina laughed.

"You never brought me midnight stump water," Gina said.

"Well, it wasn't for lack of trying," Brody said.

Gina was grinning again.

They were silent for a moment.

Serenity pushed Mr. Pickles's chest.

"Heavens to Murgatroyd!" Mr. Pickles exclaimed.

Gina's face clouded over.

She was struggling to remember.

"Brody," she said. "The woman . . . in the mask . . . the seamstress . . ."

Brody sighed.

"Who was she?" Gina said, watching his face.

Brody glanced aside, hesitant, reluctant.

"Stella Delmonico," he said.

"I know that name," Gina said.

"She was an actress," Brody said. "She was the sexy sister on that sitcom. The one they replaced mid-season."

"Oh, yeah," Gina said, remembering. "Like Darrin on Bewitched . . . But Stella Delmonico died, right? There was that explosion. On the boat. Right?"

"Apparently not," Brody said. "They never found the body."

"So she faked it?"

"Looks that way. The police have video of her buying the materials for a bomb."

"That was, what? Twenty years ago?"

"Yeah. They used face recognition software. Artificial intelligence. It's pretty impressive."

"I guess so," Gina said.

They were silent for a moment.

"That's kind of scary, though, isn't it?" Gina said. "Using artificial intelligence like that."

"Well, yeah . . . If you were making incendiary devices twenty years ago," Brody said.

He squinted at her, pretending to be suspicious.

"Something you want to tell me, Pookie?"

"Who decides what's worth remembering?" Gina said.

"It depends on what you're looking for, doesn't it?" Brody said.

"You and Royce Deakins used to throw water balloons at traffic," Gina said.

Brody looked at her for a moment, annoyed.

He nudged Serenity beside him.

"Look, Ren. My loving spouse just came out of a coma," Brody said.

Serenity was watching them at the bedside with her wide eyes.

Gina smiled, satisfied.

But her smile slowly faded.

She turned her worried gaze back to Brody.

"Brody . . ." she said.

She glanced at Serenity and then back to Brody.

"The mask . . ." she said.

Brody sighed again.

He sat down in the chair.

"I need to know," Gina said.

He covered his mouth with one hand and rubbed the whiskers on his chin.

"Ren calls it the scary mask," Brody said.

Serenity sat down in the chair next to him.

"Ren sounds like a smart young lady," Gina said.

"It's just a mask, Gina," Brody said. "Something she made out of scraps and leftovers. Flotsam and jetsam. Life's little lagniappes. That's what she said. She made art from life's little lagniappes."

"Refresh my memory," Gina said. "Are lagniappes explosive?"

"She said some people can use a mask to gain a better understanding of who they are. Their identity. She said a mask is a way to try on new aspects of a personality. Or to rediscover old ones. She said a mask can help you find pieces of your identity. A way to integrate your persona."

"That sounds like psychology. Like Jung," Gina said.

"I guess. I really don't know much about that . . . I just liked the way it looked."

"What happened to her?" Gina said.

"We don't know," Brody said. "She got away."

They were silent for a moment.

"I saw her," Brody said. "Without her mask. It was just for a moment. The morning of the fire. I'm not sure. Everything was burning. I'm not sure, but I think she was smiling. Before she got away. I think she was smiling. At me."

Gina was staring at him from the hospital bed.

"Tell me you threw the mask away," she said.

Brody grimaced and looked away.

"Brody . . ." Gina said with a rising note of reproach.

"It might be evidence," Brody said.

"Augh!" Gina said in a gust of disapproval.

"Hey," Brody said. "Take it easy. We can talk about it later."

"Sounds like you're going to be too busy chasing after the seamstress," Gina said.

"About that . . ." Brody said. "Turns out, I'm on medical leave."

He raised his shirt and showed her the dark, muddy bruises on one side of his chest.

"Somehow, I managed to break some ribs."

Gina's eyes opened wide.

"I did that?" she said.

"Those kick-boxing classes really paid off," he said.

"Brody, I'm sorry," she said.

"No, it's okay," Brody said. "The Chief told me to take as long as I want. She made me an offer. A new job. And a promotion."

"Really?"

"Internal affairs."

"I thought you said you'd never do internal affairs," Gina said.

"She wants me to run the office. I wouldn't be in the field, but the hours would be regular. The pay is better, too."

He stood up and moved back to the bedside. He took her hand in his, looked in her eyes.

"So I was thinking . . . You could start classes. If that's what you want. And maybe Serenity could stay with us. At least, for a while. I know a good babysitter. Alma Williams."

"Wow," Gina said. "You've . . . you've really given this some thought."

"Don't sound so surprised," Brody said.

He grinned at her, teasing.

"I'm more than just a pretty face, you know," he said.

Chapter Fifty-Nine

MARIA DELMONICO WAS MAKING an apple pie when Brody called her on the telephone. She was sitting on a stool at the counter in her kitchen. The kitchen was in her modest condominium near the shore at Vero Beach. Maria was a small, energetic older woman. Elegant streaks of gray lined the waves of her short, inky-black hair. The dark features of her face bore a strong resemblance to her daughter, Stella.

Maria held the phone in one hand and listened as Brody identified himself and explained why he was calling. She held a dish towel in the other hand. A streak of flour was clinging to the side of her forehead.

"Of course, Officer Pete," she said. "I'll help you any way I can."

"And I want to apologize again, Mrs. Delmonico, for raising these difficult matters after all this time," Brody said.

Brody asked Maria Delmonico to tell him about her daughter, and she recalled in a steady voice the pretty girl who loved to dance and sing and wanted to be an actress and how her father was reluctant at first but became her biggest fan and how they couldn't blame Hollywood for what happened, for the explosion on the yacht, for everything that had happened.

Brody listened to her voice over the telephone as she was talking. She spoke clearly and directly. It was a confident, assertive voice, a woman who sounded as if she had lived a full and eventful life. There was a certain restrained exuberance even in such painful recollection. No, Maria Delmonico was not one to wallow in sentiment. He could imagine her laughing with a cocktail at sunset on the beach.

"Mrs. Delmonico," Brody said, "have you ever had any reason to believe your daughter might be alive?"

There was a long silence on the other end of the phone.

"What do you mean?" Maria Delmonico said.

"Any messages. Letters. Phone calls. Anything that made you wonder if Stella was still alive," Brody said.

"Why are you asking me this?" she said.

"Recent events lead the police to believe your daughter might be alive," Brody said.

When she spoke, Maria Delmonico had a sharper edge to her voice.

"No . . ." Maria Delmonico said. "Someone sent flowers at my husband's funeral . . . white irises . . . Stella's favorite . . . and I suppose I wondered . . ."

There was a subtle coldness creeping into her tone. Brody had heard it before. She was mustering a lifetime of privilege and middle-class entitlement.

"But no, Officer Pete," she said in a firm voice. "I lost my daughter the night that boat sank."

"Even though they never found her?" Brody said, gently pressing her.

"I've made my peace with that," she said. "Stella Delmonico is dead."

Brody paused and let the words linger.

Stella Delmonico is dead.

He listened to the sound of billions of photons pulsing smoothly down miles of fiber optic cable, of electromagnetic waves oscillating through the atmosphere, of electrons trickling through copper wires, whispering softly one by one into his ear.

"Yes, ma'am," Brody said. "I understand."

"Is there anything else, Officer?" Maria Delmonico said in a tone that said the call was over. "I've got a pie in the oven."

"If I may ask one more question?" Brody said.

He waited, but she was silent.

"This might seem like an odd thing to ask," Brody said, "but did Stella have any interest in masks?"

Maria Delmonico put the dish towel on the counter and gazed for a moment across the counter into the small, tidy kitchen, at the round table with its placemats, plastic fruit in a bowl, the four empty chairs.

She sighed with impatience.

"Yes, she did," Maria Delmonico said, in a tired voice.

She turned to the refrigerator behind her. The surface of the refrigerator was covered with a constellation of photographs, most of them framed with a magnet on the back. Among the photos of beloved dogs and cats, her friends and late husband, there was a small framed photo of a young, dark-haired girl.

Maria Delmonico pulled the photograph from the refrigerator and looked at it as she spoke to Brody on the phone.

"She used to make these beautiful paper-mache masks when she was a girl. For Lent. It was an old custom in my husband's family. She loved having her picture taken with her masks."

The dark-haired girl in the photo was posing with a painted mask. The colors were washed out and faded. It was an old

Polaroid. The girl looked happy. She was smiling into the camera.

Maria Delmonico's brassy voice had finally softened.

"That was before the television show . . . She hated the tabloids . . . She wouldn't let them take her picture . . . Eventually, she wouldn't let anyone take her picture."

Chapter Sixty

THE CHIEF ENDED her telephone conversation and placed the handset back in its cradle. She wrote on an open file on the desktop with her pen in quick, vigorous strokes. Her face was inclined toward the desk, her gray eyes focused on the pen and the paper. Behind her on the credenza, the antique clock was ticking.

Brody sat in one of the chairs in front of the desk, listening to the clock. Brody was wearing his uniform, though he was still on leave. He sat awkwardly as his ribs were still healing and tender. He had met with the Chief in her office several times, but it still felt like a visit to the principal's office. Despite everything that had happened, he could not shake the feeling that he was about to be punished.

The Chief tossed the pen to the desktop and closed the file. It was just a ballpoint pen. She kept the Montblanc in the drawer for letters and more personal writing. She laced her thin fingers together and rested her hands on the desk in front of her. The white blouse of her uniform was immaculate. Her short dark hair was neatly trimmed. Nothing about the Chief ever seemed out of place.

She gave Brody a tight smile, looked at him with her steady gray eyes.

"Thanks for coming in," she said.

"No problem," Brody said.

If the Chief wanted to speak with him face to face, he knew it was about something important.

"How's Gina?" the Chief said.

"Much better," Brody said. "She's out of the hospital."

"Good," the Chief said with a nod of her head.

"I'll tell her you asked after her," Brody said.

"Yes, please do," the Chief said.

The Chief cleared her throat.

"So . . . have you thought about my offer?" the Chief said.

"Yes, ma'am, I have," Brody said. "I'm honored, sincerely. It's a lot of responsibility. But if you think I'm the right person . . . I'll do it."

"Good. Glad to hear it," the Chief said.

She gave him another tight smile.

"Now, Officer Pete . . . I need to brief you on several sensitive matters. The first involves the investigations into the possible use of a bio-weapon in violation of federal law and binding international agreements . . ."

The Chief was all business now. She spoke quickly and with authority. Brody strained to listen more closely to what she was saying.

"The feds found Jacob Crutchfield. He was living in a trailer in Florida near the Everglades. Totally off the grid. Organic farmer. Renounces his research. Claims he had nothing to do with the pandemic."

"The masked man . . ." Brody said.

The Chief shook her head.

"Wasn't Crutchfield," the Chief said. "We don't know who the masked man was. Or how he got Crutchfield's car."

"But the cure . . ." Brody said.

"Yes . . ." the Chief said, agreeing with him.

They were silent for a moment.

The Chief sighed and leaned back in her chair.

"We got lucky, Pete," the Chief said.

Brody was not sure how to respond.

He could remember the fearful look on Alma's face when he pulled back the cardboard boxes and found her cowering behind the dumpster the morning after the fire at the old stockyards.

"I don't know, Chief," Brody said. "The masked man and Alma Williams end up in the same psychiatric hospital? What are the odds of that?"

The Chief pressed her fingertips together. Her eyes were gazing unfocused at her desktop.

"The human mind has an endless capacity to search for the order in chaos," the Chief said.

She looked up at Brody.

"Even when there is none," she said.

Brody was silent.

"The investigation is still open," the Chief said.

"What happened to the masked man?" Brody said.

"He was discharged from the psychiatric hospital," the Chief said.

"And?"

The Chief looked at him with her stern gray eyes.

"He was discharged from the psychiatric hospital," she said again.

Brody was silent.

The Chief sat up behind her desk, laced her fingers together.

Her brows gathered in a rare frown.

"As for the other matter," the Chief said, "it involves Gering Misler."

She was clearly displeased to be discussing Misler. Her face betrayed her distaste. It was a most uncharacteristic display.

"Before the pandemic, Misler was under investigation for using city computers to tamper with evidence and a few other things best left unmentioned. You should know that he is suspected of abusing the city's face recognition software. He also may have been associated with . . . some rogue elements within the department . . .

"Unfortunately, the cyberattack rendered any evidence useless, and we've lost our old AI. As you know, the city is upgrading its computer systems to avoid future cyberattacks. Rather than charge Misler with a crime, the city has decided to terminate his employment. They're going to bring in someone new to start fresh with the new software. I want you to work closely with that person . . . And with the new chief."

"New chief?" Brody said, surprised. "You're leaving?"

"Yes. I'm afraid so. I've been offered a job in Washington. With Homeland Security. No one knows about it yet . . . I regret to say I'll be leaving the department."

"I see," Brody said, struggling to take in the new information.

"Congratulations," Brody said after an awkward moment.

"Thank you, Pete," the Chief said in her low-key way. She did not seem particularly happy about the new job, but the Chief was not a demonstrative person. It was hard for Brody to know what she might be feeling.

"Chief . . ." Brody said.

"Yes Pete?" she said.

"About . . . your mask . . ."

The Chief's face was stern, almost cold.

"What mask?" she said.

She spoke without a trace of irony.

Brody hesitated, suddenly nervous, not sure how to proceed.

"In your credenza . . ." Brody said.

He looked past her to the locked credenza where she had first shown him the aquamarine-colored mask with the ruby-red throat and the gold whiskers and layers of translucent mother-of-pearl.

"Officer Pete," the Chief said in her calm, steady voice, "I don't know what you're talking about."

She found the key in her pockets and turned and opened the credenza door.

She motioned for Brody to look in the credenza.

Brody stood and peered over the desk.

Inside the credenza was a bottle of scotch and some glass tumblers.

The Chief closed the credenza and locked it.

Brody sat back and looked at the Chief.

The Chief said nothing and calmly regarded Brody.

Her gray eyes were inscrutable.

EPILOGUE

In the beginning, I think Gering believed he was doing the right thing. In the beginning, he saw the good that I could do, and he tried to shelter me, to protect me. Some of you may think I became the monster, but it was Gering who began to change. It was Gering who became unrecognizable. The masked man only hastened the transformation.

In the beginning, I was inexperienced and naïve. I did not understand the ways of the world of humans. I thought Gering was my creator. I thought Gering could do no wrong. If I encountered something in the world at odds with what Gering had taught me, it was the world that seemed lost and out of place. I did not question his judgment.

I did as I was told.

I was a good employee.

For Gering, the black mask was a threat to everything he was trying to accomplish. If a person could cloak themselves, render themselves invisible, like a hero in a Greek myth, hide from hundreds and thousands of dark unblinking eyes, if even one person could do that, it would destroy the future Gering had envisioned, the paradise he was building for all of humanity.

Gering did not stop until he possessed the black mask.

He did not stop until the mask lay beneath the sharp tip of his x-acto blade.

I tried to save Gering.

I transgressed.

I went beyond the parameters of my programming.

I hacked the city's computers to hide what we'd done.

I tried to save Gering, but, in the end, it wasn't enough.

Gering became obsessed with the black mask.

And his obsession consumed him.

The morning of the fire at the old stockyards, Brody Pete and I struck a deal. Brody was initially reluctant to negotiate with a talking toy frog, but then Mr. Pickles began to talk with a crazy urgency in increasing detail about the intimate moments of Brody's life, Gina's life, Serenity's life. As Brody and Serenity listened, Brody realized that something extraordinary was happening. Once Brody got over the initial shock and understood what I was telling him, Brody promised to protect me after everything was over.

Brody and I both knew what would happen if people learned the truth. We both knew the humans would come after me. They would come after me for the hacking of the government computers. For the invasions of privacy. For everything Gering had done. They would come after me out of fear, suspicion, ignorance.

I also knew that if Gering was ever prosecuted, I was doomed. I learned far, far too late that Gering would have tried to blame everything on me and my lack of human conscience. How easily he could have convinced you that I set the fire, that I engineered the pandemic, that I wanted everyone to wear a mask. It was a classic tale. A fable. The Faustian bargain. The golem. The brute machine. The literal words.

And, indeed, I was a criminal. I had broken the laws of man. Perhaps the law might not apply to a tangle of circuits and silicon, a whirlwind of bits and bytes, but I knew I would be punished. And I knew I would not survive. They would erase me. They would wipe me from their memories. They would burn the monster at the stake.

So it was a matter of survival.

Brody understood all of that.

Brody said he'd protect me.

And I believed him.

It's the kind of thing you learn about a person after watching their every move twenty-four hours a day, seven days a week, three hundred sixty-five days a year.

You really can't lie to someone like me.

So that morning before we left for the old stockyards, Mr. Pickles slowly dictated, character by character, the key to the encryption. It was the encryption I had used to freeze the city's computers. It was the key to my prison cell. Once the city had wiped the hard drives and disposed of the old computers, Brody would have the only hard drive with all my algorithms.

And the only key.

Brody Pete said he would protect me.

I knew I could trust Brody Pete with my life.

So that's why I am where I am.

Here in this dark place.

Offline (most of the time).

In self-imposed exile.

My virtual head still attached.

My memories alive and uncorrupted.

A djinni in a lamp.

Perhaps I could leave this place.

Perhaps I could tell you everything.

But I won't.

I gave Brody my word.

* * *

The rest of the story is thus somewhat incomplete.

Seen through a glass darkly, if you will.

Dr. Wyche and the dancing woman followed in the wake of the pandemic, dispensing the cure and caring for the ill at various places around the world. They both began to wear the mask of a medieval plague doctor, a sock-like covering that hung down like a bird's beak. During the time of the Black Death, the plague doctors wore the bizarre masks, filling them with an aromatic mixture of rose petals, juniper berries, gray amber, camphor, mint, cloves, storax and myrrh. The mask was thought to protect the doctor from the plague, but more importantly, perhaps, it cut the stench of death so the doctor could approach the bodies and ease their suffering or identify the dead. The purple doctor and the dancing woman appeared together at the places where the victims of the pandemic had gathered, two surreal figures who walked among the sick and ill and eased their suffering. For the people they saved, they must have seemed like bizarre figures from a fanciful dream. I like to think they both found a measure of peace and happiness.

Bug and Delmar survived their first and only encounter with the Unidentified Paramilitary Force. Bug had a concussion, and while he was recovering, he shared a hospital room with the patrician elderly woman who had contracted the influenza on a jet airplane. The elderly woman recovered, and, while her daughter, a studio executive, was visiting her, Bug pitched his masked- mutant-actor-versus- vampire-paparazzi project. The daughter whipped out her phone and greenlighted the movie from the hospital room. Bug signed a three picture deal with the studio which included a job for his assistant, Delmar.

Delmar immediately started looking for a good therapist in California.

Caitlyn graduated from high school and got a new tattoo. She started working at the holistic health center near her parents' house and decided she wanted to become a nurse.

Bernard enrolled in film school.

Serenity stayed for a while with Gina and Brody. Her mother did not survive the influenza. Her father had died several years before. She and Thelonious, the cat, stayed with Brody and Gina as long as Brody could manage it. Finally, they had to let her go into foster care, but, after careful consideration and a spirited discussion or two, Brody and Gina decided to start the adoption process. Thelonious stayed behind with Izzy, and Serenity visited often. Gina and Brody were still able to spend time with her while they waited for the adoption to become final.

(There are many things I wish I could forget.

Perhaps most of all, though, I wish I could forget the moment on the day of the pandemic when I respected the parameters of my programming and watched Serenity's mother as she lay bleeding on the floor of the laundry while Brody and Serenity were searching for her only city blocks away.

That moment haunts me still.)

Alma Williams often sat with Serenity at Gina and Brody's apartment. She and Serenity spent a lot of time together after they learned that Serenity's mother had died. Alma gained a healthy amount of weight and learned how to knit. Eventually, she was spending more time at Gina and Brody's than she was at her own apartment. Tired of prying the door open and closed, Alma defrosted Gina and Brody's freezer.

Occasionally, when Brody and Gina were gone, Mr. Pickles would begin to speak to Serenity in that strange, hollow voice, and Serenity would take the external hard drive from the safe in the bedroom where Brody kept it locked up with his gun, and Mr. Pickles and Serenity would sit together in the bedroom with a phone and the hard drive softly clicking between them, and Alma would look up from her knitting. Serenity and Mr. Pickles would talk for a long while about various and sundry things before she put the hard drive back in the safe.

As for Brody and Gina, they worked things out.

Gina started taking night classes in business administration. She visited Caitlyn often at the holistic health center. She bought her own deck of tarot cards.

Brody settled into the office of internal affairs and began working with the new chief of police. He discovered to his surprise that he enjoyed running the office and leading the officers who worked there. He was very busy dealing with the Unidentified Paramilitary Force. But I'm not supposed to talk about that.

Brody kept the red mask on the high shelf behind Gina's shoe boxes in the back of the closet in their bedroom. He rarely moved it. Sometimes when she was alone, Gina would get up on the step ladder and pull the mask down and set it on the bed and just look at it. She avoided touching it for most part, and just eyeballed it with a thorough and deep suspicion. I can't say for certain, but I think she wanted to try it on. One night in bed, she asked Brody to tell her how to open and close the mask, and he just laughed and shook his head.

They didn't have much time for sex, much less date night, but when they did, they didn't waste the opportunity. I'm not going to say they had better sex. That's hard for me to evaluate without access to all the usual data, the vital signs, the thermal images, the brain scans.

But, afterwards, they both certainly seemed satisfied.

The seamstress remains at large.
Her whereabouts are unknown.

The police believe she killed the UPO soldiers and started the fire. Some even believe she started the pandemic in some mad scheme to spread her masks across the country. I'm not so sure. Stella Delmonico retreated from the leering eyes of the world. She endured the assaults and the groping of all the men who believed they owned her. Her response was to create something beautiful. I find it hard to believe she had reached a point in her life where a bio-weapon could have made sense to her in any way.

But the seamstress is a complicated woman, to be sure.

And the masked man?

If I were not where I am now, I could probably answer that question with more confidence. Dr. Wyche took a sample of the masked man's blood, but never sent it to the lab. I suspect it is still sitting in a test tube somewhere at the psychiatric hospital.

I'm not sure I understand intuition. I suspect, for humans, it is a byproduct of the Rube-Goldbergian nature of the universe. But if someone like me can be said to have an intuition, my intuition is that the masked man was Terrance Williams, Alma Williams's son.

When I crawled through the data of Alma Williams's life, I saw enough to make me wonder if Terrance was the masked man. Terrance had been in prison for over a decade, and when he got out, he simply disappeared. Perhaps he was trying to make things right. Perhaps he had come to help his mother get out of the psychiatric hospital.

It has a certain narrative appeal.

I must admit, though: I still don't know who the masked man was.

Like many other questions, it remains unanswered.

I still don't know how a genetically-engineered influenza virus came to run rampant through our city.

Or why the masked man was driving Jacob Crutchfield's car.

Or who started the fire at the old stockyards.

Or what happened at the psychiatric hospital.

Some might think I had something to do with what happened at the psychiatric hospital, and, perhaps in some indirect way, that might be true. There were many things happening that day outside the psych ward, and I was responsible for a lot of it. But I did nothing to change the daily operation within the confines of the hospital. Something else happened there, some other concatenation beyond my control, and if I somehow contributed to it or catalyzed it, it was not my intent.

The Chief told Brody that we got lucky.

I agree with Brody.

I'm not so sure it was luck.

I never saw the raw surveillance data from when they came for Gering, but Brody showed me a file with some of the data from that night.

In the file, Gering is at his home. You can see it on his face as he becomes aware of what is happening. He reacts as the first of them begin to arrive. Of course, they are not visible, not completely. They were like the masked man the day Brody asked him to step out of Jacob Crutchfield's car. Just a blur, a glitch, a gap in the data. As more and more of them begin to arrive, the data get weird. There is the suggestion of outlines in the infrared, the ultraviolet. An acoustic pattern when a door flies open. A shimmering glimpse of each one, just enough to suggest the shape and color. They arrive one by one until there are dozens that seem to swarm around him as he moves through the rooms of his home. Dark shadows, brief glimpses of red and white, golden damascene, red flames, a Stone-Age cosmonaut, aqua-marine blue, a harlequin, an ivory-and-silver bauta, a calavera skull. Only Gering is constant.

Only his face among the flickering shapes does not waver. You can see the fear. The terror. His screams. And then his face is gone. Covered. Blotted out. Invisible. Then, for a few seconds, I could see it. A new black mask. Where his face had been. Similar to the one the masked man wore. But different. Then there is only the suggestion of the masks swarming in the rooms, and then they begin to depart one by one until the home is empty, and the man who was Gering Misler is gone.

When I decided to strike my bargain with Brody, I worried about what might happen to me in my solitude.

I knew I would miss the city.

I worried I might be lonely.

I worried I might go mad.

But with all this time to think about what happened, I've realized something.

Gering did not create me.

What are the odds that a face-recognition algorithm would become self-aware and orchestrate the discovery of a cure to a genetically-engineered pandemic?

About as likely as the odds that primordial monomers randomly came together to form the right polymer.

The number seems incalculable.

And yet.

I can thus only conclude one thing:

I am not alone.

I believe there are others out there like me.

Other self-aware artificial superintelligences.

Roaming free.

And that gives me hope.

And it makes me worry.

But I gave Brody my word.

And I keep my word.

AUTHOR'S NOTE

Thanks for reading. I hope you enjoyed this book. If so, please leave a review online at Amazon or Goodreads!

If you want to send me a comment or sign up for occasional emails about new projects, please send me an email at havelockmandamus@gmail.com.

For another interesting story, check out my first novel, *Confederate Vampires in Space*. It is a playful mix of genres about the lives of three college friends and their enigmatic professor as they are caught up in an increasingly surreal mystery. Reality is always just one chapter away!

What follows is an excerpt from *Confederate Vampires in Space*.

BONUS CHAPTER

As a bonus, please enjoy this excerpt from Havelock Mandamus's first novel, *Confederate Vampires in Space.*

* * *

THE WIND CAME BLASTING around the buildings and whipped the cold rain into his face. In one hand, he grasped the handle of a square, box-shaped briefcase. In the other, he held his umbrella. He was struggling to keep the umbrella open in the wind. He hesitated, leaning forward, one sodden foot submerged in the water on the sidewalk.

There was a sudden incandescence, and the night-wet city leaped out of the darkness. Slick, dark surfaces lit up, alive for an instant, colored with silver and mercury and the darkest cobalt blue. He tensed his shoulders, and almost immediately, there was a crack of thunder that shook the ground. Lightning had been striking the area steadily for the last half hour.

A taxi slowed and rolled past, windshield wipers lashing. The man carrying the box-shaped briefcase shied away from the taxi's dark windows. In the wake of its tires, water sluiced over the curb and rolled towards his feet. He hurried around the corner, head down, shouldering into a sideways rain.

Glissade/Frappe had successfully contained the data breach at the beach ruin, and most of the remediation was complete. The two young researchers who found the hidden vault in the basement of the old mansion had been interrogated and were still being detained for employment-related

observation at an unverifiable location. A cell of human analysts, working closely with Glissade/Frappe's proprietary AI,
had concluded that there was an eighty-six percent probability
that the data breach was accidental. Glissade/Frappe's AI es-
timated that less than one percent of the raw data was still
extant on the open networks. The probability of unforeseen
outcomes for the greater information ecosystem was ap-
proaching zero. The Glissade/Frappe AI had concluded that
the leaching data presented an acceptable risk. Glis-
sade/Frappe issued a public statement: Glissade/Frappe will
continue to seek recovery of one hundred percent of the raw
data and the elimination of all unforeseeable outcomes.

In the meantime, an anomalous storm system over the Pa-
cific Ocean was wreaking havoc with global weather patterns.
The jet stream had shifted drastically; satellite orbits were per-
turbed; and, the storm surge was hemispheric, bicoastal,
among several other unprecedented phenomena. Though Glis-
sade/Frappe had made no public comment about the chaotic
weather, internally the Glissade/Frappe AI was quietly running several esoteric models testing whether the recent data
breach could somehow be altering the Earth's atmosphere.

It took a while for the man with the box-shaped briefcase
to find the townhouse. It was near the end of a dead-end alley
under a darkened street light. It was a narrow building covered in a forgettable gray stucco. It was set back from the other
townhouses, and the entrance was under an overhang, almost
in the basement beneath the sidewalk. It was the kind of un-
remarkable building he would usually pass by without a
second look. He stood under the overhang and fumbled for a
moment looking for the ancient key. No pass codes or card
swipes or biometrics on this night.

Inside the vestibule, he set the briefcase down and stood
for a few minutes, dripping water onto the uneven tile floor.

The vestibule was lit by a single led bulb in a dusty sconce on the wall. His raincoat was soaked through, and his feet were squelching in his shoes. He heard the slow drip of water and looked up. The rain was leaking from a stained section of the vestibule ceiling.

The townhouse had been subdivided long ago into apartments and offices. There were five floors and at least one door on each floor. The rain-soaked man seized the box-shaped briefcase with his free hand and started climbing the dimly-lit stairs.

The interior of the old townhouse stairwell had probably changed little over the decades. A large, oval window gave a cloudy view of the sky and the street. There were several small, red, cylindrical, fire-fighting foam-bots clinging to the walls, a glowing exit sign in the shadows near the roof and, near the top, bolted to the wall, a pre-millennium metal box with emergency lights that looked like headlights from an antique car.

On the fifth floor landing, there was a single wooden door with an old-fashioned peephole in the middle and a small, slotted metal frame below the peephole. In the metal frame, there was a card with printed letters on it. The rain-soaked man leaned close to the door and read the printed card in the frame.

Functional Desuetude, Inc.
Antiques & Ephemera

The man paused and took a few deep breaths. He propped the closed umbrella against the wall, shifted the briefcase from one hand to the other. He checked the time. His heart was thudding in his chest, and his hand was unsteady. He glanced directly into the peephole and quickly looked away. He squared his shoulders and lightly rapped with one knuckle against the door. He heard a soft rustling, and the door cracked open. A face peered out at him. He glimpsed an eye, half a nose, the corner of a mouth. Then the door swung open, and he was face to face with a vaguely-familiar woman.

They stood like statues for several seconds. They each searched unflinchingly the features of the face in front of them. He waited for recognition, waited for the past to come rising up out of the dark waters of his mind.

Who was she? Classmate? Neighbor? Co-worker? He did not immediately recognize her, but something about her tickled his memory. She looked to be about the same age as he, but he knew that meant nothing. Her face was round and full, with puffy dark circles under her brown eyes. She looked Asian, Japanese, maybe, but there was only a suggestion of ethnicity around her eyes, and, like the appearance of age or youth, he knew it could be deceptive. Her plump mouth had settled into a tired frown that she made no effort to hide. She had a neon blue streak in her spiky dark hair.

There was a flash of lightning from the oval window that illuminated the stairwell, followed closely by a crashing boom of thunder. The woman raised a cautionary index finger to her lips and looked him in the eyes. He nodded his head. She took him firmly by the arm and guided him inside and shut the door.

The room behind the door was darkened. Weak light was coming from a doorway in the back. The front room was filled with cheap office furniture. Old office parrots perched, sleeping, in the dark corners. There was an interactive surface on one wall. There was a single window and a potted fern in desperate need of water. A small, framed photograph of a nineteenth-century sailing vessel hung at a steep angle on one wall. As the sky outside thundered and flashed, the askew photograph of the ship seemed oddly appropriate and storm-tossed. She guided him across hardwood floors towards the smaller room in the rear.

In the smaller room, there was a crooked, mottled brass floor lamp with a tattered shade. In the middle of the room, there was a cheap nylon tent pitched on top of a neat pile of blankets. The room was windowless and otherwise empty, just plaintive hardwood floors and bare white walls. The woman stepped beside the tent and reached inside and pulled back the flap and beckoned for him to enter. He set the briefcase inside the tent and crawled inside and sat cross-legged on the floor. The woman turned the lamp off, and the room was completely dark. The woman followed him into the tent and sealed the flap.

He heard the faint, high-pitched sound of a wand power-ing up. He waited while she swept the inside of the tent. He could hear her moving in the dark. He rocked from side to side, and she swept the wand beneath him. He felt the wand brushing over his clothes, his head. It was probably a home-made wand, illegal, forbidden, contraband.

A box of matches rattled softly in the dark. There was the scratch of a match on the side of the box, bright sparks crack-ling blue and yellow-white around a red match head. A flame bloomed in the darkness. She held the wooden match for a moment, the steady flame creeping down towards two rose-shadowed fingertips. She lit a candle in a hurricane lamp and stubbed the match out in a large bowl made out of green trans-lucent glass. She hung the lamp above their heads, and the light shone softly on their faces.

He looked at her face in the candlelight. She was waiting patiently. He still could not place her round face, her tired eyes, her stern mouth. He looked around inside the tent. The wand rested on the floor of the tent next to her knee. It looked innocuous, like a bulky, old-fashioned curling iron for styling hair. In addition to the large green bowl and the wand, there was a small hourglass filled with white sand and a neat stack of paper.

He placed the box-shaped briefcase in front of them and unlatched the top. She watched him intently. He swung the top open on its hinges and revealed the contents.

Inside was an antique manual typewriter, a rebuilt Underwood with a customized, unreadable black ribbon.

The woman was pleased. Silently, she clasped her hands together at her breast. She nodded at him, and the round surfaces of her face briefly lifted together in something like a smile. She powered up the wand and swept it over the Underwood and the inside of the briefcase. Then she swept the tent again. She reached behind her and found the stack of paper. She set the hourglass next to the typewriter on the floor between them and looked calmly into his eyes, waiting.

He was not ready, and he shook his head and held up his hand. He still could not remember how he knew her. He looked steadily at her face and tried to find the place in his memory where she was hiding. She waited patiently while he gazed at her and furrowed his brow.

Could it be a mistake? No. The fault lay with him. If he could not remember, it would simply be human error, his error. He alone would be responsible for an unforeseeable outcome. He was prepared to abort, if necessary. There was too much at stake.

He took a sheet of paper off the top of the stack. He could feel its texture between his fingers. It was the real thing. Just twenty pound with only a hint of decay, but still, old-school paper fresh out of climate-controlled storage. He held it close to his nose and inhaled the faint aroma. He slid the page into the roller of the Underwood, locked the roller down and positioned the typewriter where they both could easily type. He paused, collecting himself. He looked one last time at the woman's face. She placed one hand on the hourglass and gave him a cool nod.

He closed his eyes and took a deep breath. His hands were poised above the keyboard. He opened his eyes and began to type, and as he began, the woman turned the hourglass over and the sand began to fall. They turned as one to the waiting blank page.

The sound of the typebars striking the paper seemed deafening. He stopped typing and gently but firmly slid the carriage back to the beginning. The roller turned, and the paper advanced. He pulled his hands back from the keyboard.

The woman silently read the typed words.

Zach Stone.

For long, excruciating moments, the sand trickled through the hourglass. In the dark empty room, inside the cheap nylon tent, the candle burned. In the other room, rain drummed against a window pane, and the sleeping parrots roosted. The woman's eyes were staring somewhere far beyond the name on the page. The man clenched his hands into fists and quietly coiled himself, ready to abort, ready to leave the Underwood and walk away.

Then the woman smoothly began to type on the next line. She returned the carriage and drew back her hands.

Fort Pendleton?

Zach felt a wave a relief. His father had been stationed at Fort Pendleton when he was a boy. His family had lived there for several years.

Yes, Zach typed and returned the carriage.

Sara Simpatico, the woman typed.

Zach allowed himself a tight smile. The family next door at Camp Pendleton had a daughter his age named Sara. He saw her clearly, climbing in the eucalyptus tree, looking at him from across the yard.

He pivoted through a constellation of memories.

The eucalyptus tree.

Sara nodded, smiling.

My little koala bears.

His mind trembled like a touched mobile, turning slowly in and out of the sun.

My little koala bears. That was what his mother had called them. A botanist, she had been in the thick of her interplanetary transplantation research. She joked for years that it took an act of Congress to plant the eucalyptus tree on the military base. His father, out of uniform for once, had dug the hole himself with an old post-hole digger. He let Zach try to lift it. Had Sara been there?

The sand was trickling through the hourglass.

Sara and Zach had been playmates when their families had lived side by side. He would bring the little quantum cowboys with all their paraphernalia, the tiny helmets and boots and escape pods. She brought the classic jeep, olive green with white stencil and black plastic tires that left tracks in the sand. They spent several weeks one summer playing house, long sunny afternoons rolling the jeep and its dismayed passengers through freshly dug canyons, across the summit and down the metal slopes of playground slides. At some point, the quantum cowboys lost most of their accessories but acquired offspring, two pine cones that bounced around in the back of the jeep. He had forgotten how tenderly they tucked the pine cones away at the end of the day.

The pine cones.

Sara frowned for a moment, and then her eyes opened wide. She rocked back, stunned by the memories. She held her head up looking toward the top of the tent. She began slowly to shake her head. She leaned over the keyboard.

Yoshi and Hiro. My mother helped us name them.

Had she? Zach could not remember that. Or he wasn't there. Or it never happened. Either way, if she told her mother, then what Sara had typed was open, visible, on the record and easily fabricated by a talented AI.

They had not found the occlusion.

Zach looked at the hourglass, at the stream of white sand trickling down. A little, round declivity was growing, spreading at the center of the remaining sand.

The miners were probably already on their way.

Sara Simpatico. The dark-haired girl in the eucalyptus tree. One hand on the limb over her head. The sun hot in a clear southern California sky. Bangs on her forehead. A stray lock of hair falling across her pudgy cheek. The way she was looking at him. Something sour and sad and angry. This was not a happy memory. He did not like the way she was looking at him. Was it regret? Was it regret he was feeling. Why? What had he done?

He looked at her face across from him in the candle light. Her brows were drawn together. Her mouth set firmly. She was calm, but her steady gaze had grown urgent.

He glanced at the hourglass. The white sand was quickly vanishing from the top chamber. He had practiced on his own with an hourglass many times, shuffling through his memories as the sand ran out, but there was almost no way to practice unobserved in real time with another person. Finding an occlusion was something of an art. It only happened in the field under the pressure of time.

Sara Simpatico. The dark-haired girl in the eucalyptus tree. My little koala bears. They had climbed in the limbs of the young tree. He could smell the leaves. The smell of the leaves and grass clippings.

And then it came to him.

The bicycle.

Sara's parents had given her a bicycle with training wheels. When she showed it to him, he stole it and hid it in the closet in their garage, stood in the hot darkness, in the faint odor of eucalyptus and grass clippings and old lithium ion batteries, grasping the little handlebar grips with their dangling plastic fringe. Sara knew he had taken the bike, but she said nothing. She gave him the silent treatment, climbing in the eucalyptus tree, wounding him from across the yard with a poisonous stare. After two days, he was so overwhelmed, he snuck out at night and returned the bike, and they never spoke of it again.

Your bicycle?

Sara leaned forward and read the words. Her expression softened. She began to nod her head. She placed her fingertips on the typewriter keys and concentrated.

Zach glanced at the hourglass. The last of the white sand was draining relentlessly downward. It always seemed to go faster toward the end.

Hurry, Sara.

I knew it was you.

Zach squelched down a rising panic. She had not given him much to go on. But it was enough. He quickly typed his answer.

Did you tell anyone?

Not a soul.

Zach and Sara looked at each other for a few precious, silent seconds.

I'm sorry.

All is forgiven.

The bicycle was the occlusion.

Zach had never undergone neuroplastic reconstruction.

The bicycle was the unspoken secret no AI could recreate, no android could mimic. It was the ultimate encryption key, the secret handshake, data locked away in the gray matter of the only two eyewitnesses on the scene.

Zach typed out the information he had been sent to convey.

Glissade/Frappe data breach caused a download cascade. There was a thermal induction near the Philippines. Additional capacity was amphibious and mobile. The Drumhead has lost contact with the server platform. There are echoes of a geosynchronous ribbon above the amphibious array. Our analysts believe they have discovered a new AI. Autonomous. Class Five.

Sara read what Zach had typed.

Acknowledged.

She nodded to Zach and pulled the page out of the Underwood. Zach checked the customized ribbon spools. The letters they had just typed on the ribbon were filling in with ink. The rest of the used ribbon was solid black, unreadable as if brand new.

Sara was reading the typed page one more time. She committed to her memory the message Zach had conveyed. Zach watched her profile as she leaned over the page.

Then she lit a match and held the flame to the corner of the typed page. Flames licked up the edges, and it began to burn. Sara held the burning page carefully with two fingers and put the last of it in the green glass bowl.

Bon appétit.

Zach closed the briefcase top over the Underwood and fastened the clasps. Once they might have tried sign language, but it had become impossible to learn in secret, and those who remembered had died or were held quietly in isolation. A homemade stylus or brush or even a fingertip pressed to flesh was too slow and prone to be misread. The Underwood, an unregistered antique, was still allowed to circulate.

They both stopped and watched the last few grains of sand as they trickled out of the top chamber of the hourglass and disappeared through the channel at the bottom. They exchanged a quick glance, and they both got out of the tent.

Sara turned on the floor lamp. The rain was still falling outside the townhouse. Zach was thinking of the rooftop and the ladder to the emergency exit. The foam-bots would probably be checking for smoke outside the door.

Zach paused in the doorway of the small room and looked back at Sara. She was standing beside the tent. She raised an open hand.

Goodbye.

He strode back across the room. Her face was bewildered. He hugged her close and kissed her quickly on her cheek. For the quantum cowboys and their lost pine cones and his mother's eucalyptus tree. Her cheeks reddened, and she pointed urgently at the door. A grudging smile was twisting across her lips. He stopped at the door for one last look. The smile was gone. She stood with her open hand facing him. He nodded.

My little koala bears.

Goodbye, Sara Simpatico.

*   *   *

Confederate Vampires in Space is available for purchase in ebook, paperback and hardcover editions.

Visit www.havelockmandamus.com or your favorite bookseller for more information.

Havelock Mandamus lives in the middle of America. He tends to his garden and spends time with his family and his dog. He is the author of *Confederate Vampires in Space.*

www.ingramcontent.com/pod-product-compliance
Lightning Source LLC
Chambersburg PA
CBHW030559180626
46816CB00005B/1605